SELENA FLOWERS AND THE CURSED RUBY

THE MERBLOOD SAGA

BOOK 1

ELLA ENGLISH

CONTENTS

1. Selena — 1

2. Selena — 13

3. Selena — 19

4. Selena — 23

5. Selena — 27

6. Chloe — 31

7. Chloe — 41

8. Selena — 45

9. Faustina — 53

10. Selena — 61

11. Selena — 69

12. Selena — 79

13. Selena — 93

14. Faustina — 103

15. Selena — 109

16. Selena — 113

17. Faustina — 119

18. Selena — 125

19. Selena — 131

20. Selena — 139

21. Faustina — 151

22. Selena — 157

23. Selena — 163

24. Selena — 173

25. Chloe — 181

26. Chloe — 187

27. Selena — 195

28. Aunt Ada — 201

29. Faustina — 209

30. Selena — 213

31. Selena 223

32. Faustina 231

33. Faustina 237

34. Selena 245

35. Selena 249

36. Faustina 257

37. Selena 261

38. Selena 265

39. Selena 269

40. Chloe 275

41. Selena 281

42. Chloe 287

43. Selena 291

44. Faustina 297

45. Chloe 303

46. Chloe 307

47. Chloe 311

48. Selena 323

49. Selena 327

About the Author 333

SELENA

Selena's hands trembled as she crammed clothes haphazardly into her bulging suitcase. Her stomach churned with apprehension. Today was the dreaded move to Madderly Bay. As the train pulled away from London, true panic set in. She desperately texted her dad, seeking any shred of comfort, but he was powerless to help. Selena gazed out at the fading city, leaving her home behind with a heavy heart.

"Who are you texting, Sweetie?" Selena's mum Fiona chirped.

"No one," Selena muttered, sinking into her seat. Nerves twisted inside her as the train barreled towards the unknown.

"Oh, Babycakes, you're going to love our new home! It's blissful," her mum gushed, clasping her hands in delight. "I spent the most amazing childhood summers there with Great

Aunt Ada." Her mum threw her arms wide as if trying to hug the memory. "The sun was always shining, and I'd build the most spectacular sandcastles on the beach."

Skeptical, Selena asked, "Was it really sunny all the time? We are talking about the English summer." She tried to picture it but wasn't sold on her mum's description.

"Well, maybe there was the odd drizzle." She waved her hand flippantly. "But that didn't stop me from constructing the most elaborate castles with seashell turrets and moats."

She leaned in conspiratorially. "I even made friends with a family of crabs. They were loyal subjects in my seaside kingdom."

She gazed out the window as the gloomy landscape rushed by. "Do we have to go?" Selena pleaded, turning back to her mum. "I don't want to leave London."

"Oh, don't be silly." Her mum fluttered her hands as if shooing away Selena's concerns. "You'll have the time of your life there. That charming old mansion welcomed me each evening with the perfume of climbing roses as I snuggled into bed."

Selena sighed, her doubts lingering as the train clattered on. No matter how idyllic her mum made it sound, apprehension still gnawed at Selena's stomach. She stared out at the increasingly overcast sky and let out another uneasy sigh, wishing she could share her mum's delight instead of dreading what awaited them.

Night fell as they arrived. The chilling rain and inky black sky made Selena's pulse race faster as she stepped onto the deserted platform. This foreboding place would be her new normal. Icy rain needled Selena's skin as she dragged her suitcase, struggling to keep up with her mum's vivid red hair whipping ahead. Sinister waves slammed against the slick black railings as they hurried along the harbor wall. The forceful sea reached out to her as if trying to claim Selena—as it had once before.

Panic rose in her chest. Her breath grew rapid and shallow, almost lost in the roar of the crashing surf. She quickened her pace along the narrow walkway, eager to outrun the grasping waves. But they chased her relentlessly, spraying her back with freezing sea foam.

Selena's heart raced faster with each step, the churning waves roaring in her ears. The icy sea breeze blasted her back, intent on pushing her forward into the unknown. She gripped the railing with white knuckles and forced herself onward along the cliffside path. She had to keep going or risk being swallowed by the growing darkness.

Selena tried to stay hopeful as she made her way along the cliffside path, the sea swirling below. Her mum had inherited this mansion from Aunt Ada after her sudden passing three months prior. Mum claimed the old house was "blissful," but Selena struggled to share that optimistic view, anxiety creeping in as the wind whipped her raincoat.

As Selena rounded the bend, the mansion came into full view. The tall house loomed, silhouetted against the night sky, both enticing and menacing. Selena quickened her pace, eager to get out of the cold and into the dubious shelter of the house. Suppressing a shudder, she tried to reassure herself that it was better to be inside than out here being tossed around by the elements.

As she reached the house, a shiver went down her back as she took in the narrow attic windows, which were like eyes peering down ominously. Shingles hung from the roof like gnarled teeth, hungry and waiting. Selena clenched her jaw, clinging to the hope that living here had to be better than their cramped rental flat, no matter how foreboding the place appeared.

The roof bulged and shifted under the light of the moon. It flinched at the weight of the pelting rain as if it were alive, breathing. Selena jumped at a squeak and a clank beside her. A rusty gate hung from a broken fence, waving in the wind. Her fear morphed into disgust.

Her mum had lied: this was no charming retreat but a rotting relic.

As they approached the front door, a bloodcurdling wail pierced the air. Selena froze, clutching her mum's arm. "What was that?"

Her mum chuckled uneasily as she clasped a key in one hand. "Just the wind, Sweetie, I'm sure," she promised, but Selena couldn't shake the sense something creepy lurked inside this mansion. The tall pines shuddered against the storm, concealing dark secrets and unseen eyes watching their every move. A big creak spilled from the hinges as her mum finally unlocked the door.

Her mum pushed the heavy front door open, and a strange energy burst forth.

"That's weird," Selena uttered as an unusual tingle ran down her spine.

"It just needs some fresh air!" her mum replied cheerily, flipping on the overhead light. Its dim glow only amplified her mum's excited smile. "When Great Aunt Ada left me this house, I knew our luck was finally changing. The stars have aligned for us, Selena—you'll see."

Selena rolled her eyes as her mum took a deep, contented breath. To her mum, the musty old mansion was permeated with some special, mystical aura. But to Selena, their sudden inheritance had simply come at the perfect time. They'd fallen behind on rent at the last place and barely escaped eviction by hastily packing their things and catching the first train out. This was less destiny and more dumb luck.

"There's a special energy in this place. I can feel it," her mum said, giving Selena a quick peck on the head before striding off, her boots echoing on the wooden floors as she explored further.

Selena sighed, wandering slowly behind. She loved her mum, quirks and superstitions included, but wished she could see things more clearly. This was just an old house, not some magical new beginning. Still, Selena had to admit, it beat getting tossed onto the streets.

Despite narrowly avoiding homelessness yet again, Selena felt anything but *lucky* as she looked around this creepy old mansion. Her mum told her one of her dad's rare child support payments had arrived just in time to pay for the moving van, which was coming tomorrow to bring all their stuff to the house.

"Chin up. This place could be charming," Fiona announced.

Selena trailed behind, unconvinced. Her actress mum was relentlessly optimistic, even though she rarely got roles. They were constantly doing midnight flits when the latest waitressing gig dried up, and they couldn't pay rent. Selena had lost count of how many times she'd packed her meager belongings and fled by the skin of their teeth. She considered herself an expert on living out of suitcases.

"Don't be such a Negative Nelly," Fiona trilled. "I can feel it in my bones—this will be our forever home."

Selena suppressed an eye roll. The bones hadn't steered them well so far. But she had to admit, creepy was preferable to homeless. She'd make the best of it, as always.

Fiona grabbed Selena's hand in the darkness and led her through the corridors. The airless house coiled itself around Selena, squeezing her breath out of her lungs. Her thoughts swam through her oxygen-deprived mind, creating images of monsters lingering in the dark corners that surely sheltered them. Terrified, she blindly followed her mum into the kitchen. She fumbled along the walls, trying to get her bearings. Her hand hit a light switch—*Thank God!*—but when she flipped it, nothing happened. Her mum activated the torch on her phone, making a halo of light around her bright red curls. Selena glanced up the worn, curved staircase to the blackness beyond.

"Are the bedrooms upstairs?" she asked.

Fiona nodded, leading the way. Gray-green moonlight trickled through the windows, throwing long shadows that slithered through the house like eels. Selena reached out to touch the wall as she climbed the staircase. It was wet and gooey as a frog beneath her fingers.

"Yuck! This wall's all slimy," Selena cried. Mildewy air tickled the insides of her nostrils. She sneezed.

"This one here is yours." As they reached the top of the stairs, her mum opened a door and switched on the light. The room blazed yellow. "And I'm over here down the hall." She hugged Selena tightly, enveloping her in a burst of lavender perfume and a cloud of hair.

"I need to be up tomorrow at seven to start my new school," Selena replied, sweeping her hair behind her ears. "I hope I can wake up in time…"

"I'll try to get you up, Pumpkin."

"Maybe I could take the day off? I'm so tired, and I'm not sure I'm going to be able to wake up anyway."

"Don't be silly. Just set an alarm on your phone," Fiona said, kissing her on the cheek.

Selena held her tightly. "Or maybe I could sleep with you, just for tonight?" she asked hopefully.

"No, Dinkums. Not tonight. Buck up now, you'll be fine."

"Aren't we going to change the sheets?" Selena wrinkled her nose at the bed. It looked ancient.

"Ours are in the moving van, so we can't. It's all right. It won't kill you for one night." Fiona gave a big yawn before shutting the door behind her.

Hot tears blurred Selena's vision as she stumbled to the dusty window of her new bedroom. She blinked rapidly, the old clock on the wall creaking with each tick. Only a few more hours until she'd have to walk through the doors of her eighth new school.

Selena's stomach knotted, picturing the curious stares that would follow her down the unfamiliar halls. She was the perpetual outsider, never quite fitting in. She looked down to see her feet stuck fast on the rotting floorboards.

Wringing her clammy hands, her heart pounded faster in the stillness. Selena opened her mouth, but the stale air caught in her throat. The atmosphere clung to her, heavy and close.

She slumped against the cracked window frame, forehead pressing to the cold glass. Outside, rain spat against the window. At least the gloomy weather matched her mood. With a shuddering exhale, Selena watched her breath fog the dirty pane.

Selena's chest constricted as a flood of memories hit her, drawing her back to the fateful day at the beach when she'd been four years old. The waves beckoned to her with their gentle crash against the shoreline, but she knew what lay beneath them—darkness and fear. She closed her eyes and tried to take a deep breath, but it was impossible to quell the rising panic. Images flashed through her mind like an old movie reel: the sand sticking to her feet as she stepped off the beach towel, the sudden rush of cold water engulfing every inch of her body, the desperation to keep herself afloat no matter how hard it seemed. Then, just when all hope seemed lost, a lifeguard showed up, and her lungs filled with sweet air again. Since then, Selena had struggled with crippling panic attacks whenever she found herself near water. Today was no different.

Selena gazed out the second-story window, her eyes tracing the twinkling lights scattered across Madderly Bay below. Although only twelve, she'd already changed schools eight times, never having the chance to make real friends. Would this place be any different? She pondered her fate as her eyes wandered the narrow, moonlit streets curving left toward the sea. The winding row of homes came to a sudden halt at the edge of Aunt Ada's overgrown garden, where the view of the water stretched as far as she could see.

Beyond the tangled shrubs and weeds, the land fell away into darkness with a perilous thirty-foot drop to the rocky shoreline far below. The crumbling seawall ran along the cliff's edge, the only barrier between the garden and the roiling sea.

Selena shivered, remembering her earlier walk along the narrow seawall. One misstep on the slippery surface could easily send someone plunging to their death. The churning ocean waited hungrily, ready to swallow anyone who got too close.

A glint of silver flashed in the churning sea below. Selena's stomach turned, bile rising in her throat. She was suddenly seething. How could her mother have thought living on this cliff above the ocean was a good idea?

"What was she thinking?" Selena mumbled angrily, pulse

pounding as the waves crashed against the rocks. That silver shape flickering in the depths: what was it?

Panic gripped Selena's heart with icy claws. She fumbled desperately for the curtain, pulling it closed to shut out the view. Breath coming in gasps, she stumbled back, hitting the wall.

Selena squeezed her eyes shut, wanting to block it all out. The precarious cliffside, the treacherous seawall, and the roiling abyss that called to her below. She thought of her mother's carefree smile as they'd arrived. How could she be so blind to the danger lurking within the depths?

She tightly wrapped her arms around herself as she glanced around. The pink rosebud wallpaper reminded her of the skirt of a dress in a horror movie she'd seen once. Something bad had happened to the girl wearing that dress. Selena shook off the thought, telling herself she was being silly.

She approached the antique dresser, drawn in by its intricate carvings and elegant design. As she leaned in for a closer look, a putrid odor wafted out from the worn wood. She tentatively opened one of the drawers, only to be greeted by a swarm of silverfish scurrying in every direction. With a shriek, she slammed the drawer shut, her skin crawling with revulsion. Trying to shake off the feeling, she sat on the edge of the creaky bed and ran her hand over the faded quilt. It was soft to the touch, but a musty smell lingered, making her nose wrinkle in disgust. Sighing, she got up to open the window for some fresh air. As she leaned against the sill, gazing out at the moonlit trees, the wind carried a whisper that made her spine tingle.

"You don't belong here..."

Selena whirled around, heart racing, but no one was there. She slammed the window shut and dove under the moth-eaten covers.

Despite being weary from her travels, hunger plagued her. Selena got out of bed and rooted through her suitcase until her fingers closed around a chocolate bar buried deep. She tore off the wrapper and wolfed down the candy, letting its sweetness bring comfort for a moment.

The bathroom was dingy, with chipped white tiles and a flaky pedestal sink. Selena brushed the chocolate from her teeth and stared at her reflection in the spotted mirror. Her face looked tired, and her skin was almost translucent. She looked as ghostly as this old house felt. A shudder ran through her as she flicked off the light and hurried back to her room.

She checked under the covers for spiders and, satisfied there was nothing there, switched off the light and climbed into bed. The mattress was lumpy yet soft, shaped by years of use. She sucked on her hair—even redder than her mother's—but it tasted bitter and salty, like the sea.

Outside, the wind whistled through twisted branches that scraped the windowpane. Their shapes in the moonlight made her think of claws. Selena pulled the musty pillow over her head but still heard the house creaking.

Anxieties scurried through her brain like cockroaches. Would this strange, new house ever feel like home?

Selena wished she could talk to her dad. He had always been able to calm her nerves. But her parents had divorced six years ago, and now her dad lived across the ocean in America with his new family. Whenever Selena called him, his fussy twins squalled in the background. He'd say, "Let's chat later," promising to fly her out for a visit, but it never happened.

Curling into a tight ball under the covers, Selena tried to warm herself against the chill of missing her father. Eventually, exhaustion overtook her, and she drifted into an uneasy sleep.

2

<hr>

SELENA

Selena jerked awake to a knocking at the windowpane. Her pulse hammered in her ears above the sound of heavy rain.

Tap-tap-tap.

An urgent knocking through the dark.

She lay frozen in tangled sheets, straining to see the window through the gloom.

"Let me in," a raspy voice whispered. The hairs on her arms stood on end. "Let me in..."

Heart racing, Selena forced leaden limbs from the bed. The cold floor stung her bare feet as she crept toward the window, still too afraid to look.

Tap-tap-tap.

The frantic knocking grew more insistent.

With trembling hands, she drew back the curtain. Raindrops streaked the glass, but the shadows beyond were impenetrable. What was out there in the storm, beckoning her to let it inside?

The tapping ceased. Selena's breath caught as she searched the blackness for any sign of movement. A lightning bolt illuminated two pale eyes boring into hers before plunging her back into darkness.

She leaped back with a gasp, icy fear flooding her veins. The disembodied voice hissed again beside the glass. "Let me in, Selena..."

Fearfully, Selena ran back to bed, burying herself beneath the covers as she heard scratching on the windowpane.

Tap! Tap! Tap! came louder and more insistent than before.

"Go away!" she screamed, squeezing her eyes shut and praying that whatever it was would be gone.

A piercing screech made Selena freeze. She curled tightly as more cracks and bangs erupted outside.

Where was her mum when she needed her most? Selena realized with dread that her mother had her headphones on, listening to rainforest sounds as she fell asleep like she always did. Selena was alone.

Selena's heart pounded as she stared into the darkness. Had she seen two eyes at the window, or was it just her imagination playing tricks?

Get a grip. It was nothing, just shadows and lightning.

She took a shaky breath. She had almost convinced herself it wasn't real when...

SMASH!

Shattering glass jarred her upright. Icy air prickled her skin as she stared wildly around the dimly lit room, heart lodged in her throat.

What was that? Selena's mind raced as adrenaline flooded her veins. Maybe a tree branch blown by the wind? But the eyes...they had seemed so real, boring into her soul.

She shook her head sharply.

Stop it. There's nothing supernatural out there. You're letting this creepy old house get to you.

But her pep talk did little to slow her thudding pulse. Hugging her knees, Selena strained her ears for any other sounds over the storm. She prayed her mum would wake up and check on her soon. Whatever was out there, real or imagined, she didn't want to face it alone.

The walls of Selena's bedroom quivered, picture frames rattling against the floral wallpaper. Her bedside lamp oscillated wildly, threatening to crash to the floor. Outside, a tree scraped and thumped against the window as it swayed in the wind.

Selena's heart pounded. What was happening? An earthquake?

Then she heard it—the rush of water pouring in through the smashed window. But how? She was on the second floor, far too high for flooding.

Heart in her throat, Selena peered through the darkness. The room was already half filled, icy water rising fast around her bed. Something was splashing about the flooded floorboards.

As she threw aside the sheets and stepped down, fingers

as sharp and cold as icicles closed around her ankle. Selena gasped, heart seizing as a shimmering apparition materialized at the foot of her bed.

"Don't be afraid. I won't hurt you," it rasped. Selena's stomach dropped.

The creature had a girl's face sagging with rot, framed by damaged red curls knotted with seagrass. Its skeletal arms ended in curved talons. But where its legs should be was a long, scaly fishtail, limp and studded with oozing sores.

"Let go!" Selena kicked at its icy grip, pulse pounding in her ears.

She slithered up and perched at the bed's foot, grinning to reveal a mouthful of jagged teeth. "My name's Faustina," she croaked. "Come live with me under the sea... "Don't be afraid. I won't hurt you," it rasped. Selena's stomach dropped.

"No! Get out!" Selena pressed back against the headboard as Faustina crawled closer, tail flicking.

"It won't be so bad." Faustina's pale eyes flashed. "We'll have such fun together. Do you like Scrabble?" She asked casually as if this were a normal sleepover.

Selena's skin crawled at its closeness. There was nothing human left in this being—only a rotten, shimmering husk filled with evil.

Faustina's smile twisted. "Pity," she hissed, talons grasping. "But you don't have a choice..."

Selena opened her mouth to scream, but no sound came out. Faustina's webbed hand clasped over her face, its grip like iron, forcing her down into the freezing black water.

Selena gagged at Faustina's rancid breath. "Leave me alone!"

Faustina's bony fingers dug into Selena's neck, squeezing tighter and tighter as she cackled. Selena's vision blurred as the creature's rotten face loomed above her, filling her with terror. She fought back, hitting at the heavy body on top of her, but Faustina seemed to be made of stone. As tears streamed down her cheeks, Selena tried to scream for help, but every sound was muffled by the suffocating grip on her throat.

3

SELENA

Selena struggled in vain against Faustina's iron grip, the mermaid's snarled red hair whipping her face. Fresh panic surged as Faustina's powerful tail thrashed, making it impossible for Selena to grasp the slippery scales.

Summoning all her strength, Selena grabbed Faustina's wrists and wrenched them apart, breaking the hold. Gasping for air, Selena pulled away from the mermaid's reach.

But Faustina was too quick. Before Selena could push her off, the mermaid lunged forward with lightning speed. Strong hands shot out and grasped Selena's shoulders in a fierce grip.

"What are you doing?" Selena gasped.

"Trying to turn you into a zombie mermaid, duh," Faustina replied, tail flapping.

Selena gasped. "A zombie what?"

"Mermaid. Weren't you listening?" Faustina's eye sockets flickered, glowing in the darkness like red coals. "It'll be fun. We can be BFFs."

"But how did you even get in here?" Selena cried.

"Magic, obviously." As the mermaid grinned Selena noticed her teeth were mossy yellow as well as sharp. "I raised the water level and climbed on in. I've been waiting for you to move in forever."

Selena wrinkled her nose at the rising green water swirling with smelly yellow froth. "Ugh, did you have to break my window, though?"

"Sorry about that." Faustina shrugged. "Had to make an entrance. Anyway, just hold still for a little nibble..."

She lunged toward Selena's neck. Selena shrieked and shoved her back.

"I don't want zombie mermaid rabies!"

Faustina pouted. "It's not rabies. It's a super cool gift." She leaned in. "Although I admit, the fish breath takes some getting used to."

Selena choked on the blast of rancid air. "No offense, but I think I'll pass."

"Aww, don't be like that." The mermaid flapped her tail, splashing Selena with foul water. "We'll swim with dolphins. And our matching hair will look so cute."

Selena had to laugh despite her fear. This was the strangest monster she'd ever met. But those teeth still looked plenty sharp. She had to escape.

"Um, maybe just give me some time to think about it?" She squeaked.

The mermaid clapped excitedly. "Yay, progress. I knew you'd come around."

"I'm begging you, stop the water," Selena choked on the stinky fumes rising from the churning pool. "I'll drown."

"Sorry, hazard of zombie mermaids." Faustina shrugged again. "We tend to make a splash."

With a hissed spell, she stopped the deluge pouring through the shattered window. Selena gasped in relief before meeting the mermaid's glowing stare.

"Thanks for not totally flooding my room. But did you have to break my window?"

"All part of the fun." Faustina cackled. "Now, don't move a muscle. This won't hurt...much."

She bared her mossy teeth and lunged.

"Get away from me!"

Selena recoiled from Faustina's grip, shoving the mermaid back. They grappled and thrashed, equally matched in size and strength. Selena tumbled out of bed, banging her neck against the nightstand's corner.

Faustina pounced, but Selena rolled aside just in time. The mermaid crashed onto the flooded floorboards with a wail. Before Faustina could recover, Selena scrambled up and launched herself forward, shoving Faustina straight through the smashed window into the stormy night.

Pulse racing, Selena yanked the curtains closed. She stood shaking as she listened to the wind and rain, no longer hearing the mermaid's screams. Faustina was gone. For now.

Exhausted from the struggle, Selena carefully made her way back to bed across the glass-strewn floor. She had survived the zombie creature's attack. Bruised and aching, she collapsed onto the mattress. Eyelids heavy, Selena surrendered to sleep, praying for no more horrors that night.

4

SELENA

Selena jolted awake to her mum's voice. "Sweetie! The toaster's busted. Can you fix it?"

Fiona, wearing a blue kimono, waved the appliance. Selena checked her phone. She'd forgotten to set an alarm and was now late for school.

"I don't know how to fix a toaster," she said, hurrying out of bed.

Fiona plucked a strand of seaweed off the curtain rod. "How did this get in here? And why's there glass all over?"

Selena tensed. How could she explain the mermaid attack?

"Maybe the window was hit by lightning?"

Her mum wrinkled her nose. "And what's that smell?"

"Um, just the smell of an old house, I guess," she mumbled. Better not mention murderous sea zombies just yet. "I mean, I bet no one's changed the sheets in ages."

"You look pale, Honey," Fiona fretted, pressing a palm to Selena's clammy forehead.

"Rough night." Selena changed topics. "Did Aunt Ada die in this bed?"

"No, in my room. But it was peaceful, and her last words were, 'Life comes and goes like a wave. The sea shall take me now.'"

"And how do you know? You weren't even here."

"I know, but I sensed it. I do have gifts, you know..."

Selena tuned out her mum's chatter. She had bigger problems than her aunt's demise, like how to avoid becoming fish food for a certain undead she-beast.

Fiona kept rambling about her psychic gifts until Selena interrupted.

"Sorry, Mum, gotta get ready for school." She shooed Fiona from the room and shut the door.

Alone again, Selena eyed the broken window warily. She had a feeling that trouble would return with the tides that night. And she needed a plan before then.

After pulling on her damp uniform, Selena headed down the hall. Sunlight filtered through the stained-glass coat of arms above the front door—a mermaid surrounded by seaweed. Selena shuddered, recalling Faustina's sharp teeth. A worn chandelier dangled from the center of the ceiling, tinkling its ominous melody in the current of air that blew through the room.

Paintings in gold frames hung from the wall, and she hesitated at the top of the curving staircase.

"Is there any food?" she asked.

Fiona didn't seem to hear, preoccupied with the peeling green wallpaper patterned with seashells.

Selena dashed down the stairs. In the kitchen, she slapped together a jam sandwich. Her stomach rumbled.

Fiona wandered in, still holding the broken toaster. "Babycakes, I'm auditioning for a toothpaste ad today," she announced brightly.

Selena just wanted to escape the house. "Good luck. Can you change my sheets?"

"Of course, Sweetie." Fiona fussed with Selena's messy curls. Selena squirmed but enjoyed the brief motherly affection.

Jerking free, she ran into the downstairs bathroom and splashed water on her face, trying to make herself feel a bit more human. But her reflection in the mirror, purple smudges under her green eyes and a sickly hue to her skin was a disaster—no time to fix it.

Fiona met her at the door with an enthusiastic send-off. Selena didn't share her excitement. All she wanted was to avoid mermaids and make it through the day.

"Have fun, Angel," Fiona said. "And make some new friends."

"I don't want new friends," she muttered, hurrying past the portraits of ancestors whose eyes followed her as she fled into the morning light.

SELENA

Selena ran along the coastline with a map to the school on her phone clutched in one hand and her jam sandwich held in the other. Sunbeams bounced off the surface of the sea, dazzling her. She focused on putting the terror of the previous night out of her mind. After all, her day was going to be even more awful. Her curls stuck to her sweaty forehead. The school blouse her mum had bought her from a charity shop was already too tight.

Selena's shoes scuffed against the pavement as she sprinted toward the school. She quickly finished her jam sandwich, tossing the crusts in a nearby bin.

Finally arriving at the main office, Selena was greeted by a woman with green-framed glasses perched on her nose and wild blonde curls framing her face. The woman's lips were coated in a fine layer of sugar from the powdered donut she was munching on.

"Sorry I'm late, it's my first day," Selena panted. "Could you tell me which room I'm supposed to be in? I'm Selena Flowers."

The woman let out an exasperated sigh and slowly set down her donut on a stack of papers. She brushed off her fingers, sending a small snowstorm of sugar flying, before peering at her computer screen and typing in some words. Selena's impatience grew as she waited for a response.

"Okay, follow me."

The donut woman moved slowly. Her high heels looked like they would be excruciating to wear, and she took tiny steps. Maybe because her skirt was a bit too tight. But mainly because she did not seem to be in a hurry to get anywhere. The walls were dim and musty. *Maybe everything near the sea gets tainted by salt. Maybe that's why the bottoms of the walls are streaked with white.* She passed a trophy cabinet jammed full of sports trophies. The names Andrew and Jamie jumped out at her.

"Okay, this is it," she said after they'd plodded up and down the corridors. She pointed at a glass door marked 3B.

Selena took a deep breath and stepped into the classroom. Everyone looked up and stared at her in silence. Then, all at once, they started to laugh.

"Okay, class. That's enough." The teacher turned to Selena with a kind smile and waved her over to an empty chair.

Everyone was still snickering, except the girl in the seat

next to her, whose peachy skin glistened under the harsh overhead light. She had a pointed nose and doe-like eyes that brightened as she looked at Selena.

Giving a reassuring smile, she held back a wave of chestnut hair and whispered, "It's your blouse. It's all covered with jam. I'm Chloe, by the way." She gave a sniff then dabbed a tissue to her nose.

Selena pulled her blazer closed and shrank down in her seat before pushing her hair behind her ears. The morning of Maths and English classes dragged by. Selena tried to melt into her chair while the rest of her classmates snuck glances at her and giggled.

Selena stole a glance at Chloe. She wore the regulation uniform: a burgundy blazer and light-blue shirt that fitted her perfectly. She wore a navy skirt with knee-high socks and flat black shoes, but somehow it looked so put together as if she'd strutted out of a fashion magazine.

Selena sighed, glancing down at her own jam-covered blouse. She didn't know which was going to be worse in Madderly Bay: school or home. A wave of nausea hit her as she thought of the crazed zombie mermaid who might be waiting for her when she got home. Selena had to tell her mum about it. The creature terrified her, and she feared it might return.

6

CHLOE

Chloe watched the new girl, Selena Flowers, who sat beside her. Selena didn't seem to be paying any attention to the teacher's droning voice. Instead, she kept absently twirling the same auburn curl around her finger before letting it spring back into a perfect spiral.

Chloe wondered if Selena was as miserable as she felt in this tiny seaside town. She could hardly believe she'd ended up here, in the middle of nowhere surrounded by fields of swaying grass and cows. The rolling hills were dotted with wildflowers, their golden pollen wreaking havoc on Chloe's allergies.

"Ah-CHOO!" She sneezed loudly for what felt like the hundredth time that day. Living in the countryside meant breathtaking scenery, her mum kept insisting, but Chloe found little beauty through her watering eyes. All she wanted was the busy streets and bustle of friends she'd left behind in the city.

Maybe, just maybe, together, they could find a way to bring some excitement into their lives in this dump by the sea. She decided she'd try to talk to the new girl after class.

When the bell rang for lunch, Chloe made her way through the crowd to catch up with Selena. The cafeteria was adorned with handmade posters announcing upcoming school events taped to the olive-green walls. Fluorescent lights ran across the ceiling, harshly illuminating the rows of long tables lined with uncomfortable orange plastic chairs that had gathered crumbs atop them. Leftover trays of congealed food sat forgotten.

"So, you're new, right?" Chloe asked Selena as the smell of fried fish hit her. Her stomach heaved.

"Yeah, just moved here from London."

It was hard for Chloe to hear Selena over the din of trays being slammed down on tables and the scraping of chairs.

"Me too!" Chloe exclaimed, piling her plate high with mashed potatoes and sausages. "We used to live in Peckham. I loved the hustle and bustle. But Mum said the city was becoming too hectic for her. She longed for a slower pace, so here we are in sleepy old Madderly Bay."

"Don't even get me started. Mum forced me to come to this boring town without even asking how I felt about it," Selena said against the hiss of pop cans being pulled open and shoes squeaking against the floor. "We inherited a house from my great aunt. It's massive, but super scary."

"Like ghosts, you mean?"

"Mm, yeah, maybe. I swear Aunt Ada's portrait watches me," Selena said. "Her eyes follow me everywhere. It's downright spooky."

"Okay, that's weird. But at least it's interesting." Chloe rolled her eyes and sniffed. "My parents just want to live a dull, quiet life here. Bor-ing. We've only been in town a week, and I'm already desperate for some excitement."

As Chloe and Selena wove through the crowded lunchroom, Selena muttered, "Yeah, this place is so tiny and dead, there's nothing to do here."

A girl with blonde hair and a ponytail bounced up to Selena and Chloe. She planted her feet and put her hands on her hips. "Um, I heard that," she said with a frown.

Chloe's eyes drifted to the corner of the girl's mouth where a glob of mayonnaise was stuck. She wrinkled her nose.

Beside her, Selena fidgeted with the hem of her shirt and stared down at her shoes. Her cheeks flushed pink.

"I'm Cindy, resident Madderly expert," the blonde girl announced in her high-pitched voice. "And for your info, Madderly is the sickest place ever."

Chloe glanced at Selena and could tell she was trying not to laugh at the girl's exaggerated enthusiasm.

Oblivious, Cindy kept rambling. "Madderly Academy has the best-looking guys and girls around."

This time Selena couldn't hold back her laughter. She let out an unladylike guffaw.

Cindy's face hardened. "You got a problem with my hometown?" She sputtered angrily.

Wanting to avoid a confrontation, Chloe quickly said, "No, no, Selena just gets the giggles when she's anxious. We didn't mean any offense."

But Cindy stood firm, her hands planted on her hips. "I don't care if you're new here. Diss Madderly again and you'll have me to answer to."

A cheer of "Madderly rocks!" sounded from the ever-growing group of kids who had surrounded them. Chloe clenched her teeth as more kids squeezed closer. Selena pushed her way past through the crowd and sat down at a table.

"Our teachers are the best, and we can party just as hard as anyone from London," Cindy confidently declared.

Selena let out a snort, causing heads to swivel their way.

Cindy whipped around and glared at Selena. "Hey, piggy, did you just snort?" Cindy's abrasive voice reverberated around the room.

Chloe sat next to Selena, mustering a friendly smile. "Look, we're just trying to have lunch. No need to make a scene."

Cindy sneered and turned to Chloe. "I wasn't talking to you, Princess Snooty Pants."

Chloe's gut twisted as Cindy attacked Selena. "I haven't finished with you, piggy."

Helplessly, Chloe watched an athletic boy with a smattering of freckles sidle up to Cindy. His hooded blue eyes scoped out Selena like a hawk zoning in on prey. His dirty-blond hair fell over his forehead in an artfully messy fringe that just brushed his eyebrows.

"You should try being more polite," he said with a smirk. "Cindy doesn't talk to just anyone."

"You tell them, Jamie," Cindy said, giving him a gross smile.

The blob of mayonnaise glistening in the corner of her mouth jiggled when she talked.

"Newbies always get stuffed in the bin on their first day," Cindy said with an evil grin.

Chloe laughed nervously, hoping Cindy was joking. But something told Chloe that Cindy wasn't the joking type.

Suddenly, a new boy pushed his way through the crowd. His tousled dark curls and ears that stuck out gave him a cute, roguish vibe. Though his grin was cocky, Chloe couldn't help but find him appealing.

"Ah, go easy on them, Cindy," he said. "They've still got a lot to learn."

"Dunno about that, Andrew," Cindy said. "They need to learn fast if they don't want to be eating lunch out of the bin."

For a second, Chloe thought Andrew was being nice. But then, he leaned right in Selena's face and blew a huge pink bubble. He popped it right on her nose. The sickly-sweet stench of strawberry flooded Chloe's senses.

Andrew and Cindy both busted up laughing. So much for him being nice. It was all just an act.

Strangely, Selena didn't react to the gum explosion. Chloe watched as she scraped bits of pink goo off her cheeks while everyone roared with laughter.

"Just because you're from London doesn't mean you can be all stuck up," Andrew declared.

"I'm not stuck up," said Selena, pulling a long string of gum from her hair. "I just want to eat lunch in peace."

"Hey, what's that bruise on her neck?" Cindy whooped. Howls of laughter erupted around her. "Been in a fight, piggy?"

Chloe had noticed the bruise, too, but she'd decided not to ask about it. It wasn't any of her business. She rolled her eyes and said, "That's enough, okay?" She wanted to do something to help Selena, but she also didn't want to get in trouble. Especially not on her first day. She glanced around the crowded dining room. Where was a teacher when they needed one?

"What were you in a brawl with? A gorilla?" Cindy taunted, standing close to Selena.

"I didn't fight anyone," Selena said, her eyes welling up. Chloe watched with dread, praying she wouldn't cry. "Just go away."

"Did oink-oink get too close to a lamppost? She must have been lost and wandering, huh?" Cindy continued, eliciting laughter from everyone around them.

"Will you just get lost?" Selena shouted, thrusting out her chin and curling her lips into a sneer.

"Piggy's getting angry. What do you think, Andrew?" said Jamie.

"Stop calling me piggy!" Selena yelled.

"Well, you're round like a pig. Oink, oink," Andrew said, and Jamie joined in.

Relief flooded through her, as Chloe saw a teacher striding toward them. He didn't look too pleased as Selena blurted, "Well, you could stand to lose a few pounds off your ears, Andrew. They look like satellite dishes."

"Shhh," Chloe hissed, kicking Selena under the table. "A teacher's coming."

Selena ignored her. She jumped up and screeched, "Dumbo! Dumbo the elephant," into Andrew's face.

"Alright, settle down!" bellowed the teacher as he marched over. He was tall and spindly, like a daddy longlegs in khaki pants and a tie. But it was the horrendous brown toupee perched crookedly on his head that drew the eye. It looked like a fuzzy woodland creature had crawled up there and died.

"I'm Mr. Bottomley, the headmaster," he announced in his reedy voice. "And I will not tolerate any tomfoolery at Madderly Academy!"

Chloe had to stifle a laugh at the irony of a man named Mr. Bottomley with a deceased rodent on his head scolding them about misbehavior. She could already tell this school was going to be anything but dull with characters like this around.

Chloe glanced at him, unsure whether to stare at his beady eyes behind thick glasses or the matted creature above them. "Nice to meet you, sir," she managed weakly.

"Can anyone tell me what is causing this disruption?" Mr. Bottomley said.

"They started it," said Andrew.

"We did not," said Chloe. "They keep making fun of us."

"Well, cut it out," said Mr. Bottomley. "I don't want to hear another word out of any of you. Just finish your lunch quietly, everyone." Mr. Bottomley harrumphed.

"Yes, sir," Cindy said.

His toupee slipped sideways, and he hastily adjusted it. He hurried away, his hairy companion still clinging on for dear life.

Chloe hoped that was the end of it, but before Mr. Bottomley had even left the lunch hall, Jamie reached out to touch the tip of Chloe's nose.

"You have an awfully long nose. Did anyone ever tell you that? Are you a witch?"

"I'm not a witch," said Chloe, narrowing her eyes at him.

Jamie smacked his palms downwards, flicking her tray up into the air so it landed in Chloe's lap.

"She's just too… uh… beautiful for the likes of us," said Andrew. Cindy glared at him. A blush stained Andrew's face. "I mean… too snooty. Yeah, too snooty for the likes of us," he said as he looked at the ground.

"Who do you think you are?" Cindy snapped. "Prancing around like you own the place…"

Chloe balled her hands into fists under the table. She took a slow, deep breath, trying to keep her rising temper in check.

"Back off Cindy," Chloe snapped.

Kids crowded around them, pressing in on their lunch table.

"You make quite a pair," screeched Cindy. "Porky Pig and Princess Snooty Pants."

"Don't you ever call her that again," Chloe hissed, standing up with the remainder of her tray. "Come on, Selena. I'm done listening to this."

"You don't want to mess with me, princess," Cindy snarled. "I own this school."

Chloe stepped even closer, eyes blazing. "Try me, Mayo Lips."

The spectators erupted into laughter.

Cindy's face turned red. "W-what did you just call me?" she sputtered.

The laughter swelled even louder. Cindy looked around in embarrassment as people pointed at the incriminating evidence.

"I think the name fits you perfectly," Chloe said with a smug smile.

Cindy clenched her fists, utterly humiliated. The crowd was now completely on Chloe's side, hooting and hollering.

"You'll regret this!" Cindy shouted as she turned and pushed her way through the jeering students.

Chloe watched her flee then turned to Selena with a triumphant grin. Maybe this town wouldn't be so boring after all.

7

CHLOE

"You're not fat," Chloe said, blowing her nose as they left the dining hall. "They're just upset because we're treading on their turf."

"That's easy for you to say. You're so pretty. I mean, do you have any problems at all?" Selena asked as she threw her hands up in exasperation.

Chloe sighed. Selena had no idea. "Well, honestly, my mum's a nightmare. She never leaves me alone."

"That doesn't sound so bad."

"Does your mum text you fifty times a day? Does she track your phone?"

"No, but—"

"Then you can't say it's not so bad."

"But at least your mum cares," Selena remarked.

"All mums care. They're supposed to."

Selena sighed. "I guess my mum does care a bit, but she

cares *more* about being an actress. I mean, she's like ancient, and she's still trying to catch her big break." Selena shrugged. "Maybe she needs a reality check."

"Oh, that sounds amazing," said Chloe. "I want to be an actress, but my mum wants me to be something boring like a doctor or a lawyer. She goes on about it whenever I tell her I want to act." She made a face. "Hey, what's your mum's name? Maybe I've heard of her."

"Fiona Flowers. But you won't have heard of her. The only thing you might have seen her in is a commercial where she's a crazy magician. She waves her wand and creates this ice cream called Sugar Shimmer."

"Oh, yes. I know it. It's that ice cream with edible glitter in it." She put on the same cheeky voice used in the advert and whooped, "It's glitter and fun and oh, so yum!"

"Well, believe me, one advert for Sparkle Delight does not pay the bills. I wish she'd get a normal job."

"I reckon you should always follow your dreams."

"I guess," Selena said. "By the way, you were amazing back there. Mayo Lips!" Selena chuckled. "I don't know how I would've coped with all that otherwise. Except, well, I went off on one. I do that a lot. I don't know how you kept your cool. I would have punched Cindy."

"Ha-ha. I pretend to be nice then stick in the knife later, I guess. Anyway, I'm not that nice. Sometimes, I feel like I'm going crazy with my mum watching me all the time." She cleared her throat. "And honestly, I think Andrew's kind of cute."

"But he has Dumbo ears."

"I guess."

"And he's a jerk."

"You're right. Maybe we should try getting back at them a different way."

"But how?" asked Selena.

"We'll think of something. And now it's your turn to dish. Where did you get that bruise?"

Selena paused for a beat then blurted, "I just collided with a lamppost, that's all."

"Oh yeah… that's a likely story." Chloe giggled.

"I did," Selena said.

Watching the other kids come outside after lunch, Chloe felt like she was an alien who'd never be accepted by them. She sneezed into her elbow.

"My allergies have gotten worse since I got here."

"What are you allergic to?" Selena asked, tucking her hair behind her ear.

"Cats, pollen, dust, but my shellfish allergy is the worst… Come on," she said to Selena, pulling her to the far end of the schoolyard and looking out over the railing to the sea. It was a long way down from there. Chloe shifted her gaze to the road instead.

"No way…" she said as she caught sight of a familiar face.

"What is it?" Selena asked, looking around.

Chloe gestured to the car parked across the road.

"That's my mum's car," she said, pointing at a blue Volvo. "She just can't leave me alone."

A neatly dressed woman got out of the car and hurried

across the road, right over to them.

"Mum, please. What are you doing here?" Chloe asked. She glanced back and saw Andrew and the rest watching them.

"I was so worried about you. I decided to see how you were getting on. You weren't responding to my texts."

"We can't text at school," Chloe mumbled.

"Well, I figured parents were an exception," her mum responded brightly. "Who's your friend?"

Chloe's face burned. She knew all her classmates were watching her. "I wish you hadn't come. The way you check up on me all the time is embarrassing." She heard Andrew and Cindy snicker, or maybe she'd imagined it.

Her mum's face crumpled, and Chloe reproached herself for losing her cool. "I was worried about you."

The bell rang. Chloe grabbed Selena's arm.

"Gotta go," she said, turning away from her mum. It was a relief to head back inside the school.

8

SELENA

When school let out, Selena saw Chloe's mum take her arm and lead her to the car. She didn't envy that kind of mother, but part of her wished *her* mum had showed up for her first day.

Selena dawdled along the seafront, avoiding going home. She had way bigger problems than the mean kids at school. Sure, Cindy and her crew had made fun of Selena and called her names. But that was nothing compared to the zombie mermaid who had tried to bite her. So, dealing with school bullies like Cindy suddenly seemed insignificant. Selena would gladly take name-calling over neck-biting any day. At least human bullies couldn't turn you into the living dead.

She peered into the placid water, wondering if the mermaid lurked below. A flash of scales made her spine tingle. Was that her?

What if the mermaid returned tonight? Selena considered finding a weapon just in case. Though repelled by the monster, she was also curious. If they met again, she might ask questions to understand Faustina better. How lonely was her existence underwater? Was there a cure for her condition?

Mostly, Selena hoped the mermaid stayed away for good. She was lonely, too, but not desperate enough to become an undead sea creature's companion. There had to be a better way to make living, human friends.

Selena sighed, dragging her feet as she finally turned toward home.

She walked up to the old house.

Ugh, I wish the roof tiles would stop watching me.

Inside, beyond the entry hall, the long, dark corridor's wallpaper peeled back to reveal a horrid shade of dark purple. A picture of Great Aunt Ada in her younger days hung among the portraits of her relatives in ornate gold frames. Selena had never met her aunt in person, but she'd seen her in photos. She recognized her pointy, determined chin, her red hair set in waves, and a magnificent gold necklace studded with bright rubies at her throat.

Fiona appeared beside her. "Beautiful, wasn't she?"

"Yeah." Selena peered at the painting. "That's quite a necklace."

"Yes, I remember Aunt Ada wearing it when she was alive."

"What happened to it? Did Aunt Ada leave it to you?"

Fiona laughed, turning toward her. "Alas, no. A shame since it looks like it might be worth a few quid. She sold all the most valuable things before she died. Luckily, she did leave me some of that money. So, I can pay for food and electricity… for a little while, anyway. She gave the rest of her money to a cat charity—would you believe? And now all that's left is just piles of junk." Over her shoulder, Selena watched as Aunt Ada's eyeballs spun around quickly before they came to a standstill.

Selena gasped then glanced at a painting beside it. A man with a long, greenish face and shadowy eyes peered out at her. A sneering ginger cat sat at his feet. Suddenly, the cat gave a meow, and Selena jumped. Then it turned its head the other way and hissed while the man's eyelids fluttered up and down, making the sound of squeaky bed springs.

Suppressing a shiver, Selena spun around to her mum.

"Did you hear that?" She burst out, her heart thumping hard in her chest, but her mum had moved away.

"Hear what? Oh, you've got to see the living room. It's horrid. Come on." She led Selena into another grand room, also papered with terrible wallpaper. This one was made up of lurid green and yellow stripes. Selena still wasn't sure if she'd imagined the meow. This house was driving her crazy with all its disruptive sounds. "Look at this mess." Fiona gestured to some peacock feathers arranged in a vase, weighed down by dust. "I have to get these out of here."

"Why?"

"You know very well that peacock feathers are bad luck!"

"Really?"

"Yes, I can't have them anywhere near me when I'm in a theater."

"But you're not in a theater."

"I know, but they could still derail my acting career," she said, grabbing the feathers and throwing them down on the sofa.

Selena sighed. She couldn't keep track of all the superstitions that ruled her mum's life.

"And I really need to get these out of here." Fiona gestured to an ancient gramophone on the side table and piles of dusty books that were piled up to the ceiling. "I'm going to hire a skip to get rid of most of these things."

"Good idea," said Selena, running her finger through the dust on the gramophone. "There's just way too much old stuff around here."

"You know, I love this place, but today I sensed some evil spirits hanging about." She picked up a bundle of dried sage leaves and lit it from a candle that was flickering on the mantlepiece.

Selena grabbed her mum's sleeve. "I know! I told you this place was creepy as soon as we got here."

"Now, Sweetcheeks, I know this old house has some rather troublesome spirits rattling about," Fiona said. "But let me tell you, no pesky poltergeist will put a damper on our good fortune."

She waved a bundle of smoking sage around like a magic wand. The aroma reminded Selena of summer bonfires, though it made her cough.

"Off with you, phantoms!" Fiona cried in a singsong

voice, waving the sage to and fro. She danced through the halls, Selena trailing behind.

At each new room, Fiona cleared her throat. "Begone, bothersome ghosts," she declared with a flick of her wrist. Sage smoke swirled fancifully.

Selena stifled giggles as her eccentric mum shooed away the spirits with dramatic flair. She waltzed and twirled as if performing a ritual dance.

By the time they were back in the living room, Selena felt lighter. Perhaps Fiona's spell had worked—or at least, her childlike delight was contagious.

Fiona sank onto the sofa, beaming. "This house belongs to us joyful souls now." She gave Selena a playful wink. "Let those gloomy ghosts haunt somewhere else. Our future here sparkles bright."

Selena smiled back. With Fiona's whimsical approach to life, maybe this old house didn't seem so creepy anymore.

"Anyway, how was your day? How'd the audition go?" Selena asked, hovering beside the sofa.

Dropping the still smoking sage into the vase vacated by the feathers, Fiona pulled open a book and read out the title. "*The Myths of the Deep, Blue Sea.* Now doesn't that sound riveting?" Still looking down at the book, she said, "Oh, the audition went fabulously. I think I aced it."

"That's great," Selena said carefully. Maybe her mum had aced it, but Selena wouldn't count on anything until they knew for sure. She was used to her mother's overabundance of confidence, even though she rarely booked any acting jobs.

"Yes, once I start earning again, we might be able to buy a car. Wouldn't that be nice?" She flicked through the pages.

"I guess." She didn't think it was going to happen; she had heard it all before. "Mum, something weird happened last night," Selena began, fidgeting with her hair. "Someone came into my room last night."

"Oh, heavens!" Her Mum cried, jumping up from the sofa. "An intruder? We must call the police at once."

"No, it wasn't a person," Selena said. "It was...a zombie mermaid."

"Blimey!" Mum said, her eyebrows shooting up. "A zombie mermaid? In our house? That's bonkers."

Selena blinked, confused by her mum's odd reaction. "You're not freaked out?"

Mum shook her head with an amused laugh as she plopped down on the couch. "I can't believe a zombie mermaid would have the nerve to show up here. What did they look like?"

"Well, she looked rough," Selena explained. "Her face was all melted."

"Well, obviously." Fiona waved her hand impatiently. "She's a zombie. But what else?"

"She had red hair —"

Her mother's eyes lit up. "I'm sorry you had to meet Faustina. She always was a troublemaker."

Selena's mouth fell open. "Who is she?" She asked, sitting beside her mum.

There was a pot of tea and a pile of chocolate biscuits on

the low table in front of them. Selena bit into a biscuit, but it felt like sand, so she put it back on her plate.

"Oh, Honeybunch. Where do I even begin?" Fiona said, filling two cups with tea. She wrapped her arms around Selena and hugged her tight. "I don't want to upset you any more than you already are. Maybe it would be best if you don't know."

Selena ran her tongue over her lips, but they stayed dry. "It's okay. Who is this crazy mermaid?"

"Actually...she's related to you."

Selena gawked in shock. That wasn't something she'd expected.

9

____

FAUSTINA

Far below the surface, Faustina hovered amongst jagged rocks, the eerie glow of bioluminescent tube worms and anemones lighting her scowling face. She tore a glowing pink flower from the seafloor in anger, grinding its petals between her bony fingers.

How dare Selena refuse her invitation to join her zombie squad. Didn't she realize it was an honor to be handpicked by Faustina?

No need to brush your hair or teeth down here—just drift along with the currents living your creepiest, kookiest life. Who cares about chores when you can be partying with pirates and sea monsters all day and night?

Snooping about Aunt Ada's old house had been thrilling. After so many years underwater, Faustina was curious to poke around the surface world again. But prickly Selena was no fun at all.

Faustina reminisced about her childhood in Madderly, back when she was alive. She shared a tiny, twig-woven cottage with her twin sister, Starona, more than four hundred years ago. They'd stay up giggling under the covers then race at dawn to milk their goat, Nutty. Her human parents were hazy memories now, but Starona's sunny smile remained etched in her mind. Because Faustina had turned into a zombie at twelve, she would always remain the same age.

Alas, zombie brains tended to get foggy. Lately, Faustina struggled to recall their childhood antics, or how they became mermaids. All she knew was they'd been insepara-ble...until that fateful day long ago.

Nearby, Aunt Ada perched on a spiky rock, absently petting a purple squid with patches of gold on its back. Her frail form was hunched with age even in death. Faustina sighed, feeling suddenly lonely. If only Selena would be her new friend. Together, they could explore both land and sea, a twosome of whimsy and adventure.

"What are you doing with that ugly thing?" Faustina grumbled, pointing at the squid. It turned bright red in offense.

"Why, it's going to be my new pet," Aunt Ada declared. "I'm trying to think up the perfect name. Hmm, what do you call a man with cat scratches on his head?"

"I don't have time for games," Faustina snapped.

"Claude!" Aunt Ada proclaimed with a laugh. The squid made a face. "Oh wait, I think this one's a lady. So, what's a woman with one leg longer than the other? Eileen!"

The squid stuck out its tongue in disgust.

"Ugh, even that dumb blob hates your awful puns," Faustina fumed.

"No need to get crabby, dear," Aunt Ada replied lightly.

Faustina huffed. "I just came to see how you're settling in down here."

"Oh dear, I do miss my old house terribly," Aunt Ada croaked as she stroked the grumpy squid. "Having a nice chat with friends, snuggling dear Mr. Wiggums, using my lovely teapots, especially that chipped yellow one. This gloomy underwater life is a tricky adjustment, I must say."

"Yes, that is a bummer," Faustina spoke with a hint of annoyance in her voice as she swam up to Aunt Ada. Her face was full of wrinkles and aged spots, framed by pale blue eyes. Miniature yellow fish swarmed around the falling skin flakes from her decaying cheeks. "I'm your friend, aren't I?"

"It's not the same," Aunt Ada said wistfully as the squid wrapped its legs affectionately around her neck.

"I don't want to hear it." *How could she be so ungrateful?* Faustina paused before taking a deep breath. "Well, I went to visit your lousy house the other day, and Selena's living there with her mum."

"How wonderful," Aunt Ada exclaimed, a smile spreading across her wrinkled face as she leaned forward eagerly. "Tell me, how is Fiona getting on these days?"

"I didn't get a chance to meet her. Selena shoved me out the window."

Aunt Ada gave a tinkly giggle.

"It's not funny," Faustina said, anger rearing up as she swam in circles around Aunt Ada.

Faustina did a flip into the bright orange sand at the bottom of the ocean. The zombie merkingdom at Madderly Bay was crawling with other zombie mermaids just like her. The place was saturated with their magic, turning the once frigid sea into a warm and glowing oasis, and the sand a radioactive shade of orange. It made her mad that no one seemed to understand her desire for a friend. She reached out into the warm sand, surrounded by the magical energy of her fellow zombie mermaids. The water glowed orange from all their combined power.

"Recently, I don't know what's happening, but I just can't recall a lot of things." Faustina said sadly.

"Maybe I can fill in the gaps?" Aunt Ada offered.

"I mean… I sort of remember falling out of my dad's boat with Starona and—"

"You hit a patch of magical water, and you turned into mermaids. What about it?"

"Ugh, I don't remember the specifics," Faustina grumbled with a shake of her head, auburn curls swirling around her mottled face. "I know Starona and I used to sit on the rocks, singing and combing our hair to lure sailors to their doom—you know, typical siren stuff. But the details are foggy."

She scowled, racking her mushy zombie brain for memories. An image of the wizard pirate Zlotan's angry, sunburnt face flashed in her mind, igniting her temper.

Why had he cursed her and Starona, turning them from

mermaids to zombie mermaids hundreds of years ago? Then it hit her. "Damn Zlotan!" she cried. She could see his gap-toothed sneer as he screamed curses at them. Faustina quickly shook the memory away. Dwelling on the past was pointless. Today was for doing.

"Bah, who cares how it happened?" she declared with a nonchalant flick of her shimmering tail. "I happen to adore being a zombie mermaid, even if I can't recall all the grisly details."

"Do you? Do you really?" Aunt Ada asked, squinting through milky eyes. Her knitting needles clicked.

"Of course!" Faustina declared with overblown bravado. "Who wouldn't relish aimless drifting and making new friends to nibble on?"

"Hmm, I'm not convinced, kiddo," Aunt Ada replied gently. "Mostly, it's just us ghouls, the fish, and the occasional bored sea toad passing by."

Faustina's shoulders slumped. It was true. Her underwater kingdom was achingly lonesome at times.

"Here, have you tried knitting?" Aunt Ada suggested, holding up a lumpy square of algae yarn. "It really passes the time."

Faustina grimaced. "No thanks, I'll leave the knitting to you."

"I'm making a sweater for my squid."

The squid beamed.

"That'll mean making ten armholes. Don't you have anything better to do?" Faustina said, agitated.

Aunt Ada grinned mischievously. "Well, now, you've

given me a thought. Perhaps I'll call her Decima, since it means tenth in Latin. She does have eight arms and two tentacles. Oh, and this just came to me—cats should be stopped from swallowing wool. Otherwise, they might accidentally end up having mittens."

Faustina groaned. "Oh, aren't you the punniest." She wasn't in the mood for Aunt Ada's lame jokes.

Faustina gazed at the half-finished walls of her underwater dream house in the distance. "I've been trying to build a replica of your house, you know. But it's slow going on my own."

"Sorry, I can't see too well without my glasses. I've lost them somewhere."

"It's hard work. I'm building it from rock and bits of coral. It's just taking a long time. Getting it to all hold together is the worst."

"Why not ask the other zombie mermaids for help?"

Faustina scowled. "Those lazybones? Useless, the lot of them. I was hoping to get Selena to join us down here. But she's a party pooper."

"You'll have to be patient." Aunt Ada's needles clicked away as she knitted, the squid nestled comfortably against her tail.

Faustina envied their closeness. When would she find a companion of her own? Doing everything alone was terribly dreary. She longed for someone to explore the ocean's wonders with, to share laughs and secrets. Each passing day of solitude gnawed at her, like the fish nibbling away at Aunt Ada's damaged tail.

"But I need a friend," Faustina pleaded, rocketing upwards in frustration. "It's no fun doing everything on my own."

Faustina gazed sadly as Aunt Ada peered through the eerie yellow glow of the water. Below them lay scattered bones of fish and even humans, remnants of lives lost.

"Chin up, you'll find a friend eventually," Aunt Ada replied, seeming not to grasp Faustina's profound loneliness. She then added, "I'd fancy a nice cuppa and some ginger cake right now."

Faustina was fond of Aunt Ada but transforming her into an eternal underwater companion was backfiring fabulously. The woman was a downer. All she did was bang on about her cat, Mr. Wiggums, and her teapot collection. *Hello, you've got the whole ocean to explore now, Aunt A!* But instead, it was "Oh, I wish I had some ginger cake" this and "Does this seaweed scarf bring out my glassy eyes?" that.

Honestly, it was enough to make Faustina want to rip out her own hair...seaweed...whatever flowed from her scalp these days. Aunt Ada was raining on her creepy, undead parade. Couldn't she see the goopy glass as half full? There were pirate shipwrecks to plunder, great white sharks to befriend, Atlantis myths to unravel.

But noooo, Aunt Ada just had to keep moping about her former land-loving life. Faustina made a mental note: for her next recruitment, try finding an adventurous spirit. Less likelihood of them turning into a whiny wet blanket.

"There isn't any cake. Here, try some snail crunches,"

Faustina said, slurping one down. "Mmm, yummy yellow goo."

"I'm not so sure, love... Being undead has rather ruined my appetite," said Aunt Ada, making a face as she clicked her knitting needles. "But I suppose I'll give it a go." She popped a snail in her mouth. Her eyes widened and she spat it out at once. "Ugh! Disgusting."

10

SELENA

"You've got to be kidding me!" Selena exclaimed, unable to believe she was related to a zombie mermaid. "Is this really happening? Am I going to turn into one of them?"

"Well, no. Not unless she bites you," her mother replied.

"But that's what she tried to do." Selena shuddered as she raked her hair behind her ears. "We've got to get out of here."

"How peculiar, though," Fiona said, chewing on her bottom lip. "Aunt Ada used to tell me all about zombie mermaid lore when I was a kid, and it really freaked me out. It's basically a family secret that we pass down through generations. But I don't remember her saying anything about zombie mermaids coming up onto dry land."

"It wasn't dry. She made the whole sea rise. She smashed the window so the water could come in. I almost drowned.

Why did you never tell me about her?" Selena stared at her mum, trying to take everything in.

"I suppose I never thought I'd need to tell you," Fiona replied with a dramatic sigh. "Zombie mermaids hardly ever leave the ocean, so it didn't seem relevant. But Faustina has always been rather peculiar."

"That's an understatement," Selena said, adding extra sugar to her cup of tea.

"Well," Fiona replied, delicately sipping her tea, "Faustina was a pleasant enough zombie mermaid, for the most part. Aunt Ada told me she used to be very close with her twin sister, Starona."

"So, what happened?"

Fiona dipped a chocolate biscuit into her tea. "Oh darling, the most dreadful thing!" Fiona exclaimed, popping the biscuit in her mouth. "Poor Starona was eaten by a shark, simply ghastly. And Faustina, she did not handle the tragedy well at all. She started lashing out at the other zombie mermaids, even those they had created together."

"What do you mean, 'created'?"

"Bitten, or infected, of course." Fiona paused and leaned back on the sofa. "What did she say to you?"

Selena's head was spinning. "She said she wanted to be friends, but she also tried to bite me," Selena told her mother, pulse racing with fear.

Fiona let out an exaggerated sigh, shaking her head. "Okay, Buttercup, I admit I may have miscalculated things. I knew there was some risk in coming here, but I thought it would work out swimmingly."

Selena's mind reeled, struggling to process all these strange revelations. She jumped up and placed her hands firmly on her hips, staring her mother down. "Do you have anything else you want to tell me?"

"No, not right now," Fiona said with a warm smile. "Honey bunny," she purred, "you're freaked out, so I reckon this is all you need to know for now."

"All I need to know? *All I need to know!*" Selena could feel her voice rising as anger bubbled up inside. "Mum, a zombie mermaid was in my bedroom last night. I think I deserve to know everything."

Why is she still keeping secrets? This is my life, too! I have a right to know the truth.

"And you will, in good time," Fiona replied calmly.

Selena sat down with a huff, glaring at her infuriatingly cryptic mother. She took a deep breath, trying to slow her racing heart.

"But what if she comes back?" Selena demanded. *Surely, Mum understands how terrifying this is for me. I need answers now.*

"Well, hopefully she won't," Fiona said gently, squeezing Selena's shoulders. "But just to be on the safe side, how about you sleep in my room tonight?"

"No thanks," Selena snapped, crossing her arms.

She was still fuming inside over her mother's secrecy. The thought of sleeping curled up next to Fiona like a child made Selena's anger flare hotter.

I'm not a little kid anymore. I can handle this on my own. She didn't need her mother's coddling and half-truths.

Fiona looked taken aback. "But darling, it's not safe

alone in your room. What if Faustina comes back in the night?"

"I'll be fine," Selena said curtly, avoiding her mother's worried gaze.

She stood up, signaling an end to the conversation. *Let Mum worry all she wants. I don't need her protection. Not when she treats me like a naive child.*

"Please don't be mad at me. Why don't we try to focus on sorting this place out? It's a lot for me to do on my own." Fiona gestured at the mess around them. Selena noticed the toaster on a side table with screws and a screwdriver beside it. "You could help me go through all this, Honey Bunny."

"Can't. Homework. But I promise I'll look at the toaster later. And stop calling me Honey Bunny!"

"Oh, one more thing, I keep finding handwritten little notes in the cupboards," said Fiona. She held up a pink page torn from a notebook and read, "What do you say when you want a kiss from a flower? Plant one on me. Sounds like Aunt Ada. She was obsessed with puns. Is that meant to mean something?"

"No idea," Selena said before escaping to her room.

She dumped her books on the now-dry bed. Her mum had changed the sheets, but the stench of death still hung in the room. She drew the curtains and flopped down on the bed.

Selena froze as the wallpaper rippled, green scales scuttling upwards like an army of insects. Selena inhaled sharply, pulse thrumming. She grazed the scales with tentative fingers. Razor edges sliced her skin. Beads of crimson welled up, the coppery taste flooding her mouth as she worried her bottom lip.

She stared, transfixed, as the scales continued their crackling ascent. The rosebuds on the paper writhed, vines constricting around the glittering green. Thorny stems twisted and stretched before receding back into the floral pattern.

As she peered closer, a flash of movement behind the scales caught her eye. Two milky white orbs stared back at her, clouded in death yet somehow seeing. With horror, Selena realized they were the disembodied eyes of a mermaid, its decaying flesh wedged between the scales. As she watched, transfixed in terror, the mermaid's jaw dislocated with a wet pop. Gray lips parted in a soundless scream, revealing jagged teeth frozen mid-snarl. Selena gasped and involuntarily bit her lip hard enough to draw blood. Crimson welled up as the metallic taste flooded her mouth. Hands trembling, she withdrew them, worrying her bottom lip at the grisly remnants of the zombie mermaid hiding amongst the scales.

Selena's tongue probed the cut on her lip, the pain blossoming. She glanced down. Crimson dotted her trembling fingertips. The wallpaper looked as sweet and pastoral as before, its momentary transformation erased.

Or had she imagined it all? This house was sinking its tendrils into her mind, poisoning her thoughts...

She shook her head sharply. No. It was real. There was something sinister lurking beneath the quaint exterior of this place.

And when she thought it couldn't get any worse, a high-pitched, breathless voice started whispering in her ear. "You don't belong. You don't belong." Who on earth was that? Another of the ghosts that lived in the house along with the moving paintings?

She put her hands up over her ears, but the voice kept repeating the same words over and over.

"Shut up!" She shouted, but the voice had tapped into her deepest fear. She didn't belong anywhere. Never had. Her dad had deserted her. They'd never settled anywhere, and she couldn't rely on her mum. And now even the house was rejecting her. Terrorizing her and trying to drive her away. Would she ever find a place she could call home? The voice rang tinny in her ears before fading away to a crackle.

Selena's insides knotted, bile burning her throat. Faustina's face flickered in her mind. Those flaming red locks an echo of her own, the sharp point of her chin a mirror of Selena's. Her gut twisted further at the thought.

They shared blood. This horror was family.

Selena pictured Faustina's murky eyes, sunken shadows where life once flickered. Hollow pools staring back at her, reflecting her future. How long did creatures like Faustina endure? Centuries? Forever?

Selena needed to know more, understand what cursed blood ran through her veins. But Faustina's ugly face swam before her eyes, hungry and cunning. She would return. She would sink her rotting teeth into Selena's flesh, inject her poison.

Selena's hands trembled as she envisioned her body

bloating, skin mottling gray, joints twisting. Becoming one of them—forever hunting warm-blooded prey. Trapped in a nightmare that never ended.

She wrapped her arms around herself, digging her fingernails into her soft flesh. It was not too late. Faustina had not won yet. But Selena could feel her out there in the dark depths, patiently waiting to finish what she'd started.

11

SELENA

The past week had been agony. Each night Selena tossed and turned, listening for any sound of Faustina returning. Her nails were bitten down to the quick with anxious waiting.

But as day after fearful day passed with no sign of the zombie mermaid, Selena finally began to relax. Maybe Faustina had given up. The smashed window was repaired, new bedding bought to banish bad memories.

Selena fell into a routine with her mum: microwave dinners, struggling through homework, meditative chanting and reiki sessions on the couch. During those peaceful moments, Selena considered asking more about their twisted family history. But no, better to pretend none of it had happened.

Still, it was a dark secret to keep. She had to tell someone normal, like her new friend, Chloe.

As they drifted towards the end of the schoolyard after lunch, all eyes followed confident Chloe while Selena shrank out of sight.

Selena stopped and gripped the schoolyard railings so hard her knuckles turned white. She took a deep breath and tried to calm her nerves. "I need to tell you something," she said, looking out at the choppy sea.

In her head, she practiced what she wanted to say: "The first night I was in Madderly something scary happened. I was asleep in bed when..."

But as soon as she opened her mouth, her words got all jumbled up.

"What?" Chloe seemed more interested in checking her manicure than listening to Selena's story.

"Never mind," Selena mumbled, feeling flustered and starting to cough.

A gray shape sliced through the waves and Selena jumped, Faustina's pale face flashing in her memory. The past week's terror came rushing back.

Chloe offered her a bottle of water, eyebrows raised questioningly. Selena met her eyes and took a gulp.

"Doesn't this place give you an odd feeling lately? Like something's not right?"

"Not really," Chloe replied, sounding puzzled.

I'm only confusing her more. Selena wracked her brain for the right words. "Then what do you make of that?" She nodded at the gray fin in the surf.

"Probably a shark," Chloe replied with a shrug.

Selena lowered her voice. "But what if it's—"

"Hey Porky!" Andrew called out tauntingly as he strode towards them.

Selena frowned at the hurtful name. Before she could react, Chloe cut in sharply, "Don't call her that."

Andrew rolled his eyes. "Alright, alright. I was just joking around." He turned back to

Selena. "Can't believe you haven't heard about the shark sightings in the bay this week. It's been hanging around but it's not going to do anything. Just thought you'd like to know."

"We've all heard the rumors," Chloe replied coolly. She placed a reassuring hand on Selena's arm. "Everybody knows about it. My mum never stops warning me not to go for a swim unless I want to get eaten."

"But how do they know it's a shark?" Selena asked. "Because I bet you it isn't."

"What is it then?" asked Chloe.

"Something worse," Selena blurted, her voice filled with a hint of fear.

"What could be worse?" Andrew said, scrunching up his face. "Not that I'm afraid of sharks," he mumbled, blushing and avoiding eye contact with Chloe.

Selena leaned against the cool metal railings, her eyes fixed on the sea. The sun's rays danced on the ripples, creating a mesmerizing display of light. The waves were gently lapping against the sea wall below, a soothing melody in her ears. Andrew and Chloe's voices blended with the sound of seagulls calling overhead. A rush of salty ocean air filled her lungs, mingling with the scent of seaweed.

"What do you want?" She yelled, her voice quivering with fear as she saw the gray fin flick up leaving a spray of water. It had to be Faustina, the terrifying zombie mermaid who haunted her dreams. Selena was frozen in terror, unable to move as she realized Faustina was not just a nightmare but a dangerous reality.

Jamie's voice broke through Selena's panic.

"Selena's talking to the sea. I think I recognize the language... It's whale-speak."

"Get lost, Jamie," Selena huffed, pushing him away. "I wasn't talking to a whale!"

Jamie grinned mischievously. "Don't be embarrassed. You saw a whale and wanted to chat. 'Cause you're a whale too, right Baby Beluga?"

He started making silly whale noises, causing the group of kids to crack up. Selena rolled her eyes, feeling helpless as Jamie continued with his moans and roars.

"Quit it," Chloe scolded, but Jamie just kept on whooping.

"What's in here? Whale food?" Cindy snatched Selena's backpack and opened it.

"Hey, give that back." Selena reached for the bag, but Cindy tossed it to Jamie. He unzipped it and started talking like he was on a nature show.

"Check out this humpback whale in its natural habitat. Just had a big meal, but they gotta keep eating to stay plump."

"What do whales munch on?" asked Cindy.

"Peanut butter crackers," Jamie declared, holding up an empty packet.

"Oh my god, stop!" Selena yelled.

Jamie reached into Selena's backpack and whipped out a cup of gooey chocolate pudding.

"Whale, whale, whale, what do we have here?" Andrew said, fighting back laughter.

"Breaking news guys, the humpback whale has a new favorite dessert - chocolate pudding!" Everyone burst into hysterical laughter as Selena blushed with embarrassment.

He tore it open, grabbed a fistful of the brown goo, and chucked it at Selena. The chocolate oozed down her face and splattered onto her shoes. Her lip started to quiver as she fought back tears.

"Yo, you gotta stay away from that humpback, or she might wanna chow down on you too. Whales have big appetites," Jamie said with a smirk. Selena whipped the pudding cup from his grasp and flicked some brown stuff in his face.

Selena was seeing red as Cindy pulled her hair. With an almighty roar, she mustered all her strength and pushed Cindy over. Now on top, Selena smashed a blob of pudding into Cindy's screaming face.

As Selena pumped her fist in the air, two knees slammed into her back from behind. The force of the tackle drove the air from her lungs as she face-planted into concrete.

"Look at her squirm like a worm on a hook," taunted Andrew from behind.

Chloe appeared, shoving him off by his shirt collar. "Get off her, you jerk."

Selena wiped pudding from her face, struggling to catch her breath as a wave of pain and dizziness crashed over her. She rolled onto her back to see Jamie looming above, brandishing a fistful of gooey chocolate pudding.

"Pudding fight!" Jamie shouted gleefully before smashing the pudding directly into Selena's hair. She spluttered as globs of it dripped into her eyes and mouth.

Her vision blurred with unshed tears of humiliation. Selena swiped fiercely at her eyes as she jumped up, seething with anger and humiliation. She spotted her backpack laying nearby and got an idea. "Eat this, Jamie!" she yelled.

With all her might, Selena launched the bag like a missile. Jamie laughed harder at her pathetic throw, not realizing the danger. At that moment, Mr. Bottomley came storming over, face red as a tomato.

Selena watched in horror as her backpack collided with Mr. Bottomley's head. "Timber!" cried Andrew.

With a muffled "Oof!" the headmaster toppled over. His glasses skittered off as the kids erupted into giggles.

Mr. Bottomley flailed on the ground like a turtle stuck on its back. "Get it off!" He yelled, yanking Selena's backpack from his head. Suddenly, his toupee slipped free in the struggle.

The bald man leaped up too fast, still clutching the bag. But his toupee had taken on a mind of its own. The children howled to see it wiggle across the ground like a furry earthworm escaping the dirt.

Finally stopping under the swings, the toupee laid there curled in on itself. The kids laughed at Mr. Bottomley's exposed head flashing in the sunlight. Red-faced, he clutched at the spot where his hair had fled.

"This yours, sir?" Jamie asked, barely containing his laughter as he picked up the wig.

Mr. Bottomley scowled, jamming the toupee back on his bald head. He crawled about until he found his glasses.

"Who started this fight? I could hear it all the way in my office," he bellowed, spittle flying.

Trembling, Selena pointed at Jamie. "He did, sir! He took my pudding!"

"No way, she went nuts."

Cindy spoke up sweetly.

"Sir, I saw what really went down. Chloe and Selena were laying into Jamie, calling him thick as a brick and all sorts of mean names. It really hurt his feelings."

Mr. Bottomley frowned at Chloe and Selena. "Is this true?"

"No way!" protested Selena.

But Cindy continued spinning her tale: "Jamie was just trying to stand up for himself. Then things got out of hand when they started lobbing pudding at him. It was total chaos."

Mr. Bottomley wiped his forehead in frustration. "Chloe, Selena - my office. Now."

Selena and Chloe shared a hopeless look. Jamie smiled innocently while they were blamed for everything. It was so unfair. Selena scuffed her shoes, resentfully following the disheveled Mr. Bottomley. His ridiculous appearance barely improved her mood. They were sure to be punished.

Once they were in his office, he sat behind his desk, fingers steepled as he gazed at them sternly over his glasses.

"I understand you're new here," he began, voice stern and accusing. "However, that is no excuse. Fighting will not be tolerated at this school."

"But we didn't start it," Chloe protested.

"Just keep out of trouble. That's all I ask. I don't want to have to call your parents in." As he put his fingertips on the desk and leaned forward, the toupee became perilously close to falling off again. Selena bit her lip to stop a laugh from escaping.

"I will be watching you both," he said. "If you follow the rules, you won't get in trouble."

"We promise we'll behave," Chloe said.

"Excellent," he replied, leaning back in satisfaction. "Now get to class, both of you." He waved his hand dismissively. "And I don't want to hear another peep out of either of you."

Selena followed Chloe down the hallway, still freaking out from what happened in the yard. As they walked, Chloe turned away and sneezed into her elbow. "What a mess that was. I thought he was gonna call my mum for a minute."

"I know, I totally lost it," Selena said with a sigh. "But Jamie really pushed my buttons calling me a whale. And Andrew egging him on didn't help."

Chloe's face got all soft when Andrew's name came up. It was no secret she had a major crush on him. "For sure, they crossed a line. But you know Jamie loves riling people up. Don't let him get to you next time, kay?"

Selena frowned. It was easier said than done when her worries felt so close. "What about Andrew, though? You're always making excuses for him."

Chloe blushed a little. "I know, he can be annoying. But he's sweet too sometimes. Don'tcha think people deserve second chances?" She looked at Selena meaningfully. "Don't you?"

Her friend's thing for Andrew only made Selena's worries bigger that she might lose Chloe to the popular crowd. The thought of facing school alone freaked her out. But she didn't want to seem lame, so she put on a brave face and shrugged. "Not him. He's had way too many chances if you ask me."

12

SELENA

The next day, Selena dragged her feet as she and Chloe walked the beach after school. She dreaded returning home, unable to bear another empty conversation with her mum about Faustina. But confessing the truth to Chloe still felt too risky. Selena was trapped with no one to confide in.

As they passed a group of men in "Fishery Conservation" jackets, Selena overheard snippets that made her blood run cold.

"Pretty sure we'll catch it today..."

"Can't risk a shark attack..."

The men abruptly stopped talking when they noticed the girls. With urgent haste, they rushed to their boat and fired up the motor.

Selena's pulse quickened. They had to be talking about Faustina. What if the men caught the mermaid or worse?

Selena imagined Faustina captured in a tank, poked and prodded. She shivered.

Chloe gave her a puzzled look, noticing her distress.

"I hope they don't kill it," said Chloe. "It's got a right to live, too."

"I don't think they would. Their jackets said 'conservation,' so that means they're not supposed to kill the animals, right? They're trying to locate it and help it go farther out to sea."

Chloe kicked at the wet sand. "Did you get in any more trouble from yesterday? I've been worried sick Mr. Bottomley will contact my mum, but so far, I think I'm safe."

"Don't worry about it." Selena waved her hand dismissively. "If he was going to do anything, he would have done it by now."

Selena watched the men in the boat who kept a steady distance behind a silver-gray fin that poked through the surface of the water.

"Are you listening to me?" Chloe asked.

"Sorry." Selena turned to take in Chloe's cross face.

"You look like you're zoned out," Chloe said. "What's up? Why do you get so freaked out by the sea? Are you really that scared of sharks? You know they can't come on land, yeah?"

"Thanks for the news flash. I feel so much better." Selena grinned to hide her anxiety. The tingly feeling had returned, convincing Selena the mermaid was close. Even though she wanted to tell Chloe everything, she couldn't. It would make her too vulnerable. Better just to lie. "Honestly, this house we're living in is weirding me out. Want to come check it out? I swear it's haunted."

"Okay, why not?" Chloe said.

As Selena led Chloe up the cobblestone street of the seaside village, she wound a strand of hair anxiously around her finger. Her eyes darted between the charming storefronts, taking in vibrant hues of robin's egg blue, buttercup yellow, and rosy pink.

She paused outside the bakery, inhaling the scent of cinnamon rolls drifting through the window. It only sharpened her nerves rather than soothing them. In that moment, a woman with wavy gray hair and a flour-stained apron caught sight of them from inside.

"Hello dears," she called warmly. "I'm Mrs. Thompson. Are you new to town? I don't believe I've seen you before."

"We just moved here from London," Chloe replied as they entered the shop.

"Well, welcome. Come in and grab a treat. I just took a fresh batch out of the oven."

Inside, Mrs. Thompson proudly arranged a platter of biscuits. "Help yourselves, loves. I always think there's nothing better than a homemade bake."

Selena took a biscuit, thanking her along with Chloe. They each took a bite, chocolate chips melting in their mouths. For a moment, Selena relaxed into the cozy bakery atmosphere, forgetting her troubles. But her dread only deepened at returning home.

Soft white light flooded the entrance hall, and patches of blue and yellow from the stained-glass window above the door poured in. As Selena stared up at the coat of arms, she was sure the mermaid flicked her tail. She glanced over at Chloe, not daring to ask Chloe if she'd seen anything.

As Selena led Chloe down the shadowy corridor, doubt crept in. Had she made a mistake allowing Chloe into her eerie home? Selena tensed as the portraits seemed to shift on the walls. The canvases creaked and groaned as if the subjects were alive.

"Did you hear that?" Selena whispered, pulse quickening.

"Hear what?" Chloe asked uneasily.

"The portraits—they're moving," Selena gasped as a painting caught her eye. "Look."

Selena pointed to the portrait of the man with the ginger cat curled at his feet. His face was twisted and distorted, his lifeless gray eyes rolling wildly.

Just then, a deep, rumbling purr echoed through the room. The painted cat was now gazing at her with sharp green eyes and purring menacingly. The unnatural sound sent a chill down Selena's spine, frightening her.

"Woah. Freaky!" Chloe exclaimed, jumping back from the portrait.

Selena shuddered. She could almost see the painted figures climbing out of their frames, their unseen eyes tracking her every move. This was a mistake. How could she have let Chloe come here, exposing her to the lurking horrors of this house?

Chloe leaned in to study the portrait, tilting her head as she inspected every detail. Her eyes were wide with fascination. Was she really intrigued or just pretending so she wouldn't hurt Selena's feelings?

Selena balled her hands into fists. What if she freaked Chloe out for good? Would Chloe still want to come over and be friends? Or would she tell everyone at school that Selena was a weird freak who lived in a haunted house?

No, please. Don't let me lose my only friend. Selena tried to steady her breathing as anxiety threatened to swallow her whole. Selena's heart pounded as Chloe turned to her with wide eyes. She had to change the subject before Chloe got scared off for good.

"I've got goosebumps," Selena said with an exaggerated shiver. She forced a grin, hoping it seemed like she was playing it all up as a joke. "This old house is so creepy. What about you?"

Chloe glanced back at the portrait uncertainly. "Um, yeah, kinda..."

Selena's stomach dropped. Was that fear in Chloe's voice? This wasn't working. She had to keep things light.

"So, hey, you wanna go grab a snack?" Selena asked, already edging toward the kitchen, which was at the end of the corridor. "I've got popcorn and chocolate and pretty much anything you could ever want to eat."

Chloe turned back to Selena, seeming to relax. "Ooh, yes, chocolate. Good idea. Lead the way."

Selena exhaled in relief as they headed down the corridor. Disaster averted, for now at least. She just needed to keep Chloe away from the supernatural stuff. Surely, they could have a normal friend sleepover like everyone else...right?

Chloe sneezed. "Do you have a cat? I mean a real one?"

"No, but maybe Aunt Ada had one? I don't know."

Selena gulped. A high-pitched giggle wafted into the corridor.

"I think my mum has a visitor," Selena said, pushing open the creaking door to the library. The room's gold wallpaper shimmered in the dull light.

Selena's jaw dropped as she saw her mum up a rickety ladder, handing a dusty leather-bound book down to none other than...

Mr. Bottomley?

What is he doing here? Probably blabbing about her getting into a fight at school. Dread weighed heavy in her stomach.

Fiona peered down at them from atop the ladder. "Oh, hi, Honey Bunny." Selena cringed at the nickname. "Who's your friend?"

"This is Chloe," Selena said as Chloe tilted her head, causing a wave of chestnut brown hair to fall away from her face, revealing sparkling brown eyes.

"Do call me Fiona," she said, waving at Chloe. The chunky turquoise jewelry adorning her wrists and neck clanked together with the motion. Fiona smiled warmly at Chloe as if they were already old friends.

Her fiery red hair was swept up in a loose bun, with curly tendrils framing her face. She wore a flowing purple blouse and floral maxi skirt paired with wildly clashing striped leggings. The eclectic style should have appeared haphazard, but Fiona somehow pulled it off flawlessly.

Perched atop the ladder, she moved with innate grace and poise, utterly at ease. Her luminous skin and piercing green eyes lent her an otherworldly beauty. Selena felt drab standing next to this vibrant character who was her mother. As Fiona's jewelry clattered loudly, Chloe gave an uncertain wave back.

"Oh, I couldn't," said Chloe. "My mum says I shouldn't call grownups by their first names."

"As you wish." Selena's mum turned to Mr. Bottomley with a smile that nauseated Selena. "May I introduce you to this delightful gentleman…"

"Hi, Mr. Bottomley," Selena said weakly, feeling queasy. She rushed to the window and threw open the curtains, desperate for fresh air. Sunlight flooded the room, glinting off Mr. Bottomley's smeared glasses. He held up a hand to shade his eyes, mouth twisting in irritation.

Selena noted how he angled his body away from her, toward her mother. His shoulders were tensed, jaw tight. He avoided meeting Selena's gaze, instead casting furtive glances at her mum.

"Do you know each other?" Fiona said from the top of the ladder.

As Selena stepped over to her mum, Mr. Bottomley turned his back slightly as if to block her from the conversation. The way he hovered near her mum made Selena deeply uneasy.

Mr. Bottomley grasped her mum's hand as she

descended the ladder. "What a gentleman," her mum purred, smiling coyly. Selena grimaced.

Her mum settled on the ratty sofa, and Mr. Bottomley handed her the old book, which was bound in red and gold.

"Of course, we know him. He's the headmaster at our school."

"Oh, how wonderful," Fiona said, clapping her hands together.

"Not really," Selena mumbled under her breath.

Her mum gave an eager nod. "You're probably wondering how we met."

Selena and Chloe exchanged uneasy looks.

"I was in the garden when I got a call from my agent—"

"And I was trimming my hedge when I heard someone in distress," Mr. Bottomley interjected, inching closer.

Chloe turned to Selena with wide eyes. "Wait, Mr. Bottomley is your next-door neighbor?" she whispered.

Selena pulled a face. Her shoulders slumped as the realization set in. Just her luck. The tyrannical headmaster who had gotten them in trouble earlier lived right beside her. She would have no escape from his watchful eye, even at home.

"I admit, I howled." Her mum made a dramatic sad face. "Can you believe I didn't get the toothpaste advert?"

"Simply tragic," Mr. Bottomley said, plopping down beside Fiona. "You're such a talented actress. I can't fathom it."

Selena rolled her eyes. *Yeah, right.* Her mum's biggest acting credit was an ice cream commercial. Still, Mr.

Bottomley gazed adoringly as if Fiona were a Hollywood starlet.

"Oh, aren't you a dear," Fiona said, fluttering her eyelashes. Selena fake gagged. "Anyway, he leaned over the hedge, and I told him what happened." Fiona made an exaggerated pouty face, causing Mr. Bottomley to nearly swoon off the couch.

Selena focused on the red book Fiona had placed on the table, partly to avoid watching this romance train wreck. Was the book...glowing?

"She was in a bit of a state," Mr. Bottomley said.

"Selena, get this. Mr. Bottomley is going to fix our toaster," Fiona announced.

"Please, call me Roger," he insisted in a suave voice.

Selena tried not to vomit. If her mum started dating her headmaster, she was boarding the next spaceship off this planet. Selena walked over and stared up at the towering bookshelf. Over the past few days, she'd combed through most of the mansion's library, searching for clues. She'd skimmed the endless books about antiques, bird watching, and poetry. But nothing useful came up about the mystery surrounding the deranged mermaid.

Selena's gaze landed on the red leather book her mum left on the table. She hadn't noticed it in her previous searches. As she reached for it now, a tingle shot through her fingers. This was no ordinary book—she could sense it.

Selena opened the crackling pages, traces of warmth still lingering on the yellowed parchment. Intricate maps marked with strange symbols sprawled across each page. She traced some sketches of mermaids that felt like they might provide some answers.

Ignoring the chatter around her, she clutched the red tome to her chest. Its mysteries called to her. She had never felt a book hum with such power before.

"Chloe, look," Selena whispered eagerly, beckoning her friend over. She pointed to the cryptic markings. "Treasure maps?"

Chloe's eyes widened. "Whoa..."

Selena's pulse quickened. This book was the key; she was sure of it now. She just had to decipher the clues within its magical pages.

Selena's mum laughed that high, fake laugh Selena hated. "Now Babycakes, I don't think you should be looking at that old book."

Selena squeezed the red leather binding. Why was her mum always keeping secrets from her? She was so sick of being left in the dark.

"Why not?" Selena asked, matching her mum's tense tone.

"It's not for you, Muffin. Give it here." Her mum held out her hand impatiently.

Selena reluctantly handed it over, anger boiling inside. It wasn't fair. This could be the key to unlocking the mansion's mysteries and her mum just snatched it away.

"Run along now. Mr. Bottomley and I need to talk." Her mum was already turning back to make goo-goo eyes at Selena's headmaster.

"Let's go," Chloe whispered, pulling Selena toward the kitchen.

Selena stomped off, frustration gnawing at her gut. There had to be a way to get that book back and find out its secrets. She was so tired of being left in the dark. But she'd show them. One way or another, she'd uncover the truth.

***

Selena flopped onto her bed, spilling popcorn across the covers. She grabbed a handful from the bowl and munched anxiously.

"If my mum starts dating Mr. Bottomley, I'll just die," she said through a mouthful. "Can you imagine if kids at school found out? They already think I'm crazy without knowing my mum's dating a man with a dead hamster on his head."

Chloe giggled as she popped a few kernels in her mouth. "They won't find out. I won't tell them."

"Of course, they will. Everyone spies on everyone here." Selena shoved another fistful of popcorn in her mouth. "My life will be over if this gets out."

"Calm down," Chloe said. "They just met. And he's old enough to be her dad. Eat some more popcorn and don't stress."

Selena sighed and grabbed another handful. The salt and butter soothed her nerves, even if just a little. She was thankful to have a friend like Chloe who didn't think she was a complete freak. At least not yet.

The doorbell rang. Selena hurried out of her room and to the top of the stairs to see who it could be. Chloe followed.

"That'll be the Chinese takeaway," Fiona said, rushing to the door. "I was so emotionally drained after not getting the audition that I couldn't face the hassle of cooking. Chloe, you'll stay for dinner, won't you?" she shouted up the stairs. "And Roger? I insist."

Roger was staring at the portraits that lined the walls.

"I'd be delighted. You know, some of these portraits might be worth something."

"Really?" Fiona's eyebrows shot up.

He ran his fingers over a chest of drawers. "There might be one or two valuable pieces here, too."

"I didn't know you were an antique buff."

"There are a lot of things you don't know about me," he said, laughing. He pulled open a drawer and pulled out a scrap of paper. "What kind of alcohol do flowers drink? Rosé. What's that meant to mean?"

"I think it's one of Aunt Ada's puns."

"Well in reply, I'm going to say, 'You had me at Merlot.'"

"Oh, very good, very good." Fiona giggled.

Selena and Chloe came down the stairs and followed her mum into the kitchen. She got out bowls, put them on the kitchen table, and started dishing out rice, kung pao chicken, and sweet and sour pork. Selena didn't want to sit down to dinner with them, but she was starving.

Luckily, Chloe broke the ice straight away and started gushing about the Sparkle Delight advert.

"It's just so funny," she said, leaning forward while she

shoveled food into her mouth with chopsticks. "You're hilarious."

"Sometimes, one has to do things just to pay the bills, you know."

Fiona jumped up and opened a bottle of wine then poured a glass for herself and Mr. Bottomley. He was staring at Fiona weirdly as he ate.

"I know what you mean," he said, gulping down the wine. "I started out as a classics scholar, but in the end, I had to become a teacher to put food on the table."

"Wow. I love Greek poetry," Fiona gushed while glancing sideways at Selena, who was gobbling food. "Hunger is insolent and will be fed," Fiona said, putting another spoonful of rice in Selena's bowl, and Mr. Bottomley guffawed.

"I love Homer, too," Mr. Bottomley said. "What are the chances?"

"So do I," Selena said, nearly choking on her food as she tried not to laugh. "Homer Simpson's hilarious, but Lisa is my favorite character."

Mr. Bottomley guffawed like she'd told a great joke. Puzzled, Selena stuck her chopsticks straight up in her bowl of rice.

"Um, I think he meant Homer the Greek poet," Chloe whispered.

Selena's face turned redder than a stop sign as she realized her mistake.

Selena's mum hurried over. "How many times have I told you not to stand your chopsticks up?" She grabbed them.

"It's terrible luck!"

"When she travels, she brings back superstitions instead of souvenirs," Selena muttered to Chloe.

Mr. Bottomley waggled his eyebrows and held out his glass for more wine.

"Both to the rich and poor, wine is the happy antidote for sorrow," her mum quoted, topping him off.

"Euripides?" Mr. Bottomley said, chewing enthusiastically on his chicken.

Selena wondered how much longer she could endure this dinner.

Suddenly, Mr. Bottomley's face broke out in weird red splotches. Selena and Chloe exchanged an uh-oh look.

"You okay, sir?" Chloe asked. "Your eyes are bugging out."

"It's...my...throat," he rasped.

Chloe jumped up. "Are you allergic to something?"

"Peanuts," he choked out.

Selena's mum freaked. "There are peanuts in the kung pao!" She ran around in circles shouting, "Should I call 9-9-9?"

"Wait, I have an EpiPen." Chloe grabbed her backpack. "I carry it for shellfish attacks."

She jabbed it into Mr. Bottomley's thigh. He yelped, then face-planted into his dinner plate.

13

SELENA

After Mr. Bottomley had been revived and he and Chloe had gone home, Selena snuck into the library. She found the forbidden book peeking out from under a pile of magazines where Fiona had tried to hide it. The pages were stained, and some were almost worn through, especially the maps. Generations of fingers must have traced the lines around the coastline of Madderly Bay, Scarville Caves, and the Crystal Cove.

Selena studied the strange symbols and letters scattered across the maps. They looked like some kind of code or ancient language. She traced her finger along the coastline, imagining buried treasure awaiting discovery. What secrets did this book hold? Why had her mother tried to hide it away?

She paused at a drawing of a jeweled necklace—the

same one Great Aunt Ada wore in her portrait. Selena read the description:

This necklace originated from treasure seized from the pirate Zlotan's ship in 1608. Zlotan, a wizard, put a spell on the necklace and gave it great powers. In the right hands, it can do great good. Any powers possessed by the wearer will be amplified. She who is good when wearing the necklace unleashes good. One who is pure of heart can truly harness the healing power of the necklace. Yet she who is evil when wearing the necklace will cause great harm. And beware, only by being buried can the necklace's powers be fully blocked.

The ruby necklace was stolen from the pirate Zlotan by mermaid twin sisters Faustina and Starona. These girls eventually became zombie mermaids after a curse was cast upon them by Zlotan. The necklace has appeared over the ages in and around Madderly Bay, but its present location is unknown.

Faustina is a typical mermaid in that she can breathe under water and give this power to others, has mermaid mind control over people, and can make the sea rise, but combined with her zombie element, she has magical powers that surpass those of the humble mermaid, most significantly the ability to view what others are doing by getting inside their heads and seeing what they can see. Faustina has a strong connection to the necklace and can sense when it is near. Her magical powers and those of the necklace have always been closely entwined. On her own, Faustina has powers that fade over time, so she needs the necklace to replenish these powers. If the necklace is taken from her while she is wearing it, her powers will have seeped into it, giving the wearer additional magic powers.

Selena sat on the sofa, using her phone to snap photos of the strange book's pages. She was so absorbed in her task that she didn't notice the ominous smell creeping into the room at first. Without warning, a noxious blast hit Selena's nostrils, making her gag and recoil. The stench was like rotten eggs mixed with stinky cheese, times ten.

Wrinkling her nose in disgust, Selena looked around for the source of the nasty odor. It reminded her of Faustina's rotten breath that time she'd burst into her room and had blasted her undead fumes onto Selena's face. She sensed there was someone in the room, but when she turned to look behind her, there was nothing there. An icy puff of air on her earlobe made her jump. Quickly, she rubbed her earlobe before shoving the book back under the magazines and hurrying into the kitchen. Was the spirit of Faustina in the house, or was it some other ghostly relative? Questions whirled in her head as she spooned cocoa powder into two cups. Maybe her mum would have an answer to what kind of a family she had been born into. She poured milk into a saucepan to heat it as she placed two mugs on a tray and made some cinnamon toast—her mum's favorite.

As she carried the tray up the stairs, water sloshed behind the walls. But it had to be her imagination, right? The sea was just where it should be, gently lapping the beach, not crashing against the house. She should be used it. There were things happening in this house all the time. Creaks and whispering sounds. The sound of water sloshing, dripping, and running like a fast-moving stream under the floorboards. Things she couldn't explain but freaked her out. The sloshing got louder and louder until there was a long hiss, like a wave crashing on surf. Then a pop before the water rush disappeared into thin air. Gulping, she opened her mum's door.

"Oh, I feel so awful. Do you think Roger will forgive me?" Fiona said when Selena came in.

"I'm sure he will. Anyway, it wasn't your fault."

"I hope so." She glanced at the tray. "This is such a lovely snack. You're so thoughtful."

Selena sat on the bed and bit into the crisp, buttery toast. "Mum, I was thinking. I'd like to know more about my family."

A dark shadow crossed her mum's face. "I don't think you're ready."

"Well, I need to know. What if Faustina tries to attack me again?"

Fiona flopped back onto a pile of pillows and waved her hand dismissively. "I think we've seen the last of Faustina. I mean, she hasn't been back, has she?" Fiona said as she cracked her knuckles, her eyes darting around the room.

"No." Selena let out a sigh. "But she might."

Fiona shook her head, resting her hand on Selena's arm. After taking a sip of hot chocolate, she asked her daughter, "What else do you want to know?"

"More about Faustina."

Fiona shrugged in exasperation. "She's been alive for hundreds of years, living with other zombie mermaids. Not causing humans any harm, as far as I know." Fiona paused, and her eyes clouded over. "I wonder why she's so fixated on you."

Selena wondered about that, too. Anxiously, she nibbled

at the toast. "Is it because I'm family? I mean, am I meant to feel flattered she's singled me out?"

"Maybe?" Fiona said.

"Because I don't," Selena said as rage stirred in her. She pulled at her hair. "I feel like she chose me because I'm some sort of freak like she is."

Her mum's eyes grew wide.

"Don't ever say that!" she said, her voice rising an octave. "Don't ever say you're a freak. I don't know what's gotten into you. Look, she's pretty immature. She's only twelve years old, you know. Once you become a zombie mermaid, that's it. You stay the same age forever."

"I wouldn't mind being twelve forever. As long as I never have to go to school again… I'm guessing zombie mermaids don't go to school," Selena said, smiling.

"That's where you'd be wrong. Faustina and sister started an underwater school called Undead Academy, back in the day, and they also started the zombie merkingdom. They were a brainy bunch who…" She searched for the words.

"… also liked to suck people's brains out?" Selena giggled.

Fiona laughed. "I suppose so. Aunt Ada told me that after she lost her sister, Faustina became bitter and started to hate the school. At some point, she smashed it to pieces."

Selena started to feel uneasy again. Faustina was bonkers.

"Ever since she was cursed by the wizard pirate Zlotan, she's not been right in the head. You know, I'm beginning to wonder if Faustina might also have come here that night to see if she could find the ruby necklace."

"Why would she do that?" Selena gasped.

"The necklace protects anyone who wears it... so nothing bad can happen to them. But it's also filled with dark magic."

"What?" Selena tingled with excitement at the mention of the magical necklace.

"Selena," she said in a grave tone. "That book—stay away from it. Forces you don't understand—powers beyond your control. Meddling could bring consequences."

Her words hung heavy in the darkness of the room. Selena shivered but said nothing.

Fiona fixed her with a piercing stare. "I'm serious. Black magic is dangerous. You're too young to cope with it."

"Y-you're right," Selena stammered, though her mind spun with possibilities.

Selena's heart pounded as she considered her next move. She had to know the book's secrets, no matter the cost.

After kissing her mum goodnight, Selena crept to her bedroom. Moonlight filtered through the curtains, casting an eerie glow across the room. She lay very still, staring up at the shadows dancing on the ceiling. Her mind raced as she replayed what she had learnt from her mum.

Faustina. A long-lost ancestor. One who had tried to bite

her that first night. One who had infected so many, turning them into aquatic creatures like herself.

Selena pondered the implications. *If one infects another, does that make them family?* She shuddered at the thought. *No, that can't be right.*

Faustina was linked to her by blood, no matter how distant. But she was not family. Not anymore. Selena hoped to never lay eyes on her again.

Feeling like her head would explode, she texted Chloe the photos of the book's pages.

Selena: *Mum just freaked me out. Told me I'm related to a zombie mermaid.*

Chloe's reply came through: *Zombie mermaids? I think your mum is pranking you.*

Selena quickly typed back: *I don't think she wants me to find this necklace.*

Chloe: *Why not?*

Selena: *It has magical powers.*

Chloe: *SRSLY?!*

Selena: *Yeah, I think she wants to find it for herself.*

She sent Chloe the map, the images, and the text about the ruby necklace, then immediately panicked. Why had she just gotten so excited and sent Chloe the pictures? Why had she blurted out she was from a family of zombie mermaids?

Chloe texted back: *I don't get it. Zombie mermaids are just a made-up thing, right?*

Selena: *That's what I thought until I saw one. She came in* through my window that first night. All slimy with bits of flesh hanging off her.

Chloe: *What if that was just like… a super vivid dream… or something.*

Selena: *She was cray. Said she was lonely. Wanted to bite me and turn me into a zombie mermaid.*

Chloe: *Unbelievable.*

Selena: *I know! She wanted me to live with her under the sea. I fought her off, then I fell on a nightstand, and that's how I got that bruise.*

Chloe: *Tbh this is a lot to take in.*

Selena nodded to herself. Chloe wasn't wrong.

Selena: *The thing is, Mum reckons Faustina is evil. And she might be trying to get into the house to find this magical ruby necklace. But I want it, too.*

Chloe: *Too weird!*

Selena: *IKR? The necklace can stop anything bad from happening to you ever again. And right now, I need that protection. Mum says I shouldn't look for it. That the magic can be dangerous.*

Chloe: *SRSLY?*

Selena: *Yeah. And it looks like it's buried somewhere on the map.*

Chloe: *Cray. Maybe your mum's right and you should stay out of it. Sounds dangerous.*

Excitement rushed through Selena.

Selena: *I kinda wanna try and find it though. Like what if I wore it? Then just because I wanted to be popular, the necklace could make me super popular? Then I'd stop getting bullied.*

Chloe: *IDK*

Selena: *Maybe the necklace will give me the power to do anything I want??*

Chloe: *Don't do anything stupid.*

Selena: *I won't.*

Chloe: *Yeah, for sure it would be great if you weren't getting bullied, but letting loose that magic could go sideways. Let's think about what your next move should be. Just promise you won't start digging around trying to find that necklace yeah?*

Selena lay awake, unable to sleep. All she could think about was Faustina—that malevolent, undead mermaid with nothing but time on her hands. Would she stay put at the bottom of the sea? Selena doubted it.

She tossed and turned, imagining she could hear water rushing within the walls, picturing Faustina slithering up the pipes. Selena peered anxiously into each dark corner, wondering if a pair of glowing eyes stared back.

The wind howled outside, branches scratching against the windowpane like long, bony fingers. Selena pulled the blankets tight but still couldn't shake the feeling that Faustina was out there, lurking in the inky blackness of the night. Waiting. Watching. Ready to strike again.

14

FAUSTINA

A few days later, Faustina slid through the water, belly grazing the sandy bottom. Up ahead, Selena and Chloe sat on the beach, faces glued to a phone.

Faustina's fangs ached to sink into soft flesh. No more playing nice. Today she would attack, rip, tear. Go for Chloe, too.

She eased closer, straining to hear their voices.

"Look, spots where the necklace could be buried," Selena said.

Faustina froze. They'd found clues to the lost mermaid treasure. Rage and excitement churned inside her. How did they have that information?

Faustina squeezed her eyes shut and concentrated hard. It took all her energy just to summon a spell. She waved her algae-covered arms slowly, fighting to get the magic flowing in her weak zombie body.

With a pop, Faustina pushed into Selena's mind. An image flickered in her brain - she was seeing through Selena's eyes now. The girls were looking down at a phone. Faustina squinted, trying to make out the screen.

An image appeared: a photo of an old book from the Undead Academy, its pages marked with treasure maps.

Glee flooded Faustina. That necklace could revive her, sharpen her mind to its old cunning. She had to have it.

A memory stabbed through Faustina's foggy mind. Hundreds of years ago, she had pored over the sea-stained treasure book's pages that had once been in the library of the Undead Academy. Now, seeing through Selena's eyes, it all came rushing back.

Fantastic creatures swam across the map: writhing sea serpents, fish-tailed mermaids, human-legged fish. Faustina trembled, barely containing her excitement.

Then the creatures stilled, transforming back into colored ink markings. The image winked out as Faustina's magic depleted.

She swore under her breath. The brief glimpse had revived so many memories. She ached to hold the book itself, turn the crinkled pages with her own gnarled hands.

Faustina roared in anguish, thrashing her scaly tail. Centuries hiding in this weakened form had eroded her once mighty magic. The necklace would restore her. But she had to find it first.

As they discussed symbols on the beach, Faustina

strained her fading hearing. Their chatter seemed on the brink of revealing the necklace's secrets. But then her vision blackened entirely.

Panicked, she raked her claws across the sand at the bottom of the sea. No! She had come so far. With a primal scream, Faustina tapped into reserves even she didn't know remained.

Magic exploded behind her eyes in a blaze of color. Her vision refocused through Selena's, just in time to see Chloe pointing at a yellow starfish symbol.

"Looks like it's in the cemetery," Chloe pointed out. "What do you think that means?"

"Beats me. But most of the symbols are on the beach," said Selena, running her fingers across the screen of her phone. "I reckon we should head to these spots near the Scarville Caves. Are you coming with me?"

Chloe hugged her knees, staring out at the dark waves. "I don't know…"

Do it! Faustina screamed inwardly, barely able to contain her excitement.

Selena shivered and tucked a strand of hair behind her ear. "I'm kinda freaked out by the ocean. I almost drowned when I was a kid."

"No way, seriously?" Chloe gasped, hands flying to her mouth.

"I can't handle it alone, so I need you there with me."

Chloe dragged a stick through the pebbles. "I'm getting weird vibes about this. Like we're messing with things we shouldn't."

Mess with everything! Faustina wanted to shout. *Snag that necklace.* She imagined its shimmering power, its juice zapping through her and giving her a jolt of life (well, as much life as an undead mermaid can have).

Selena clasped her hands in a plea. "Please? I can't do this without you."

Chloe wavered, gaze bouncing between Selena and the foreboding sea. She sighed, shoulders slumping. "Okay, fine. But we stick together, got it?"

"You're the best." Selena grinned and hugged her friend.

Faustina's tail lashed hungrily, the scent of humans thick in the air. Selena smelled of succulent roast lamb, Chloe like a juicy steak ready for devouring. Faustina's mouth watered. Just one little bite.

With a splash, she burst from the waves, claws outstretched. Selena's head jerked up, eyes scanning the water. She leapt to her feet, yanking Chloe with her.

"I've got a really bad feeling. Did you hear that?"

Chloe brushed pebbles from her skirt, frowning. "Hear what?"

Selena hugged herself, gaze fixed on the now calm surf. "Let's get out of here."

Faustina watched from behind Selena's eyes, as Selena and Chloe quickly packed up their things on the beach. Faustina's head swiveled from side to side, trying to pinpoint the source of every sound. Waves crashed onto the shore, seagulls screeched in the distance, and the girls' voices floated over it all.

Chloe shoved her hands in her pockets as they walked along the pebbled beach. "How are we gonna do this?"

"Yeah, I know it won't be easy. But we'll go at night so no one sees us searching. And..." Faustina, inside of Selena, felt her shiver. "I can't be near the ocean alone after dark."

Chloe squinted at the calm waves lapping the shore. "But we won't even go in the water. What's the big deal?"

Selena wound a hair around her finger nervously. "I know it's irrational. That's why it's a phobia."

"So, you never swim?"

"Only if I can touch the bottom. Otherwise, I panic."

Chloe touched her arm. "That's awful."

Selena clasped her hands. "Will you sneak out and help me look?"

Chloe bit her lip. "What if my mum catches me?"

"She'll be asleep. Please, I have to figure this out."

After a pause, Chloe sighed. "Okay, fine. I'll try."

Useless. Faustina sank underwater. But maybe the girls would surprise her and find the necklace after all. She could bide her time a little longer.

Soon, the necklace's power would be hers. These humans were merely pawns in her quest to reclaim her former glory.

15

SELENA

As Selena and Chloe approached the auditorium the following day, the sounds of chatter leaked through the doors.

"Who's even teaching drama now?" Selena asked. "Ms. Buckingham quit."

Andrew barged past with his friends, yelling over his shoulder, "No surprise there. Buckingham looked like she was going to lose it every time we had class."

Cindy smirked as she sauntered by. "Pretty sure you drove the poor woman to tears on the daily."

Chloe crossed her arms. "At least he shuts up occasionally. Your voice is like nails on a chalkboard."

"Ooh, snooty's crushing hard on Andrew," Cindy taunted in a singsong voice.

Chloe scowled, cheeks reddening. "You wish."

Inside the auditorium, Selena froze. Her mum waved at them from the teacher's desk.

"Mum? What are you doing here?" Selena hissed through gritted teeth.

"Surprise. I'm your new drama teacher," Fiona said, a grin plastered across her face.

Selena cringed inwardly. This year kept getting worse.

"You could have warned me. This is so embarrassing." Selena wished she was invisible as she sat down in one of the rows of chairs.

"Sorry. It was a last-minute thing. Roger needed someone to teach drama, so I stepped in to save the day. Now, it's time to get started." Fiona clapped her hands dramatically. "Children! I have wonderful news. We will be performing the gripping tale of *Zombie Island*."

A few kids perked up but most slouched lower in their seats.

"What's it about, teach?" Cindy asked.

"Why, only shipwrecks, rival gangs, and zombies lurking in every shadow." Fiona crept up behind Jamie and grabbed his shoulders. He yelped.

Selena cringed. "Mum, tone it down."

Fiona threw her arms wide. "Picture this: A ragtag group of kids, shipwrecked and stranded on a deserted island."

She pantomimed shivering and huddling together. A few students giggled.

"On this island, they split into rival gangs, engaged in epic battle."

Fiona pretend dueled with an imaginary sword. More laughter broke out.

"But then, a threat emerges. Zombies lurking in the shadows."

She lumbered around like a zombie, arms outstretched. The kids roared with laughter.

Selena flinched. "You're being ridiculous."

"Nonsense! To truly capture the drama, we need authenticity. Since we're talking nineteenth century, we need hand-sewn period costumes, elaborate sets..."

Fiona trailed off, staring into space as she envisioned extravagant props.

Selena rolled her eyes. "It's a school play, not Broadway."

But Fiona was lost in her theatrical vision, babbling on about theatrics and artistry. Selena prayed she didn't try to get the kids reenacting shipwrecks. This was going to be a long year.

Selena crossed her arms in defiance. "Well, you can count me out. No way am I acting in some dumb zombie play."

"No escapesies!" Jamie said in a singsong voice.

Selena scowled and fiddled with her hair. "There's gotta be a way to get out of this."

"I'm afraid not," Fiona cut in. "Participation is mandatory for all students, no exceptions." She put her hands on her hips. "And Selena, you shouldn't discount your talent. I'd like you to audition for one of the main parts."

"I'd love a main part, too, Ms. Flowers," interrupted Chloe. "I've always wanted to be an actress."

"Wonderful! Let's start the auditions right away. Chloe, you'd be perfect as Gracia," Fiona said, passing out the scripts. "And Selena, I see you as the fierce warrior, Helena, who battles against the zombies."

Selena made exaggerated gagging noises. Jamie and his friends snickered.

"A warrior? She's too chicken to battle a teddy bear." Jamie flapped his arms and clucked loudly. The other kids guffawed.

"I am not," Selena shouted, face burning. But her protests were drowned out by the rooster impressions and "bawk-bawk" chants now spreading through the room.

Fiona whirled around, nostrils flaring. "That's enough everybody. And you!" She pointed at Jamie. "One more cluck and it's the headmaster's office."

Jamie put on an angelic face.

"Sorry, Ms. Flowers, no more chicken noises from me."

Selena gritted her teeth. The other kids were still snickering. She wanted to disappear.

"I hope not. Okay, let's get going. Selena and Cindy, let's start on page sixteen where Zamorda says 'Yeah sure, blood tastes great, but honestly, I think the crunchy fingernails are the best part.'"

The rest of the class glared at Selena. The sooner she got the audition over with, the better. Selena started to read.

16

SELENA

Chloe got the part of Gracia, much to her delight. Selena was less thrilled about playing Helena. All she could think about was following that treasure map.

A week crawled by. Finally, Chloe agreed to sneak out that night to meet Selena on the beach. The map said one of the marks for the treasure was located behind one of the Scarville Caves so that was where Selena planned to go.

Selena found a shovel in the garden shed and carried it down to the beach on her own. As Selena made her way across the bend in the coastline known as Crystal Cove, she could feel her heart pounding in her chest and her palms growing clammy against the shovel's handle.

She located the spot where she would dig, but she didn't want to start without Chloe. She hid in the mouth of the cave for ten minutes that felt like ten hours before texting Chloe.

Selena: *Where are you?*

She watched as two figures came toward her through the darkness. They went down the beach right to the place Selena had seen marked on the map. They started digging. Selena stared at them. She was surprised anyone would dig in the same place she'd planned to. It was annoying and extremely odd. Her heart pounded. What did she do now? She hoped Chloe would show up so they could decide what to do together. Should they wait for the people to disappear?

Selena: *There are two people here digging in our spot.*

Chloe: *Do you think they're digging for the necklace?*

Selena: *How could they know this is one of the spots on the map? Nobody even knows about it.*

Chloe: *What else could they be doing?*

Selena: *Digging for lugworms? It's fishing bait.*

Chloe: *Would they dig in the middle of the night?*

Selena: *IDK*

Selena twisted her hair impatiently.

Selena: *When are you gonna get here?*

Selena waited for what seemed like forever, watching the diggers. Finally, her phone buzzed.

Chloe: *Sorry, can't get away. Mum is watching.*

Perfect. Chloe wasn't coming, and Selena was stuck in a cave, unable to leave without the diggers seeing her. Selena put her phone back in her pocket, wondering what to do. She watched the figures on the beach. They were right where she was supposed to be. Then one of them spoke, and Selena's stomach dropped.

"I have to find this necklace," came her mum's voice. "You know how it is, my little Pookie Bear. I have this huge talent, but I can't catch a break. I know once I wear the necklace to auditions, my luck will change."

"Of course, it will," Mr. Bottomley agreed. "And according to the map, it should be right here. We just need to dig a little deeper."

"I think I see a glint of something."

They both dug furiously, tossing more sand onto the growing pile.

"Oh, that's only an old can," said Mr. Bottomley.

"Phew. Something stinks," said Selena's mum. She waved her hand in front of her nose.

Selena texted Chloe.

Selena: *Crap! It's Mum and Mr. Bottomley!*

Chloe: *Are you kidding me?*

Selena saw green smoke coming off the water, and her skin crawled. The mermaid was there somewhere. She wanted to run, but if she did, her mum would see her.

Just then, Fiona screamed. She pointed to where a zombie mermaid burst out of the frothing waves, seaweed dangling from her mottled green skin. She dragged herself onto the moonlit beach, her fishtail slapping against the wet sand.

Selena texted Chloe. Her fingers flew frantically over the screen.

Selena: *Omg! There's a zombie mermaid coming out of the sea.*

"Get it away from me, Roger." Fiona shouted. "Do something."

For a moment, Selena wondered if her mum was just pretending to be afraid. After all, she knew as well as Selena the horrors of what a zombie mermaid was capable of.

But then she saw the true terror in her mother's eyes as the creature's rotting jaws snapped near her flesh. No one could feign that level of panic.

The mermaid sprang onto Selena's mum, her claw-like nails sinking into Fiona's face. Fiona let out a blood-curdling scream as the mermaid's nails raked down her cheeks.

In the moonlight, Selena caught a glimpse of the mermaid's fiery red hair. How many zombie mermaids could there be with hair that shade of red? Selena's mind raced, her thoughts disjointed with fear. Her mum had told her there were other undead mermaids in these waters. It was probably Faustina, but even if it wasn't, it was still a threat to her Mum.

Every instinct screamed to save Mum. But intervening meant facing the creature herself. Selena trembled at the thought of pitting her small frame against the snarling mermaid. How could she ever win against an undead creature intent on spreading zombie poison?

Moreover, Mum didn't know Selena had learned about her search for the mysterious necklace. And something told Selena her mum didn't want her to find out she was looking for it too.

But most of all, Selena recalled her childhood fear of

drowning. Emerging from those dark waves, only to have the mermaid drag her back down forever... No, confronting the zombie was a death sentence.

Selena's heart pounded as she watched the mermaid's jagged teeth snap perilously close to her mum's throat. She wanted to cry out, to beg Faustina to stop, but could only bite her lip in silent terror.

As Fiona screamed, Mr. Bottomley ran at the mermaid with his shovel and knocked her on the side of her head. The mermaid flopped to the beach, staring up at him. Mr. Bottomley kept hitting her, but she didn't budge. She just stared at him with glazed eyes and a creepy skeletal smile. Why wasn't she reacting? Maybe zombie mermaids didn't feel pain.

Fiona scrambled desperately up the sandy slope. Behind her, Mr. Bottomley pushed the shovel into the mermaid's chest with a sickening squelch.

Selena raised her phone and started taking photos of the mermaid. Zooming in tight, she got her in the frame and clicked. Yup. It *was* Faustina.

As Mr. Bottomley drove the shovel deeper into Faustina's side, black blood spurted from the wound, coating his hands, releasing a foul stench. The lifeless body twitched, and then Faustina threw back her head and shrieked, the sound piercing Selena's ears.

Wrenching the shovel free, Mr. Bottomley stumbled backwards. Faustina gnashed her pointed teeth, her face contorting with rage. She lunged for Mr. Bottomley, claws grasping.

He turned and fled up the beach. Weighed down by her rotting fish tail, Faustina could only drag herself a few feet before falling back. She screeched in frustration, her cries echoing through the night.

Mr. Bottomley scrambled up the sandy bank, not looking back. Selena watched wide-eyed as Faustina struggled to pursue him, her long nails gouging furrows in the sand. But the mermaid could not make it far from the water.

Howling in defeat, Faustina finally ceased her efforts. She glared balefully after Mr. Bottomley before sinking below the waves once more. Selena shuddered with relief as Mr. Bottomley joined her mother safely on the road above. For now, they had escaped the mermaid's wrath.

17

FAUSTINA

The next morning, Faustina floated by the crab shell couch, paying no mind to Aunt Ada nibbling on a sea slug. Faustina felt...well, not exactly pain where Mr. Bottomley had stabbed his shovel into her the night before. After all, she was a zombie mermaid—no pain receptors anymore.

But there was an odd, tingly numbness in that spot on her side. And a faint detachment, like her undead flesh didn't quite fit together there.

Faustina shrugged, her seagrass hair drifting in the current. No big deal. Just an occupational hazard when you were an undead, magical creature. She'd cope somehow. Maybe stuff the hole with algae and hope it stayed put.

"There you are," Ada called out in her grating voice. "Where did you disappear to last night?"

Faustina suppressed an eye roll. What she got up to was none of Ada's business. *Nosy old bat.*

"Developing a taste for the cuisine?" Faustina asked wryly, deflecting from Ada's probing.

Ada just shrugged and kept chewing. "It's growing on me."

"So, what do you think of your new library?" Faustina asked. She gestured proudly around the room she'd worked on feverishly all night. No need to mention how the battle with Fiona had sparked her creative side.

Aunt Ada held up her hand. "Hang on a minute, I'm chewing."

"I struggled at first to make it on my own," Faustina explained. "The pieces wouldn't stick. But then I remembered your advice. Get help."

Ada swallowed. "Are you feeling alright? You seem...worked up."

Faustina blinked. "Never been better. I was up all night constructing this marvelous dwelling." Faustina tumbled through the water doing somersaults.

Ada put a hand on Faustina's shoulder. "You should take care of yourself, dear. You need rest."

Faustina shrugged off her concern with a laugh. "Rest is for the weak. I feel more alive than ever."

She waved her arm around the library walls, made of woven glittering stones.

"Look how brilliantly they shine, just like the gold in your library back home!" she said.

A few skull spiders skittered by, their red bony legs

tapping on the floor. Faustina reached down and gently pet one's skeletal head as it crawled up her arm.

"Who would've thought?" she said proudly. "I had the great idea to get my clever little friends to spin all these rock pieces together into threads. Now our home is almost done thanks to their hard work."

Ada nodded, eyeing the spiders warily.

"I have to admit you've done a good job. This *does* remind me a bit of my old house." Ada patted the sofa constructed from crab shells. "But you haven't answered my question about where you were last night?"

Faustina undulated through the water, plopping herself down on the sofa.

"You don't wanna know." She flopped back, and her hair fanned around her face.

Faustina fidgeted on the sofa, barely able to contain herself. Should she tell Ada how she'd raked her nails down Fiona's face, reveling in her screams?

She knew Ada would likely scold her violence. But Faustina was fit to burst with exhilaration recalling her savage assault.

Aunt Ada sat gingerly and cocked her head. "Please tell me you haven't been doing something you shouldn't have?"

Faustina sprang up, unable to hold back any longer. Pumping a fist in the water, Faustina yelled, "Yup. I attacked Fiona last night."

Ada gasped, hand clenching over her mouth in horror. "No!"

Faustina zoomed up from the sofa and did a backflip.

Aunt Ada reached out for her as she slithered past, but Faustina moved at a dizzying speed, and she ended up with a handful of rotten scales.

"You must stop this madness." Ada cried.

But Faustina was too consumed with bloodlust to listen. She pouted. "It was one measly scratch. No biggie."

"But it might be enough," Aunt Ada said, biting her lip.

Faustina smirked, envisioning Fiona transforming into one of them. "My venom must have entered her wounds. She could join us soon."

She cackled and slapped her tail, excited. Ada swam closer, eyes flashing.

"And leave Selena motherless?" she snapped. "I can't believe you attacked her."

Faustina shrugged. "It might take ages. We'll just have to be patient."

Ada grasped Faustina's shoulders, nails digging in. "You will stay down here," she commanded. "No more trouble."

Faustina wrenched away. "And who recruits new blood if I'm stuck down here like a saint?" She swam inches from Ada's face, teeth bared. "Why not you? You might find you have a talent for it."

"I doubt it. My only talent is puns, as you know," Ada replied. She'd been unleashing oceans of puns since her transformation. "How do zombies introduce themselves? Pleased to eat you!"

Faustina groaned. "No more. It's not punny—I mean funny."

"Alright, I know this is serious." Ada munched another slug pensively. "But I'm cray-sea about puns."

Faustina pouted again. "I didn't mean to hurt Fiona. I was swimming about when I saw her with that guy she calls 'Pookie Bear.'" She sneered in disdain. "They were digging for the necklace, if you can believe it."

Ada sat up, intrigued. "Really now?"

"That Pookie Bear is so lame," Faustina ranted, throwing up her hands. "Fiona can do better. Maybe she'd be happier down here with me instead."

A pang of longing pierced Faustina's chest. She pictured having Fiona as the mother she'd lost—those twinkling green eyes, the faint freckles across her nose. Faustina could almost feel her warm embraces, soft as a marshmallow. The ones she missed so much from before she turned.

"Maybe Fiona could be a replacement mum," Faustina added softly, a rare moment of vulnerability surfacing. For an instant, she was that little girl again, craving her mother's affectionate hugs and goodnight kisses.

But then Faustina shook herself. Fiona was just a means to an end—a potential recruit for her undead army. She didn't need maternal love, only power and control.

Faustina hardened her heart once more. She had no time for sentimental longings. Her goals were all that mattered: finding the necklace and building her underwater empire. With Fiona by her side or not, she would have her vengeance against the living world.

But Ada sighed. "She was only scratched. You may wait forever. In the meantime, stay put."

Faustina shrieked, "You can't control me!"

She torpedoed from the library, eager to track down Fiona. She'd make that Pookie Bear pay for trying to find her necklace and gouging her guts. And soon, Fiona would join her under the sea.

18

SELENA

As Selena woke from a restless night's sleep, her skin was bruised and tender. She'd had a vivid dream that Faustina had come in her room and tried to bite her. She could still feel Faustina's rancid breath and sharp teeth against her neck, sending a shudder down her spine. Faustina kept whispering, "Don't fight this. Soon you'll be where you belong."

Selena's mouth was sour and dry as she went over to the window and opened the curtains. As sunlight streamed in, her skin gave off heat and pulsed unnaturally, as if infected. Was Faustina still inside her? Was the rotting mermaid just in her head, or was she actually slithering about under Selena's skin? She frantically scratched her arms, hoping the horrific crawling sensation would go away. When it didn't, she raced downstairs and splashed icy cold water on her face, desperate to purge Faustina's malignant presence.

Her mum was up early, clattering dishes around the shadowy kitchen. Selena wanted to tell Fiona about the harrowing dream, but hesitated, not wanting to worry her mother when something far worse was happening to her.

Selena stared at the heavy makeup caked on her mum's face. Was she trying to hide those awful scratches from Faustina? Selena shivered, remembering the attack.

The floor suddenly creaked, as if someone invisible stood there. An icy breeze blew in, carrying the stench of rot. Selena's heart raced. Was Faustina lurking nearby?

As her mum sipped coffee, Selena studied her closely. Her skin had turned an unhealthy gray, and she sported dark circles under her eyes. When her mum smiled, her lips cracked and bled. Selena gulped as a rotten smell drifted from the cuts.

"Hey, you look different." Selena raised her eyebrows before slowly smoothing back her hair with a trembling hand. "You're wearing a lot of makeup."

Selena searched her mum's face desperately. But all she saw was the creepy change happening. Dread filled her.

"I'm trying to cheer myself up a bit."

"Is anything wrong?" asked Selena.

"No, just lots of stress to do with the play." Fiona smiled sweetly and sipped her coffee.

When Selena stared closely at her mother's eyes, they were bulging and bloodshot. When her mum patted Selena's hand, her skin turned clammy. Selena jerked her hand away.

"What is it, Snookums?"

"I don't know," Selena said, worried her mum had been

bitten. "I'm freaked out about being in the play. I'd rather not do it."

"Nothing I can do, Sausage. It's part of the school curriculum. And I know it could be such a success if only I had the money to do it properly. As I said, we are woefully in need of funds."

Selena wondered if her mother had been searching for the necklace for good luck or if she planned to sell it. It was true that a chunk of cash might be the best thing that could happen to them. Selena peered at her mother's face, which was shifting into a gray, sickly hue.

"Mum, do you feel ill?"

"Now that you mention it, I do feel peaky. It's the worry, you know, of having no money." Fiona wandered to the window and stared out over the sea.

"I'm sure things will perk up. At least you have the teaching job."

Fiona shrugged. "I guess every little bit helps. I just have high expectations for this play."

"I wouldn't worry about it. No one expects that much."

Fiona whirled around. "I'm a well-known actress putting on a play, so people are going to expect this to be an amazing production."

"What do you mean 'well-known'?" Selena chose her words carefully, not wanting to hurt her mum's feelings. "Not everyone's going to recognize you from that Sparkle Delight advert."

"Look, I don't expect you to understand my passion for

theater, but I have to put on a good production. I have a reputation to protect."

"So, where are you going to find the money to put on this fancy production?"

"Like I said right when we got here: our luck is going to change. A windfall is imminent, believe you me. In the meantime, I'll sell some more of Ada's antiques. Roger thinks he's identified a William and Mary walnut chest of drawers. It's worth a fortune!"

"Look, until you get it valued by an actual expert, I wouldn't get too excited." Selena felt her mother's forehead. "Mum, you're not well. You're ice cold."

Fiona's laughter rang out, shrill and disjointed. Selena shifted uneasily. This wasn't her mother's usual warm, melodic laugh.

"How can I be ill if I'm cold?" Fiona asked, eyebrows drawing together as she tilted her head. Her smile remained frozen in place, at odds with the bewilderment in her voice. "Wouldn't I be hot, feverish, or sweating buckets, or what?"

Selena studied her mother's pale, clammy skin and too-bright eyes. This broken record of a laugh, her confusion at simple logic...it was unsettling. Like Fiona wasn't quite herself anymore. Like something dark had slipped in, wearing her mother's face.

Selena stared at her mother, hardly daring to believe what she was seeing. Was this really happening? She desperately hoped it wasn't true, but the signs were unmistakable: her mum was starting to turn into a zombie.

Selena knew she needed to find that necklace and fast.

Its magic was the only thing that could prevent this horrifying fate from befalling her mother. Or herself.

"Mum, I really think you should see a doctor. You might be ill," Selena said hopefully. Maybe it was just some strange sickness that modern medicine could cure.

But her mother shook her head. "You know I don't like doctors, dear."

Selena tried again. "Well at least spend the day in bed and rest."

"That sounds lovely, but I simply can't. My mind is too active, buzzing with thoughts. And we have rehearsal later, don't forget."

Selena pulled out her phone, hands trembling. She texted Chloe.

Selena: *Mum was attacked last night by that mermaid!*

Chloe's response came quickly.

Chloe: *OMG! Are you serious?*

Selena's thumbs flew over the keypad.

Selena: *Yeah...I think she's turning into a zombie.*

Chloe: *Ugh! That sucks. What are you gonna do?*

Selena: *Find that necklace. Maybe it can reverse the process before it's too late?*

Selena didn't know if the necklace could prevent zombieism, but it was her only hope. She had to find the necklace. It would fix everything. It had to.

19

SELENA

Selena drove her shovel into the sand, gritting her teeth as she flung aside rocks and old trainers. Three desperate weeks had passed since Mum first got sick, but Selena was still no closer to finding the magic ruby necklace that could save her.

Beside her, Chloe hacked at the ground, sending showers of sand over her shoulder. She'd slipped away while her overbearing mum was distracted, determined to help Selena search.

Together, they were digging at one of Selena's spots on the map. Selena's breath came in panicked gasps as the surf swirled around her feet. She loathed the ocean. Only the thought of curing her mum kept Selena from fleeing the hated water.

Whenever Selena shuddered, Chloe squeezed her hand

reassuringly. "We'll find it," she promised. But Selena saw the doubt in her friend's eyes.

On they dug as shadows stretched across the beach, the necklace still frustratingly out of reach. Selena channeled her mounting terror into fierce shovel strokes. She would not, could not stop until she found the one thing that could save Mum.

Finally, Chloe paused, wiping her brow. "Are you totally sure your mum was even scratched by Faustina?"

Selena huffed in annoyance. "Yeah, I showed you the pics of the attack."

Chloe grimaced skeptically. "But those were so blurry. You can't see anything."

"I know the pics weren't great," Selena admitted with impatience. "But you believe me, right?"

Chloe avoided her gaze, shrugging uncertainly.

Anger and hurt flashed through Selena. Why was her best friend doubting her? Couldn't Chloe see how dire this was? Selena's voice trembled as she said, "Mum's all the family I have. What if Mum becomes a zombie or vanishes into the sea forever?"

Chloe shifted, mumbling unconvincingly, "I'm sure that won't happen..."

Selena's heart sank, a profound sense of isolation washing over her. She couldn't tell anyone else about her mum's condition. They'd never believe such a crazy story. Chloe was the only one who knew, and now even she was having doubts.

Selena felt utterly alone in her fear for her mother. No

one else could understand the creeping dread she felt each day as her mum grew weaker. Only she believed Faustina's scratch would turn Mum into a zombie.

Blinking back tears, Selena attacked the sand once more. She had to keep trying. The necklace was her only hope of saving Mum and proving she was right. She dug fiercely, refusing to be defeated. Not by the doubts of her best friend, not by anyone. Her mum's fate depended on her alone.

When she got home, Selena crept in through the back door and took a quick shower to wash off the sand stuck to her arms and feet.

In the kitchen, her mum was sitting, staring down at the play that was open in front of her. She'd been attending rehearsals with her face slathered in makeup, acting like nothing was wrong. But it had worn off, and her skin had a greenish, clammy pallor crisscrossed with unhealed scratches.

"How do you think the rehearsals are going?" Selena asked, sitting opposite her.

Her mum scratched her face. "I guess it's not too bad," her mum said with a sigh. "But I don't know why Andrew and Jamie have got to be so mean to you all the time. Yeah, they're zombies, but they're acting like total beasts."

"I'm sure they'll get it eventually," Selena said, sighing.

"And I've still got to figure out how to get money for the show..." her mum muttered.

But Selena wasn't really listening. She was mesmerized and freaked out as she watched her mum scratching. She wondered how her skin must feel after being poisoned like that. It was probably an awful sensation if she couldn't stop clawing at herself.

Selena shivered, unable to look away from the angry red marks her mum was leaving on her cheeks. She wished she could make the itching stop, could heal the damage done by Faustina's venomous nails. But all she could do was keep searching for that necklace before the scratching got any worse...or turned into something far more monstrous.

At rehearsal the next day, Selena was sparring with Andrew. She held a wooden prop sword painted to look like it was carved from sea rock. Andrew had an identical prop weapon. They were practicing a fight scene.

Selena bounced on her toes, gripping her wooden sword eagerly. She loved these rehearsal battles. It made her feel like a true sword-wielding warrior heroine.

Andrew lunged, and Selena parried his blow. She then went on the attack, driving him back across the stage with a series of fierce strikes. Andrew stumbled, struggling to defend against her onslaught.

With a cry of effort, Selena slammed her wooden blade down towards Andrew's shoulder. He yelped dramatically as her sword connected then collapsed to the floor, feigning injury.

A crash made Selena whirl around. Her mother swayed where she stood, hands clutching the side of the stage. Before Selena could move, her mother's knees buckled, and she collapsed.

"Mum!" Selena rushed over and jumped off the stage, heart pounding. Her mother's skin had turned clammy and pale, with a faint greenish tinge. Selena grabbed her shoulders. "Mum, can you hear me? We need to get you to the hospital now!"

How long did it take to turn once infected? Would it be too late? Selena blinked back tears as she shook her mother gently.

Her mum's eyelids fluttered open, revealing bloodshot eyes. "No...no hospital," she murmured. "Just need...food..."

Cindy peered over Selena's shoulder, eyes wide. "Your eyes are all red, Ms. Flowers. I reckon you should see a doctor."

Fiona smiled weakly as Selena led her over to a folding chair and gave her a bottle of water. Her skin was pale and clammy, with smudges under her eyes.

"I'll be alright dear, just need to rest a moment." She gulped down water. Selena patted her mum's trembling hand and handed her a granola bar. Selena gave her hand a supportive squeeze as Mum took a small nibble. She chewed slowly, and Selena could see the effort it took. After several exhausted chews, Mum finally swallowed, and gave a sigh.

Selena bit her lip. Couldn't her mum feel the iciness under her skin? See the redness in her eyes? One of the scratches on her cheek was turning black around the edges.

But her mum just kept smiling that placid smile, insisting all was well and that the rehearsal should continue.

Chloe leaped onto the stage, launching into her zombie battle scene. Selena tried to focus, but her eyes kept darting back to her mum. Chloe always transported Selena when she performed, her intensity and passion shining through. If only her mum still had that fire.

But now her mum's eyes were glazed, distant. Her breathing grew more labored as she slumped in the chair. The same vital energy that once enthralled audiences was slowly draining away. And there was nothing Selena could do but watch helplessly as the zombie infection took hold.

Selena knew she was a lousy actress compared to Chloe. When it was her turn to rehearse with Jamie, she stuttered and forgot her lines.

"Okay, let's take that line again," Fiona said. "What's the matter, Selena? Try to focus."

Jamie recited his line, "You can fight all you like. At some point, you have to sleep. Then we will get you. We will chomp into you, and you will turn zombie."

"On the contrary," Selena replied. "We'll take turns sleeping. You'll never get the chance to—*ouch*!" She started hopping around on one leg. "He just stepped on my foot. Ow!"

Her mum rubbed her temples, looking exhausted. "Guys, I know you're trying, but this isn't working. Jamie, sweetie, you've gotta be more careful with your cues. This whole rehearsal is just a mess, though. No one seems focused."

She sighed, her voice softening a bit. "Look, I get it.

We're all stressed, and this play is a beast to tackle. But it's not going to come together if we keep stumbling through these rehearsals. I need you all to bring your A-game, stay sharp, and work together. We can do this. I know you have it in you. But I need you committed, not just phoning it in. Can you do that for me...please?"

Jamie looked down, abashed. "Yeah, sorry Ms. I'll try to do better."

The rest of the rehearsal sputtered along halfheartedly. Selena's stomach churned with worry about her mum, but she didn't have a clue what to do. Sure, she could drag her to the hospital, but would they even know how to treat a zombie infection? Of course not, because no one believed zombies were real outside of movies and books. Selena was completely alone in this mess. Everything rested on her somehow finding that necklace, and the vague hints in the old book that it could give powers to do good if worn by the right person. She had zero guarantees it would work, but what other options did she have? This magical necklace was her only glimmer of hope to heal her mum and stop this nightmare of an infection from spreading further.

Selena's mum's eyes were glazed. Selena imagined the infection oozing through her veins, destroying her humanity bit by bit. Selena shuddered. She had to find that necklace, and fast, before her mum was too far gone.

Selena wondered if her mum was still searching for the necklace, too. After all, it was the only thing that might cure her or at least stop her from turning undead.

That evening, she texted Chloe.

Selena: *Worried about Mum. I know she said not to meddle, and I might unleash something evil, but I don't care. I NEED to find that necklace. I know we've checked out most of the sites, but I'm getting frantic because I haven't found it. I'm going to check out another spot on the map tonight. Do you want to come help?*

Selena's phone vibrated.

Chloe: *Can't make it tonight. My mum told me I have to stay in. Sorry!*

Selena had to thank Chloe's controlling mum for making things even harder.

Was she chicken, like Jamie had said, or could she do it alone? She was running out of time.

20

SELENA

It was Saturday morning. Selena lingered nervously in the doorway of her mum's bedroom, not wanting to come closer. Her mum's face was a ghastly sight. The deep scratches she'd clawed into her skin were now oozing yellowish pus. The putrid wounds turned Selena's stomach.

Her mum sat at her vanity, applying layer after layer of concealer and foundation. But no amount of makeup could mask the grotesque transformation that was taking place.

Fiona's skin had taken on a lifeless gray pallor, her eyes sunken back into darkened sockets. The gashes on her cheek were deteriorating; the flesh around the edges was blackened and peeling away to reveal festering tissue underneath.

Selena shuddered, bile rising in her throat. The putrid stench coming off her mother was overpowering. This couldn't be ignored or hidden anymore. Fiona was decomposing right in front of her eyes.

"Mum, please..." Selena managed to choke out. "Let me take you to the doctor. We need help."

Fiona didn't respond, didn't even glance her way. She just kept caking on more foundation like a ghastly cadaver automaton.

Selena slowly backed out of the room, heart pounding. She had seen enough. Her worst fear was being realized: her mother was turning into a zombie before her eyes. And she was utterly powerless to stop it.

"Come down for breakfast soon, okay, Mum?" Selena said softly, trying to keep her voice from shaking.

She went to the kitchen and scrambled some eggs with trembling hands, forcing herself to focus on the sizzle of the pan instead of the nightmare unfolding around her.

When Fiona shambled into the kitchen, Selena had to stifle a gasp. In the harsh sunlight, her mother's deterioration was even more horrifying. Her mum's movements were stiff and jerky.

Selena quickly served up the eggs, but her own appetite had fled. She watched, repulsed, as her mother ate ravenously, bits of egg dribbling down her chin.

Abruptly, Fiona looked up, a strange glint in her cloudy eyes. "We should visit Aunt Ada's grave today," she said.

Selena shrank back, unnerved by this sudden proclamation. "Oh...okay," she managed weakly.

Her mother nodded. Selena tried not to cringe as her mother's cracked fingernails raked over the raw, seeping gashes on her cheek. The wounds pulsated and oozed more sickly yellow pus each time Fiona scratched at them.

It was a gruesome, involuntary impulse, like an itch deep under the skin that couldn't be satisfied. Selena could tell it caused her mother pain, but Fiona seemed oblivious, locked inside her deteriorating mind.

As the jagged nails tore at the gray flesh again, a chunk came loose and hung grotesquely off Fiona's face. Selena looked away, bile rising in her throat. She wanted to scream at her mother to stop. It was only making the horrific decay worsen.

But she held her tongue, knowing it would do no good. The infection ravaging Fiona's body was driving her now, erasing her humanity bit by bit. She was powerless to control the grizzly compulsion.

Selena's heart ached, missing her vain, theatrical mother who would never have harmed herself in such an awful way. That woman was slipping further and further away with each scratch and tear at her own ruined flesh.

"It's time we paid our respects, don't you think?" her mum said.

Selena twiddled with her hair and chewed her lip, because the last thing she felt like doing was visiting some creepy cemetery. The starfish symbol in the book flashed up in her brain that she'd seen on the map of Madderly at the cemetery. What did the symbol mean? She didn't know, but maybe the necklace had once been buried in the cemetery.

A possibility dawned on her. Perhaps the necklace had been buried there with Aunt Ada. It was a long shot, but any lead was worth investigating at this point.

"Yeah okay," Selena said carefully, heart racing. This

could be a pivotal clue, the one that finally led her to the necklace.

Fiona seemed satisfied and went back to eating. Selena was focused now on one thing only—the possibility of uncovering the necklace that could save her mother.

Once at the cemetery, she'd find a way to investigate that starfish marking without raising suspicion. She just prayed the necklace was there and that its magic wasn't too late.

It had taken them all day to finally reach the cemetery. Fiona had gone back to bed for hours before summoning the strength to rise again, her deterioration slowing her down.

When they finally arrived, dusk was falling, casting long shadows between the tombstones. Selena supported her mother's frail body as they shuffled down the overgrown paths, searching for Aunt Ada's grave.

They found it as darkness descended, a simple headstone next to a mound of earth, neglected and forgotten. Fiona grasped the urn planter at its foot with pallid fingers.

"Aunt Ada was such a strong, powerful woman," her mum said. "But she had a turbulent life. To be honest, I don't think she's passed on to the other side. In the house… I… I still feel her. Don't you?"

"Yes. Well, maybe. The portraits in the hallway keep moving."

Fiona nodded. "It's still her grave. She deserves it to look nice. I'm going to make it so pretty." She sighed. "Guess nobody visits her since we're her only living relatives. If only she'd left us all her money instead of that cat charity...our problems would be over."

Fiona frowned at Selena. "To be honest, our family history isn't really something to brag about. And I hope Faustina doesn't show up again."

Selena noticed her mum's lip twitch strangely as she said it, and there was a weird sparkle in her eyes. She wondered if the zombie curse was making her mum say strange stuff. She needed to cure Fiona fast before she went totally off the rails.

Methodically, her mum began digging holes in the earth on the grave for the marigolds they had brought, the trowel scraping loudly in the eerie silence. Selena shuddered as she watched her mother's rigid, mechanical movements.

"I hope she doesn't visit again either," Selena said, planting the marigolds. A chill wind blew, and Selena sensed something there with them. Aunt Ada's spirit maybe? "That first night totally freaked me out."

Fiona brushed off her dirty hands. "Faustina's gone off the deep end, no doubt." She knelt on a soft heap of earth and took Selena's face gently. "I could never stand to lose you, not now. You're the most important thing ever to me, Peaches."

Selena tried not to flinch from her mum's cold touch.

"And what about you?" Selena said, her forearms getting goosebumps. "I've been wanting to talk to you about something. Because you look so ill."

"What is it? You can talk to me about anything."

Selena took a deep breath. She had to tell her mum the truth. "I was there on the beach that night you were attacked. I saw everything, Mum. I'm sorry I didn't tell you before."

Fiona tensed, avoiding her daughter's gaze. "So. you saw it all then?" She said quietly.

Selena nodded, blinking back tears. "It was so scary, Mum. What's happening to you? You could really be turning into...into one of them." She gestured at the ugly gashes marring her mother's face. "You keep scratching at your wounds like they're infected or something."

Fiona wrapped her arms around herself, eyes distant. "I don't feel quite right, dear, but please don't worry. I'm not going to turn into a monster."

An uneasy silence fell between them, filled only by the wind and rustling leaves. Then Fiona shuddered and went back to halfheartedly poking at the dirt around the flowers.

Selena hesitated then continued gently, "Maybe you're right, Mum. I know you don't want to think about it. But what if you *are* changing? Isn't there anything we can do?"

She took a deep breath and added, "Like, if we found that magic necklace, maybe it could heal you, stop the infection from spreading?"

Fiona paused her work, glancing down with a conflicted expression.

"You didn't find it that night with Mr. Bottomley," Selena pressed on. "But you can't give up, Mum. We have to keep trying, for your sake."

Her mum was quiet for a long moment. Then finally, she nodded, and Selena saw a spark of her old self flash in her eyes.

"You're right, Sweetie. We'll keep trying." Fiona met her daughter's gaze. "Okay, I admit I'm worried," she said with a sigh. "I've been racking my brain about where the necklace could be. It's been buried in different spots around Madderly over the years."

Fiona patted the dirt around the flowers as Selena traced Aunt Ada's name on the tombstone. "I've checked some of those places already, but no luck yet. I know I need that necklace to stop myself going full zombie mermaid. But what if we never find it?"

Selena squeezed her mum's hand, ignoring the icy coldness. "Don't worry, we'll figure it out," she promised.

Fiona dug around in the earth with her trowel. Selena wondered if she was looking for the necklace in Aunt Ada's grave under the pretense of planting flowers.

"You don't want to meddle with the necklace," Fiona said. "Promise me. Promise me you won't."

"I don't know if I can—"

"I can't explain how I know, but believe me, it's a bad idea for you to find it."

"Mum, I know you're warning me off, but I have to find that necklace—I just have to. It's the only thing that can help with..." Selena hesitated then confessed. "Mum, I've been miserable ever since we moved here. The necklace feels like my only hope." Her scalp itched like crazy, and she yanked her hair back in frustration.

"What do you mean miserable?" Fiona asked, looking worried.

"I'm getting bullied a lot. I was hoping if I found the

necklace, wearing it would give me like a force field. To protect me, you know?"

Selena sighed, hating to tell her mum this. But the bullying was making her life awful.

Fiona clutched her hand. Selena peered into her mum's bloodshot eyes. The black withered trees bent back and forth in the chilly wind, and Selena shivered.

"I know. I saw Jamie pick on you in drama class, but you never seem to want to talk about it when I try to broach the subject."

Could this conversation be any more excruciating? "That's because it's embarrassing."

"Do you want me to speak to Roger? We can have a meeting and get it taken care of."

"I don't know if I want to make a fuss," said Selena. "I think they're getting tired of picking on me anyway."

"Let me know if you want me to talk to him, Sweetie," Fiona said. Her face was ghostly pale. The red scratches were like worms on her face. "I knew living near zombie mermaids was a risk, but Aunt Ada never said they came into people's homes."

"I get it, Mum. I guess Faustina is pretty out there."

Fiona gave a long sigh and shook her head. "Maybe I didn't think it through. I was short of cash, and when Aunt Ada left me her house… I thought things were going to be amazing."

"Have you ever thought of just selling the house?"

"Yeah, I have. But the thought of making that kind of

decision just seems like too much right now. My brain feels like it's turned to mush."

"It's okay. Just concentrate on finding the necklace and getting well," Selena said. "Come on, let's water the plants. We'll make it look as nice as we can."

Selena filled the watering can at a nearby tap and watered the newly planted marigolds. She went over to the stone planter at the foot of Aunt Ada's grave, which had a rose bush of tiny yellow roses in it.

She thought of the flower puns Aunt Ada had left around the house. Had she been leaving clues for Selena? Mr. Bottomley had read out a pun: What kind of alcohol do flowers drink? Rosé.

Could the yellow starfish symbol have actually been a rose? It was possible.

Selena plucked off some of the withered leaves, watered the bush, and pressed down on the earth inside. As she did, a jolt of electricity pulsed through her. She jumped back with a yelp.

"What is it?" Fiona cried.

"I think I got bitten by a bug."

"Yuck. Let's get out of here. I hate bugs."

While her mum packed up the trowels, Selena shoved her hands back into the crumbly earth. Her fingers hit something hard and cold—something with heavy stones.

Selena grabbed it and slipped it into her pocket. This had to be it.

On the bumpy bus ride home, Selena discreetly pulled

the necklace from her pocket to examine it up close. The rubies glinted mysteriously in the low light.

There were five large oval stones the shade of fresh blood, encircled by intricate filigree carved from some silvery metal. Each stone was perfectly polished to a mirrored sheen, as though they contained their own hidden seas within.

As she turned the necklace over in her hands, the rubies cast a scarlet glow across her skin. It was like holding a small, beating heart in her palm.

The silverwork was painstakingly fine, each twist and curl wrapping possessively around the precious rubies. Tiny unknown glyphs were etched along the metal, no doubt spelling out magical properties and secrets she couldn't decipher alone.

Selena had never seen or felt anything like it. Power thrummed beneath the flawless crimson surfaces, awaiting release. No wonder such a treasure had sparked greed and tragedy for generations. She just hoped its abilities could also kindle hope.

Around her, passengers stared and whispered as Fiona picked at her decaying face, muttering under her breath. Selena's face burned as a young boy pointed and cried out in disgust.

Fiona was deteriorating quickly from the zombie curse. Selena had intended to the give the necklace to her mother, but what if she lost the necklace in this confused state? Its power was too precious to waste.

Selena pictured the necklace burning away the creeping

rot, healing her mother fully. But she couldn't hand it over, not yet.

She had to protect its magic and use it carefully. The necklace was their only hope against Faustina, the vengeful zombie mermaid who started Fiona's curse. And it could shield Selena from the bullies who tormented her.

Once she unlocked its power, the necklace would protect them and put an end to the zombie curse on her mum. She just needed a little time to make a plan.

Guilt twisted inside at deceiving her mother. But Fiona might give the necklace away right now. Selena had to be strong.

As Fiona's fingernails scraped at peeling skin, Selena shivered. She would hide the necklace at home for now. Its magic still offered a chance to save them both.

FAUSTINA

Faustina's tail thrashed wildly as she patrolled the coastline, unable to contain her anticipation. She could feel it—the ruby necklace called to her from somewhere on land. It sang a siren's song only she could hear, beckoning her to reclaim what was stolen centuries ago.

Mine, it whispered in her brain. *Mine.*

She remembered the surge of power that had coursed through her veins when she'd first seized the magic necklace from the pirate, Zlotan. How she and her twin sister, Starona, had ruled the mermaid kingdom, commanding fear and respect. Faustina had guided the young mermaids in their education, encouraging them to bond as a community. They were happy in those days...before the shark attack that took Starona's life and Faustina's sanity.

In her grief, she'd retreated to a lonely cave still wearing the necklace, only to wake and find it ripped from her neck. The other mermaids claimed a thieving squid had snatched it in the night, but Faustina never found proof. For centuries she'd searched the coastline while it passed from owner to owner, always eluding her grasp. Until it fell into the withered hands of Aunt Ada.

That doddering old fool had no concept of the power she held. She flaunted the necklace without an ounce of respect. The thought of Aunt Ada misusing her treasure made Faustina's blood boil.

Losing her twin had shattered Faustina into jagged pieces. She went crazy—she could admit that. Soon enough, none of the other mermaids would talk to her, and swimming around for hundreds of years on her own had put her in a foul mood. Yes, it could be fun eating sailors or sucking their brains out, but that didn't happen often enough. Honestly, most mermaid zombies weren't good company. They had a one-track mind: to infect humans. Fun while it lasted, but it got old. Fast.

If she was going to be undead forever, she wanted to find some other things to do. *In-bite* some new people into the party. Suddenly, she was spewing silly puns, just like Aunt Ada.

If only she could regain the necklace; its magic might restore her. She imagined the clarity it would bring, the absolute control over mermaids and humans alike. No more would she drift aimlessly. With amplified speed and strength, she could feed more ravenously than ever before.

Perhaps it would even make her likable enough to befriend Selena, her flesh and blood. Faustina had hoped civilly inviting the girl to her underwater home would suffice. When that failed, she turned her focus to Selena's delightfully dramatic mother, Fiona. Sooner or later, she would make that vibrant woman one of them.

Faustina knew the ruby necklace was the key to everything she desired. With its magic enhancing her own powers of control, she could bend anyone to her will, puppeteering humans and merfolk alike. Her mind would finally be free of the relentless fog that had dampened her thoughts for decades.

She could make people follow her whether they wanted to or not. She even hoped it would give her the powers of superhuman strength and speed. To be able to hunt and infect people in a larger radius. She hoped it would make her more likable, too.

As she swam about, she saw a few zombie mermaids bobbing about. These days there was no ruler, and it was basically a free-for-all. Once Faustina had been like royalty and demanded respect, and now she was no more important than Aunt Ada's squid. That hurt.

She recognized a bunch of them from her school days back when Undead Academy had still been open. Sometimes, she felt bad for letting her temper get so out of control that she'd smashed up the school. Lately, all Faustina could think about were the good old days, when she and Starona had ruled over all the zombie mermaids together.

They'd earned the right to be in charge by being gutsy

enough to steal the enchanted ruby necklace when they were young. Sure, some of the mermaids had complained that Faustina and Starona didn't deserve to rule just for taking the necklace. But hey, no one else had dared to swipe it.

Faustina thought she and Starona had been pretty fair leaders, too. As long as the mermaids obeyed, they didn't get tossed in zombie jail or anything. But then Starona had to go and get eaten by a shark, leaving Faustina to rule alone.

Eventually, the loneliness drove Faustina nuts. She missed her sister. Ruling the kingdom just wasn't the same without Starona by her side.

Fiona was up there turning into a zombie mermaid, but it was happening too slowly for Faustina's liking. That was what happened when you only scratched the surface of a person's skin. It was Faustina's own fault for not getting a good bite. Still, she was running out of patience.

Of course, she could lure Fiona into the sea and be done with it. One of the perks of being a mermaid was controlling people's thoughts. But for the moment, she was reigning herself in. Because she didn't just want Fiona; she wanted the necklace. Until Fiona had it, she was more useful to Faustina on land.

Faustina knew the ruby necklace would give her all the power she'd ever want. She just had to be patient until she got it back.

For now, she was happy to control Fiona from afar, watching as she slowly lost her humanity bit by bit. It was the best horror movie ever.

Faustian cackled to herself. That necklace would be hers again soon. And once she had it, she'd rule the zombie mermaids forever. No one would dare challenge her then.

2 2

SELENA

Selena tiptoed down the stairs on Sunday morning, wincing as each creak of the steps echoed through the silent house. Reaching the first floor, she peeked into the kitchen. Her mum sat motionless at the table, staring blankly into her full cup of tea. The room was dark, the blinds still drawn over the windows despite the morning sun outside.

Selena's heart pounded, pulsing in her ears. She had slept deeply last night, soothed by the rhythmic crashing of ocean waves. But the necklace hidden under her bed emanated a power she did not fully understand. A force field, she hoped, to keep evil and bullies at bay. Yet its abilities remained unpredictable. If her mum discovered it, how would she react? Selena worried that Fiona might manipulate her into handing it over.

Taking a deep breath, Selena steadied her nerves and

stepped into the kitchen. She had to believe the necklace would protect her, at least for today.

Selena froze as her mother's hollow voice echoed through the silent kitchen.

"It's no use, Angel-face. Without that necklace, I'm powerless against the forces at play." She gripped her mug with white-knuckled hands, taking a long, slow sip. "I must speak with Aunt Ada. A séance is the only way."

The toaster popped, startling Selena. She fumbled to catch the toast before it fell.

"Mum, no," she pleaded, her own voice sounding small and distant. "You don't know what you might unleash."

Her mother's smile sent a chill down Selena's spine. "Oh, but I do have power, my dear. More than you know."

"I may believe in zombie mermaids, but you can't go messing with the spirit world."

Her mother's séances with the dearly departed were dubious enough. It had been another way to make a quick buck. That had been bad enough, but when she'd communicated with dead cats, that had been downright absurd.

Selena recalled one of those sessions, her mother emitting plaintive meows, squeaking in her best impression of a feline from the great beyond. "Don't fret, I'm having a ball up here! Unlimited steamed salmon, catnip fields to romp through. And get this—I can bat cups off the counter to my heart's delight."

Selena suppressed an eye roll. As if the cats could suddenly speak English instead of meowing. Though she had to admit, her mother's portrayal of that chatty calico named Nibbles had been oddly convincing.

"I mean, maybe you do have powers, Mum, but you have to be aware there are some dangerous forces around here. Maybe we should leave them alone. I mean, have you seen what happens in this house? The pictures move in their frames, and the walls leak goo. It's totally haunted."

"Aunt Ada is laughing at us," Fiona said darkly. "I need to talk to her. To try to get her to stop these bad things from happening, like Faustina attacking us. Can't she try to tame her?"

"How about we just leave this house and go back to London? Ever since we got here, things have started to go wrong. The bullying—"

"Don't you think I want to? But right now, I'm contracted to finish this play. We need to stick it out for a few more weeks. Are you sure you don't want me to have a word with Roger about the bullying?"

Selena remembered how Mr. Bottomley had instantly blamed her for the last fight she'd been in.

"No. It's okay, Mum. I think I can handle—"

Someone tapped on the kitchen window. Selena pulled up the blind, and Mr. Bottomley's face loomed into view. He grinned and waved.

Selena's mum hurried out into the hall and opened the door. "This *is* a lovely surprise."

"I thought you might like some muffins," he said. "You aren't looking well." He followed her through the hall and into the kitchen. "I noticed you've looked a bit peaky the last few days."

Selena stifled an eye roll. Peaky was an understatement. Her mum's face was leaking gross, yellow gunk nonstop. It was nasty.

"Oh, I'm fine, just under the weather," her mum lied as she hurried into the kitchen, carrying a giant basket of muffins. "You're so sweet to check on me."

Selena tried not to gag as her mum flashed him an innocent smile. Mr. Bottomley gazed at Fiona all moony-eyed. Selena wanted to smack him. How could he not see how sick she was? Love really did make you blind.

"It's what any good neighbor would do."

Why did he keep popping 'round? Selena buttered her toast. He obviously didn't care that she'd almost killed him with the peanuts. *Were they dating or not? Actually, better not to think about that one. I don't want to know.*

"I'm going out," Selena said, getting up as Mr. Bottomley settled himself beside Fiona at the table. "I feel like a walk… get some fresh air."

"Okay, darling. Don't go too far."

As she looked at her mum, she could see something had changed. She had a little color in her cheeks, and she didn't look like she was about to keel over. Even the wounds weren't quite as gruesome as usual. The necklace. It was already working. She wasn't going to lose her mum to the sea—to Faustina—anytime soon.

Although, she might be losing her to Mr. Bottomley, who was feeding Fiona bits of muffin right in front of Selena.

"I'm going to have the séance next Sunday at seven," Fiona said, turning to Selena. "I need you to be there. And invite anyone you know who is in touch with their spiritual side."

"I don't know any people like that…"

"That sounds intriguing," Roger said, leaning toward her mum. "I've dabbled in the spirit world once or twice myself, you know."

"Really?" Fiona said, raising an eyebrow and leaning across the table to place a hand on his arm. "Then you must come, Pookie Bear. I insist."

"I would love to see you in action," Roger said. "What do you think, Selena? Do you think your mum has a real psychic gift?" He seemed genuinely curious.

"I don't know what to think," Selena hedged. She didn't want to call her mum out as a fake psychic in front of Mr. Bottomley.

"Well, I believe in you," Mr. Bottomley said, feeding her more muffin. "You know I'll always be there to support you."

Blech! Did he have to be so nauseating? And had she just called him Pookie Bear again?

"Thanks. You don't know how much that means to me. That *someone* believes in my psychic powers." She glared at her daughter, but Selena ignored her.

At the moment, she was more concerned with getting out of there before she had to watch more of the sickening display.

"Okay, I'm leaving now," Selena said, heading for the

door.

"Tell your friends to join us at the séance," Fiona called after her.

Selena gave a noncommittal wave as she headed out the door. There was no way she was doing that. She didn't want anyone knowing about the séance. She was already a laughingstock. No point in making it worse.

23

SELENA

Selena watched as her mum tore through the dusty boxes stacked precariously high in the musty library. Her wild red curls had come loose from their bun and now framed her face like a fiery lion's mane.

It had only been a few days since Fiona had grandly declared that she wanted to hold a séance to contact Aunt Ada from beyond the grave. Ever since, she had been on a mission - flinging open drawers, overturning chairs, tossing old clothes, yellowed books, and odd trinkets across the threadbare Persian rugs.

"The Ouija board is here somewhere, I just know it!" Fiona cried theatrically, tossing a moth-eaten shawl over her shoulder. She stood in the center of the chaos, hands on her hips, surveying the room like a queen overseeing her kingdom.

Selena leaned against the dark wood paneled walls of the

library, adorned with faded gold patterned wallpaper, and sighed. Her mother's obsession was growing out of control. But she knew better than to get in Fiona's way when she was on one of her missions.

Fiona flung aside a moth-eaten fur coat and dug deeper into one of the boxes. "I've looked through all the stuff that was delivered from our old flat. And it's not here."

Selena sighed. "Mum, I told you, having a séance is a bad idea."

"Nonsense!" Her mother emerged from the mess, smears of dirt across her face. "We must make contact if we're to recover your Aunt Ada's necklace."

She began opening and overturning more boxes in her zealous search. Selena cringed at the chaos unfolding.

"Please, let's think this through," she tried again, but her mother was no longer listening. She was possessed by some manic spirit, tearing through the room for her mystical board.

"Maybe you're getting a sign from the other side."

"What is it?" her mother said, pulling a long cobweb out of a box.

"That you shouldn't hold the séance," Selena said, cocking her head to one side, "because you can't find your Ouija board."

Selena wished the only thing that would happen during this séance was Aunt Ada's spirit revealing Selena had taken the necklace. But that was impossible because the necklace had vanished days ago.

Selena had stashed it under her bed, too nervous to actually wear it yet. Her mum's warnings echoed in her mind. Still, the allure of its power called to Selena.

Finally, she'd worked up the courage to put it on. But when she checked under the bed, the necklace was gone. In its place were strange black splashes.

Someone must have taken it. Probably her mum. But Selena didn't know how to ask about it without revealing she'd had the necklace all along.

Now here they were, about to hold a séance. Selena shivered, wondering what they might conjure without the necklace's protection. She had to get it back before they contacted forces beyond their control.

Fiona stood in the center of the room with her arms outstretched, the bangles on her wrists clinking together. Selena looked down at a glass of water on the table, which started to ripple. The photos in their frames shook. The walls were vibrating, Selena realized. It was the same as when the house had shaken that first night when Faustina had crashed into her room. Except this time, it was happening without the waves pounding against the house.

A strange energy swirled around the room. A cold, deathly atmosphere settled heavily on her shoulders. All the air was sucked out of the room in a whoosh. Selena gasped for breath, and her hand went up to her throat. Her mum's eyes blinked.

SPLASH.

"What is it, Mum? What's happening? Did you hear that splash?" She glanced up at the ceiling.

"There's a Ouija board up in the attic. I'm getting the sense —"

There was the splashing sound again.

Selena's mum grabbed her wrist. Selena wanted to escape the room and the horrible energy. "Be a darling and go up and look for it, would you?"

"What? You think I want to climb up into that creepy attic when I heard a splash. There's someone up there."

"Don't be crazy, no one's there. I just need that Ouija board," Selena's mum begged. "I need to start dinner. I was thinking of Spaghetti Bolognese."

Clearly, her mum was bribing Selena with her favorite meal, but it was a welcome change from the microwave dinners she usually made. "Fine. It's a deal."

Selena's stomach churned as she trudged upstairs to her bedroom and pulled down the ladder that led to the attic. Maybe there was no one up there. Maybe the splashing sounds were just something to do with the fact that this whole house was haunted. Although that didn't give her much comfort.

A smell of sulfur hit her in the face. Green clouds of it rained down on her so thick she could hardly see as she climbed the ladder. It was the same scent that had come from Faustina that first night she'd tried to bite Selena. A strong breeze raced through the attic, and she could see one of the windows was broken; shards of glass littered the floor. She hesitated. *Had someone broken in recently?*

Selena's fingers brushed the cobwebby wall, looking for the light switch. When she flicked it on, nothing happened.

She let her eyes adjust to the darkness, then she crept across the floorboards, which squeaked with every step. Mice scampered away as she maneuvered through piles of boxes, dusty and covered in cobwebs, full of old Christmas decorations and children's toys.

Selena rummaged through the boxes and found old black and white photos of a young Aunt Ada, looking stylish in hats, evening dresses, and elaborate jewelry. Among the photos were curved pieces of paper, metallic and shimmery. Examining them more carefully, she realized they were fish scales. More fish scales were scattered on the floor, mixed in with the mouse droppings. She gulped.

She set aside the photos and dug through the boxes more quickly, determined to find the Ouija board and get out of there.

The taste in her mouth was gritty with dust but bitter, too—salty and acrid. Waves of green smoke swirled in the moonlight. Finally, she found the Ouija board, but as she got up to leave, a clawfoot tube at the far end of the attic caught her eye. How weird to have a bath in the attic.

Selena froze as a sloshing sound came from the bathtub, followed by an eerie chattering. Her heart hammered in her chest.

As she crept closer on trembling legs, a mermaid's tail rose from the bathtub and splashed back down. Selena screamed, the Ouija board slipping from her numb fingers.

She staggered back, terror flooding her veins like ice. But morbid curiosity drew her forward again. Hands shaking, she peered over the tub's edge.

The face that surged up had sunken features, with a hollow nose and eyes. A rotting visage. Selena choked back bile, paralyzed by shock and horror.

The face leered up at Selena, lips rotted and peeling back to reveal jagged, broken teeth. Her hair was a tangled, matted mess, brittle strands falling out in clumps.

Fish scales flaked off her wizened skin in patches, revealing oozing sores and growths. Her sunken eyes were filmy white, pupils long faded.

As she opened her mouth, a foul stench wafted out—the smell of decay and death. Her raspy breaths gurgled wetly in her throat.

Webs of seaweed were tangled around the mottled green and purple flesh of her decayed tail. Remnants of a seashell bra barely clung to her skeletal chest.

She reached toward Selena with one gnarled hand, sharp claws extended from each bony finger. The mermaid's head lolled grotesquely to the side as she cackled, spewing putrid black liquid from her rotted gums.

"Selena," the creature said in a soothing, melodious tone, sliding out of the bathtub and hitting the ground with a wet thump before slithering toward her. "Great to meet you at last. I'm your Great Aunt Ada."

Selena wanted to close her eyes and pretend this wasn't real. But no matter how hard she wished, the zombie mermaid thing was still coming at her through the dark, dusty attic.

Selena's heart felt like it would pop right out of her chest. There, crawling towards her from the creepy bathtub, was something that looked kind of like her Aunt Ada but WAY scarier. Selena screamed.

"My dear, don't be afraid!" Her scales shimmered in the moonlight as her horrible, claw-like fingers reached out to her. Selena gasped at the ruby necklace clasped around her sinewy neck.

"How did you get that?" Selena said.

"Decima got it for me." She gestured to a creature scrabbling out of the bath. Its legs kicked out in all directions, shimmering like long worms in the darkness.

"Oh, my God!" Selena shrieked, clapping a hand over her mouth.

"It's okay. She's very friendly. She found it under your bed. I wanted to see what it felt like, wearing it again." She touched the rubies at her neck and sighed. "Marvelous. Just marvelous. But don't worry, you can have it back."

A stab of guilt went through Selena for thinking her mum had taken it.

Aunt Ada's corpse-like fingers fumbled with the necklace clasp. Finally, it opened, and she extended the necklace toward Selena.

Selena flinched as their hands met, Ada's skin icy and brittle. Selena lost her balance and fell back, legs burning against the rough wood.

Frantically crab-crawling away, she sent mermaid scales and mouse droppings skittering. But Ada kept sliding closer, mouth opening and closing with wet clicks.

"There's nothing to be scared of," Aunt Ada rasped, foul

liquid dripping down her chin. She held out the necklace in rotting hands.

Selena reached for it hesitantly. Suddenly, Ada lunged, her claw-like nails grazing Selena's arm.

Selena cried out, stumbling back in terror. One scrape was all it would take to seal her fate. Her heart hammered wildly as Ada let out a chilling cackle.

With trembling fingers, Selena grabbed the necklace and snapped it closed behind her neck, the warm stones humming against her skin. This was her only hope now.

"Wait," Ada muttered, eyes clearing briefly.

Picking up the Ouija board, Selena scrambled down the ladder, pulse racing. Above, Ada's tail scraped ominously.

Frantically folding the ladder, Selena slammed the trapdoor shut. She clung to the necklace, its power coursing through her.

Selena checked her wrists. Luckily, Ada's claws hadn't broken the skin. One scratch could turn her. For now, she was still human.

Aunt Ada wailed and beat upon the trapdoor, but the lock held firm. Selena staggered back, relief washing over her. But she knew the barrier wouldn't contain Aunt Ada for long. Could Aunt Ada smash through it with magic or force? The latch rattled against itself, but it held. For now.

She sat on her bed, panting. The pink-flowered walls of the room were closing in on her. She had just managed to stash the necklace under the bed when her mum ran in, eyes wide with panic.

"Are you all right? I thought I heard a scream."

Selena ran over and flung her arms around her. "Oh, Mum…" She glanced up at the trapdoor.

Fiona recoiled as a splash of vile liquid fell through the attic trapdoor, striking her face.

"Ugh, what's that?" she cried out, wiping the foul substance from her forehead. The oily ooze reeked of rot, clinging to her hands, even as she tried rubbing it off on her shirt.

More drops dripped down, pooling slime on the floor. Fiona stumbled back.

"It's Aunt Ada. She's up there," Selena whispered, voice trembling.

Fiona's eyes darted around the room, finally fixing on the attic trapdoor. "That's impossible," she breathed. "Ada was buried, you saw the grave…"

Her voice trailed off as the truth sunk in.

Slowly, Fiona sat on the edge of the bed. Her body began to tremble, hands clenching the blankets.

"She's one of them now…a zombie?" The word caught in her throat. Selena nodded grimly.

Fiona's gaze landed on the Ouija board lying discarded on the floor. "But the séance," she murmured. "I have to make contact…"

"Mum, Aunt Ada is right upstairs," Selena cried. She hesitated before adding, "You could just…go talk to her."

A hysterical giggle escaped Fiona's lips. "Oh sure, pop in for a chat with the undead mermaid. What if she bites?"

Selena shifted uneasily at the thought.

"Maybe we should go eat dinner and think about what to do next," her mum said, and they headed downstairs.

"I'm sorry, Mum," Selena said, pushing her spaghetti around her plate ten minutes later, "but I don't think I can sleep tonight thinking about Aunt Ada. I would feel a lot better if you went and talked to her."

"You're right, Angel. I do need to talk to her," her mum said, slurping up her spaghetti. "Will you come with me?"

"I'm too scared," Selena replied, her stomach churning. "I thought she was going to attack me just now. But I also really want to know how exactly she ended up in our attic, splashing around the old bathtub as a zombie mermaid."

Her mum nodded. "Me too. It's just so bizarre. Will you come with me? We'll keep our distance from her, I promise."

Selena let out a long sigh. She was terrified to get near Aunt Ada again, with her pale green skin, tangled seaweed hair, and sharp teeth. But she had to know what happened.

"Alright, I'll go. But we better have a quick escape plan if she tries to take a bite out of us!"

"Deal," her mum said, giving her hand a squeeze.

SELENA

The attic stairs creaked under Selena's feet as she ascended into the gloom, torch in hand. Its weak beam barely cut through the all-consuming shadows.

"I don't know about this," Fiona whimpered from below, hesitation evident in her quivering voice.

But Selena pushed on, her breathing growing shallow with each heavy footfall. Piles of forgotten relics loomed on either side, mysterious shapes within swimming in and out of the torch's fading glow.

Then she saw it. A metallic gleam in the distance, reflecting the light with an ethereal sheen. She stumbled forward, dread coursing through her veins. The object came into grim focus—an ancient bathtub, filled not with water but with a viscous silver liquid.

A mass floated upon the surface, gray tendrils drifting

lifelessly. Selena's heart turned to stone in her chest. Through the ripples, two glassy eyes peered back, gazing endlessly into her soul.

A gurgling chuckle emanated from the tub, bubbling up from its depths. "Welcome, dears. I've been waiting..."

At first, Fiona's face went completely blank, then her eyes bulged wide as she recoiled backwards nearly toppling into a pile of moldy boxes. When Fiona spoke, her voice came out squeaky like she'd inhaled a mouse, her hands fluttering around her face in dismay. Eventually, Fiona turned a sickly green hue, letting out a noise like a dying teakettle.

"Aunt Ada, it's been so long..." Fiona stammered, unable to mask her shock and horror.

Ada chuckled, sending swirling bubbles across the tub's grimy surface. "I know, I'm quite the sight now, aren't I? But really, being an undead mermaid isn't so bad."

As Ada spoke, Fiona stared open-mouthed, her face frozen in an expression of utter disbelief and revulsion at the nightmare before them. Selena feared her mum might join Fiona in losing what little contents remained in her stomach. How could Aunt Ada be so cavalier about her monstrous transformation? They had to get to the bottom of this dark mystery, and quickly.

"I'm sorry I scared you before, Selena. I only wanted to give you a hug," Aunt Ada said.

Fiona kneeled by the tub, leaning in close. Selena watched her mum carefully. Fiona's expression had changed from fearful to fascinated.

Selena nodded at Aunt Ada, relieved the threat seemed past. She had to know: "How'd you become undead?"

"It was a few months back," Aunt Ada began. "I'm just sitting in the garden, having tea with Mr. Wiggums in my lap—he's my darling cat, you know. When all of a sudden, this wild red-headed mermaid comes surfing in on a massive wave."

Ada gestured dramatically with her hands. "I'd never laid eyes on her, but I'd sure heard the stories. Faustina, she called herself. My supposed long-lost relative. Well, let me tell you, she was not easy on the eyes." Ada grimaced. "I was shaken, I tell you. Mr. Wiggums was hissing up a storm, had to lock him inside away from her."

Selena leaned forward eagerly. "What did she say?"

"She starts going on about how we're family, she's been searching for me. Talking a mile a minute with this crazed look in her eyes. I tell you I was terrified." Ada shuddered.

"She was going on about 'Oh Auntie, lovely to see you! Let's put the past behind us' and whatnot. Hmph! This is the same mermaid who went bonkers a while back, destroyed the undersea school in a fit of temper. Read all about it in some ancient books here. Total loose cannon, that one."

Ada shook her head. "Anyway, she's going on about trying to make friends, but no one likes her, boo hoo. Then she comes out with, 'Hey, as an old lady with only a cat, would it kill you to let me finish you off?'"

Selena gasped. "No way! She asked if she could kill you?"

"I know, the nerve. I told her, Faustina, I've got my cat, my books, my knitting. I'm fine. But she wouldn't let up, going on about making me an underwater house and how I looked like a wrinkled apple."

Ada cackled. "So, I'm like, not on your nellie. No thanks, got to stay for Mr. Wiggums. She started going on about how she's had centuries to reflect on things. Apparently, she regrets going nuts and smashing up the Undead Academy in a fit of rage. Some sob story about working through her anger issues."

Aunt Ada rolled her eyes. "Said she was still hot under the collar about sharks on account of one eating her sister. But she's trying to be more zen and forgive, blah blah blah."

Ada let out a raspy chuckle, but it sounded more like a tire losing air, a long, wheezy hiss through rotted vocal chords. Black goo bubbled up between her cracked gray lips with the exertion, dribbling down her chin.

Selena cringed at the sight and stench of the viscous fluid. She didn't think she'd ever get used to Ada's zombie mermaid traits, the way foul slime and various gases seemed to leak continuously from her aunt's decomposing body.

"Sorry dears, this body isn't what it used to be," Ada gurgled, her milky eyes flashing with dim humor. She swiped at the goo trailing down her jaw but only succeeded in smearing it across her mottled green skin.

"You were saying about Faustina?" Selena's mum prompted gently, though her face had gone pale.

"Ah yes, that two-faced fish," Ada rasped, bits of black sputum flying from her mouth. "I told her hey, good on you for self-reflecting and trying to change your ways. Holding grudges only hurts you in the long run. So, I thought we were having a pleasant chat and sipping tea. But before I could blink, she'd got me in a headlock. Sunk her fangs right into my neck. I barely got out a scream before I blacked out."

Fiona shook her head in disbelief. "Good grief, what a psycho!"

"Tell me about it. At least I got Mr. Wiggums set up with a good foster home before completing my zombie mermaid transformation. Didn't want him snacking on my brain, you know." Ada chuckled.

Her mum's eyebrows shot up. "Wow. When Faustina sets her mind on something, she doesn't mess around. Then what happened?"

"Ugh, Faustina would NOT leave me alone," Aunt Ada groaned, flapping her tail in the water. "She just kept appearing and bothering me, going on about 'Come live with me in my underwater lair! We'll start a school for the undead' Honestly, I think that mermaid has a few screws loose."

Fiona shook her head. "She's a real character, no doubt. So, how'd she manage to pull you down under the sea?"

"So there I was, lying in my coffin in the living room, when Faustina comes and yanks open the lid." Ada made a popping sound. "And let me tell you, it scared me to death...again. Next thing I know, she's grabbing me by my hair and tugging me to the ocean. I mean, I guess it beats rotting away on land."

"She dragged me under the sea, then buried the empty coffin to fake my death. Devious fish, that one," Aunt Ada replied, her fanged teeth flashing in the light.

Selena's mind whirled as she pictured Ada getting pulled into the dark depths. To be buried alive under the waves...it must have been terrifying. Yet Ada spoke about it with an amused glint in her milky eyes.

Fiona clicked her tongue. "You've been to hell and back, Ada."

"That's one way to put it," Ada said with a raspy laugh. "But the ocean is as much heaven as hell. The wonders I've seen down there..." Her gaze grew distant, lost in memory.

Selena felt awe hearing about Ada's adventures. She couldn't imagine the magical creatures and sunken secrets the ocean held.

"So why come back on land?" Selena asked curiously. "Don't you like being a zombie mermaid?"

Ada sighed. "Oh, I do, don't get me wrong. Faustina built a fabulous replica of this house underwater. But after fifty years here, this old place just feels more like home. I'm too old for the whole brain-sucking, human-biting thing. I just want to enjoy my retirement in my tub."

"Ugghh, brain sucking doesn't sound good," Selena said, scrunching her nose.

"You got that right, kiddo," Aunt Ada replied. "Once you go full zombie, you get this never-ending hunger for flesh and brains. Got to get that hit of sweet, sweet brain chemicals. But let me tell you, the brain cravings are real." She let out a monstrous burp, her rancid breath making Selena gag.

"Being constantly starving sounds like a major downer," Selena said, fanning the air.

"You get used to it but chasing down your next meal gets old real fast," Aunt Ada said. "That's why I came back on land. Conjured up a monster wave with my mermaid powers and rode it right back here. I'd rather just soak in the tub than keep up that brain-sucking grind."

Fiona nodded weakly, her skin looking paler and clammier. "Faustina's gone off the deep end. She scratched me, too. I'm slowly going full mermaid zombie."

Aunt Ada clicked her tongue. "Oh, you're looking positively undead, my dear."

"I need that ruby necklace to stop the transformation. Any idea where it is?" Fiona asked desperately.

Aunt Ada pursed her lips. "Hmm, if I recall, I think Selena had it last. Isn't that right, dear?"

Selena's face turned beet red and she could feel the heat rising in her cheeks. "No, Auntie, you're mistaken," she protested, nervously fidgeting with her hair.

"Am I? Yes, maybe I'm getting muddled," Aunt Ada said slowly, her milky eyes narrowing. "I'm feeling awfully tired now, my dears. I need to take a little nap."

She sank back under the murky water, her eyes closing. Soon there was nothing left but a cluster of bubbles where Aunt Ada had just been.

25

CHLOE

On Sunday afternoon, Chloe's stomach churned with a mix of excitement and anxiety as she thought about the séance happening later that night. Communicating with the dead, it seemed thrilling but also incredibly dangerous. What forces might they end up unleashing if this worked? Part of her didn't want any part of meddling with the spirit world. But another part of her tingled at the thought of doing something her mum would majorly freak out about.

She flopped back on her bed, weighing it all in her mind. Her phone pinged with a message from Selena. Chloe grabbed it, feeling her curiosity spike again. Having Mr. Bottomley there would be beyond weird, but she had to admit she was fascinated by the whole thing. Maybe they'd actually make contact tonight.

Selena: *The séance is canceled.*

Chloe gulped. She sat up on the bed and typed.

Chloe: *Why?*

Selena: *It's too freaky to explain. I've got something to show you. Trust me, you gotta see it yourself.*

Chloe: *Is this about zombie mermaids again?*

Chloe liked Selena. They had become really tight, but there was something that bothered her. Selena kept going on about zombie mermaids, but she never showed any proof. The photos she took of the zombie mermaid on the beach were super blurry.

What if Selena made it all up? It sucked for Chloe to think that way, but the lack of evidence made her doubt. What if Selena just wanted to add some drama and mystery by pretending mermaids were real?

Selena: *Yeah, there's one in the house right now. If you see her for yourself, you won't think I'm nuts.*

Chloe: *I DO want to believe you, but I really don't want to see a zombie mermaid.*

Selena: *Come on, please. Can you do this for me?*

Chloe: *OK, but you owe me. BIG time.*

Later that evening, Chloe found herself at the Flowers's house. She walked in and peeked through the door of the drawing room where Selena's mum and Mr. Bottomley were curled up together on a blood-red velvet sofa, whispering to each other.

"It's so weird seeing them together," Chloe said.

Selena made a face as she beckoned for Chloe to follow her up the stairs. "Tell me about it."

"So, what's the story with this zombie mermaid? If I have to see her, let's get it over with."

"Okay. She's in the attic. And… she's my Aunt Ada."

Chloe's eyes widened. "No way! The one who just died? But she's who you were doing the séance for."

"Right. My mum met with her yesterday, so she realized there was no point in doing the séance since she's undead rather than dead, you know?"

Chloe didn't know, and part of her wanted to just go home. But she knew the situation was even harder for Selena. She couldn't let her down. She shrugged nonchalantly as if she ran into zombie mermaids every day.

"I guess not, but I don't know if I want to see her. What if she attacks me?" said Chloe, following Selena up the stairs.

"Honestly, I don't think she will. She's *nice*. The total opposite of Faustina."

"Yikes, I don't ever want to meet Faustina," Chloe said. "But I trust you that Aunt Ada won't hurt me, so okay."

Selena pulled down the ladder and grabbed a torch.

"Now, don't freak out when you see her. She's a nice lady, but her face is pretty gross, like a dried-out toffee apple with caramel dripping off it. But it's not her fault, being undead and all."

Chloe's stomach turned at the description. She paused on

the ladder. "Look, I believe she's up there. I don't think I have to meet her, do I?"

"No, you don't. But I want you to. I want to prove to you that I'm not making all this stuff up."

Chloe nodded. "Okay. I get it."

At the top of the ladder, Selena pushed open the trapdoor and paused. "Do you hear that sloshing?" Then she switched on her torch. "She's in the bath."

Clouds of dust filled the air and tickled Chloe's nose. She gave a big sneeze. "I can't hear a thing." She coughed as Selena shined her torch around the room, throwing long shadows against the walls.

There was a squeak and a rustle of papers. Selena grabbed Chloe's hand and pulled her through the trapdoor. Chloe gulped and stood, frozen, her fingers laced with Selena's.

"What are we waiting for? Let's just get it over with," Chloe said, dizziness washing over her. "I see a bathtub. And what's that smell? Ew, I think I'm gonna hurl."

"Come on," Selena said firmly, tugging her along.

They inched forward as Selena swung the torchlight over the dusty piles of forgotten family treasures. But when they got to the bathtub, there was no mermaid inside. Just a bunch of shiny scales floating around. Black water had sloshed over the sides, leaving dark puddles on the floor.

"I swear she was here," Selena said, staring at the tub. Moonlight coming through the window made the inky water glitter.

Chloe gripped the edge of the tub as nausea hit her hard.

The walls seemed to bend and sway around her. She was seriously about to hurl.

"She's gone now," Chloe managed to say, though her voice sounded far away, drowned out by her pounding pulse.

Selena plunged her hands into the thick black liquid. "Maybe she's hiding under here."

Chloe gagged, bile burning her throat. "Selena, stop! That water...it looks strange. And it smells awful."

The rotten stench clogged her nose and mouth. Chloe's head spun as she watched Selena's hands disappear into the dark pool. She imagined it seeping into Selena's skin, staining her forever.

"It's okay," Selena said. "It's just zombie blood. She must be down here somewhere."

Chloe bolted for the attic's trapdoor, nearly tumbling down the ladder in her haste to get away from the tub. She raced down the steps and out the front door into the night.

Bent over and gulping air, Chloe's mind spun. Selena's bizarre tales were one thing, but that tub of zombie blood had seemed so eerie. Was this some kind of prank? Chloe couldn't be sure anymore.

She quickened her pace as questions filled her mind. Had there really been a mermaid in that tub? Where had it gone? The black liquid was so strange and unnatural looking.

By the time Chloe reached home, she had almost convinced herself it was just a dramatic setup by Selena. Her friend did love taking her weird stories too far. Chloe crept inside and upstairs.

As she lay in bed, doubts plagued her. Chloe replayed the scene again and again. Was there time to create a trick that elaborate? Or could Selena's wild tale actually be true?

Chloe shivered, pulling the covers tight. One thing was certain: she wouldn't know for sure unless she worked up the courage to go back there. But the thought of facing that bizarre black water again made her veins turn to ice.

26

CHLOE

The next day, Chloe sat on her own to avoid Selena. From across the cafeteria, Selena looked at her with a hurt expression.

Cindy sat beside Chloe, beaming. "It's okay. I knew you'd get tired of porky eventually. You made the right choice."

"It's not that—" began Chloe, but Andrew had joined them and was already prattling on about how he'd been on his dad's fishing boat over the weekend, and a shark had swum right up to it.

"It was so freaky," Andrew said. "The shark's mouth was poking out of the water. It had these massive teeth, and I was, like, waving my arms and screaming, 'get away from me!'"

"Wow, sounds like my worst nightmare," Cindy said, tossing back her hair.

"It was pretty cool. It was an ugly-looking creature with these bits of skin hanging off it."

"Gross," Cindy said, eyes wide.

Chloe wondered if it had been a shark or a zombie mermaid. Or if Andrew had fabricated the whole thing to impress her, which she guessed was kind of cute. Chloe couldn't shake the memory of Selena fishing about for a zombie mermaid in the bathtub. And what was all that about Aunt Ada being in the attic? Had Selena lied about all of it? Chloe didn't know what to think.

She and Selena were outsiders. London transplants who were different—separate—from everyone else. They hadn't known each other for years like Cindy, Jamie, and Andrew. That was what bonded them. Chloe had seen a kindred spirit in Selena and was sorry Selena's mum was out there. Selena deserved better, even if her mum *was* an amazing actress. But the other day in the attic was just too much. She needed a break from Selena to get her thoughts straight.

Chloe watched Selena out of the corner of her eye spooning mac and cheese into her mouth. Jamie strutted past her.

"Oink, oink," he snuffled.

Chloe stood up. Okay, Selena was weirding her out, but she was still her friend. Jamie had no right to pick on her. But as she stood, her phone vibrated in her backpack. She pulled it out. Selena.

Selena: *I forgot to tell you. It's a long story but I have the ruby necklace!*

Chloe was shocked. Her mind was reeling. Was it true?

Selena: *What should I do with it? Maybe I should wear it, see if it'll change my life?*

Chloe sat back down, trying to take it all in. Cindy tried to sneak a glance at her phone, so Chloe placed her hand over the screen. To be honest, she wanted to forget about Selena and her problems. The phone vibrated under her hand, and she looked down.

Selena: *Why are you ignoring me?*

The bell rang for the end of lunch, and crowds of kids swarmed toward the door, so she didn't reply. She didn't know what to say anyway.

Something warned her that Selena was trouble. But Selena was her friend. Even though she was obsessed with that necklace being the answer to all her problems, Chloe was sure that Selena really needed a friend. They had been there for each other since the beginning, and Chloe wasn't going to stop being by Selena's side just because things were getting hard.

By the time she got home from school, she'd decided to reply. She reached for her phone when the doorbell rang. Chloe answered it to find Andrew outside.

"Who is it, Chloe?" Her mother called from inside. She was busy, as she always was, scrubbing the house from top to toe.

"It's just some kid from school," Chloe called back to her mum, trying not to sniffle too loudly. She turned to Andrew. "What do you want?"

He shrugged. "I just figured we could hang out or something. Since you and Selena are fighting now, I mean."

Chloe rolled her eyes. "We didn't fight. We just...disagreed about stuff."

"Oh, gotcha. Well, sorry for making fun of you and Selena." He shuffled his feet awkwardly. "I guess that was pretty lame."

"Um, yeah it was." She crossed her arms.

"So anyway, wanna take a walk?" Andrew asked, shoving his hands in his pockets.

Chloe giggled. "What, like a date?"

His ears turned bright red. "I guess..."

Before Chloe could respond, her mum came to the door with a headscarf wrapped around her hair. She looked Andrew up and down with a total judgy face.

"Chloe isn't allowed out right now," she snapped, pulling Chloe into the hall.

"Sorry," Chloe managed before the door closed. Andrew's apology wasn't worth much, but still, she would have liked to get out of the house.

"I don't know what's gotten into you," Chloe's mum said, hands on her hips. "Haven't I told you not to hang around boys alone?"

Chloe folded her arms, irritation boiling up. She was so sick of her mum being so overprotective all the time.

"He just showed up out of nowhere. I didn't even invite him," Chloe argued.

"Hmm, I'm not sure I believe that, but just stay out of my way," her mum replied. "I've got tons of cleaning to do."

Chloe opened her mouth to respond, but her mum cut

her off. "And don't walk on my freshly mopped floor! How many times must I tell you? Shoes off in the house."

Chloe's dad sat at the sofa in the adjoining living room looking at the TV, pretending not to notice them. Her mum was busy spraying and wiping the glass sliding doors until they sparkled.

Chloe peered through the spotless glass into the back-yard. Past the garden was the steep seawall that plunged down to the ocean. She was still steaming about her mum when a dark shape caught her eye.

Something slithered across the lawn towards her. It looked like a massive snake but way bigger than snakes were supposed to get. Chloe watched in horror as the creature crept closer. She could see its rotten fishtail with shards of bone sticking out.

"Mind if I change the channel to cricket?" Chloe's dad asked casually.

Chloe couldn't find her voice to reply. She just stood frozen, mouth hanging open. Her mum had her back turned, washing dishes and didn't see the terrifying thing approaching.

Chloe's mind raced. The creepy creature slithered right for the window. She could see now it was a zombie mermaid, leaking nasty greenish smoke as it slid through the flowers. Its tangled gray hair whipped around its face.

Chloe waved her arms wildly. "Mum! There's something in the garden, look."

Her mum swung around from the dishes and froze. Her

eyes bugged out as she took in the mermaid. She let out a scream, dropping the teacup, which shattered on the floor.

Chloe's dad was glued to the cricket match, oblivious to the chaos.

As the mermaid slammed into the glass, Chloe's mum shrieked, "Graham, look! Something's out there. Where are my glasses?"

"C'mon England, you got this!" Chloe's dad shouted at the TV, fist pumping. "Glasses by the sink, dear," he added distractedly.

"What on earth is that thing?" Chloe's mum asked, panicking.

"I dunno, never seen it before," Chloe lied. She couldn't very well say *"Oh, yeah Mum, it's a zombie mermaid, no biggie."*

"Should we call the police?" Her mum cried.

At the word "police," Chloe's dad finally glanced up. "Good lord," he yelled, jumping to his feet.

"We've got to get upstairs. It might smash the window," Chloe's mum cried.

Chloe watched in horror as the mermaid slid down the glass, its hollowed-out nose leaving a trail of slime. Its mouth gaped open, black drool bubbling out.

"Where are my glasses?" Chloe's mum shrieked. "Graham, have you seen them?"

Chloe's dad just gaped as the mermaid slobbered all over the freshly cleaned windows.

"I'm hiding upstairs," Chloe's mum yelled, dashing away. "Do something, Graham."

Chloe's dad jumped up and banged the glass. "Go away! What are you, a manatee?"

Chloe shuddered. "There aren't manatees here, Dad."

Luckily, his banging worked. The mermaid peeled off the window and slithered back down the lawn. Chloe's dad hugged her, and she buried her face in his chest.

"It's leaving. I think it's going," Chloe's mum called from upstairs. "I'm ringing the police."

Chloe watched the mermaid slide down the garden towards the seawall and disappear. A few minutes later, her mum and dad sipped whiskeys, her mum looking freaked out and her dad patting her hand, saying it would be okay.

The police came and took statements, promising to investigate.

Upstairs, Chloe texted Selena.

Chloe: *I saw a zombie mermaid in our garden!*

Selena: *WHAT?? What did she look like?*

Chloe: *Gray hair; no nose. Drooling black stuff.*

Selena: *That's Aunt Ada! Do you think she was trying to bite you??*

Chloe's hands shook as she replied.

Chloe: *IDK she seemed insane. What if she'd attacked my parents?? What do we do??*

SELENA

Selena couldn't help feeling a bit relieved. Chloe finally had proof of the zombie mermaids, though Aunt Ada's attack was troubling. What had made her act so aggressively, trying to bite Chloe's family? Would she come back? Anxiety churned in Selena's mind all night.

In the morning, Selena put on the ruby necklace, the metal warm against her skin. As soon as she slid the blouse of her school uniform over it, she felt the necklace's power course through her. An electric jolt filled her with confidence and energy.

At school, Jamie, Cindy, and Andrew barely glanced her way. Maybe they were tired of tormenting the new girl. But Selena preferred to think she was shielded by the necklace's invisible protection, even as the gold made her skin itch.

While washing her hands in the bathroom, Selena braced herself as Cindy approached. Usually, Cindy had some nasty remark ready. But today she just smiled and said, "Hey, how's it going? You look happy. Something good happen?"

"Oh, um, I guess I'm just in a good mood," Selena replied, surprised. Did the necklace make her outwardly radiate happiness, too?

The world felt topsy-turvy with Cindy being nice. But she was right. Selena did feel better, tiny seeds of joy sprouting inside.

After school, Selena sat at the bus stop and took off the necklace to stop her skin from itching. With the cool rubies in her palm, she ran her fingers over the smooth stones. The necklace was bringing her good luck.

When Chloe came up and saw the necklace, her hand flew to her mouth. "Oh wow, why do you have that out? It's gotta be worth a fortune."

"It was irritating my skin, but it totally made me feel amazing," Selena said, slipping it into her backpack. "Cindy was even nice to me—so weird."

Chloe nodded. "My mum is acting really strange now. She's normally totally obsessed with cleaning, but when I left her this morning, she was sitting and staring out the window, gripping a broom and mumbling about a 'fish demon.' Do you reckon you can use the necklace to make Aunt Ada leave us alone and stay in the ocean?" Chloe asked desperately.

Selena shook her head helplessly. "I don't know how to control its powers. I think the necklace just does whatever it wants."

Absorbed in their tense conversation, neither girl noticed Andrew and Jamie approaching until it was too late.

Before Selena could react, Jamie grabbed her backpack and shoved his hand inside. He fished around for a moment before yanking out the ruby necklace.

"Well, well, what do we have here?" Jamie said with a cruel smirk. He held the necklace up, the rubies flashing in the sunlight.

Selena jumped to her feet. "Give that back, it's mine!" She shouted, lunging for it. But Jamie laughed and tossed it to Andrew.

"Not anymore, loser," Andrew said, sneering. "Finders, keepers."

Andrew tossed the necklace back to Jamie. Clutching it, Jamie raced to the edge of the sea wall, the angry ocean below.

They all raced after him.

"Does this belong to fancy Miss Snooty?" Jamie taunted, waving the necklace at Chloe.

"Give it back, it's Selena's!" Chloe shouted, lunging unsuccessfully as Jamie dodged away.

Jamie held the necklace to his neck, making the rubies sparkle. In a mocking, high-pitched voice, he said, "Ooh look at me, I'm Selena the Queen Piggy. Bow down and curtsy to me, pesky peasants."

"Take that off, you jerk," Selena yelled, swiping for it. Jamie elbowed her hard, still doing the silly imitation of her voice.

"Bad manners. Curtsy to Queen Piggy or no jewelries for you." He sneered.

"I won't curtsy. Give it back!" Selena shouted.

"Hmph, I don't want your germy jewelry anyway," Jamie said in his normal voice. He pretended to be grossed out by the necklace then pulled back his arm to throw it into the crashing waves below.

"No, don't!" Selena cried, reaching out too late. She watched helplessly as it splashed into the waves. "You idiot," she shouted at Jamie.

Andrew shifted nervously. "It was just some junky necklace, right?"

"No, it wasn't," Selena yelled, panicked.

The boys raced off along the coast, whooping and screaming, leaving them to stare down at the gray churning sea below, crashing against the seawall. Selena's stomach lurched, and she struggled to breathe. "I've got to get that necklace back," Selena moaned.

When she had found the ruby necklace, she decided to keep it for herself rather than tell her mum. Selena hoped to use its power to stop the bullies that taunted her daily.

Selena also wanted to figure out how to use the necklace to save her mum from the zombie curse that was slowly changing her. She was crossing her fingers that the magic could put a stop to it before it was too late. But now the necklace was gone, lost forever.

"It's gone, Selena. Now it's at the bottom of the sea. There's nothing you can do," Chloe said gently.

Selena shook her head, eyes brimming with tears.

Without the necklace, she was powerless to stop her mum's fate.

Chloe put a hand on her shoulder. "I know it's hard, but maybe this is for the best. That necklace's power was unpredictable. It was too dangerous."

But Selena wouldn't accept it. The necklace had been her only way to protect her mum. Now it was lost, and with it any chance of stopping the horrific transformation.

Selena gazed down at the crashing waves, heart aching. The necklace was down there somewhere, swallowed by the cold, merciless sea. And along with it, any chance of stopping her mum's horrific transformation.

"It's no use dwelling on it," Chloe urged. "The necklace is gone for good. We'll...we'll find some other way to handle your mum's illness, okay?"

Selena barely heard her. She kept staring at the dark, churning water, hollow despair threatening to swallow what little hope she had left. The sea had taken everything from her—her necklace, her chances of saving Mum. And there was nothing she could do but accept that bitter fate.

When Selena got home, she found her mum busy on her laptop in the drawing room, brows furrowed.

"Everything okay?" Selena asked halfheartedly.

Her mum sighed. "Just trying to balance our finances. We need money to live on, but I wanted funds for the play, too..." she trailed off, shaking her head. "If only we had that necklace. It could've solved everything."

Selena's heart ached at the mention of the necklace. Thanks to Jamie, it was gone forever. Their one hope of stopping the zombie curse consuming Mum, lost to the waves.

Selena couldn't bring herself to tell Mum it was gone. The words stuck in her throat. It would just double Mum's stress and despair.

"Yeah, the necklace..." Selena mumbled instead, eyes downcast. She felt empty inside, totally defeated.

Slumped on the cushy red couch, Selena chewed her thumbnail nervously. Mum thought it could've saved them. But now it was gone and with it any chance of breaking the curse claiming Mum, stopping her from becoming one of the soulless mermaid horrors like Faustina.

The bitter weight of failure crushed her spirit. The necklace should be around Mum's neck now, not lying uselessly on the seafloor. If only Selena had guarded it better. Instead, their hopes were sunk, just like the ruby necklace by the cold, uncaring sea.

AUNT ADA

Night after night, Faustina bugged Aunt Ada big time to go up on land, chomp some poor human, and drag them down to join their undead crew. But Aunt Ada didn't want to harm anyone. That went against everything she believed in.

Still, Faustina would not let it go. She kept rambling on about recruiting new members and teaching mind control. She went on and on, every day, about all the awesome stuff they could do with a bigger group. Her huge enthusiasm started wearing Aunt Ada down after a while.

Finally, Ada just exploded. "Enough already. Fine, I'll bite someone if it'll get you off my tail!"

Faustina clapped her hands, her yellow eyes glinting. "Yay! I knew you'd cave."

But when Aunt Ada returned empty-handed after trying

to bite Chloe and her parents, Faustina lost it. "I asked you to bring fresh zombie blood, but you didn't even try!"

"Yeah, so, I kinda have an issue," Aunt Ada said, not looking Faustina in the eye. "Humans just smell nasty to me. Like rancid fish sticks."

Faustina looked shocked. "So what? They taste amazing. Don't diss it 'til you've tried it."

Aunt Ada grimaced. "Alright, fine. I don't have the guts for chomping necks. I know you love it, but it's just not my jam."

Faustina did a backwards flip, outraged. "Not your jam? What kind of lame zombie are you?"

Aunt Ada held up her hands. "Look, I only did it as a favor because you wouldn't stop hassling me about it. I figured I'd give it a shot, but then I saw the terrified looks on those people's faces...well, I felt pretty crummy."

Faustina shook her head in disgust. "Crumminess? I can't believe you're my aunt. Where's your zombie pride?"

Aunt Ada shrugged helplessly. She was hoping her niece would cut her a break. Fishing was more Aunt Ada's speed than fishing humans out of their houses for a quick bite.

Aunt Ada cringed. "Please dear, try to understand," she started gently.

But Faustina wasn't having it. "I thought you were finally getting your zombie on. But I guess you're still stuck in the olden days."

Faustina started to swim away when Aunt Ada called out desperately, "Hey, did you hear the one about what zombies eat for dessert?"

Faustina paused.

"Eye scream," Ada delivered the punchline with awkward jazz hands.

Aunt Ada saw the corners of Faustina's mouth turn up slightly, even as she tried to stay grumpy. "Wow, that was terrible," Faustina said, shaking her head at Ada's awful joke. But Aunt Ada could tell Faustina was struggling not to laugh.

Ada breathed a sigh of relief. Crisis averted, for now at least. She'd have to keep Faustina distracted with some lighthearted humor whenever she started with her zombie recruiting talk again.

Today Aunt Ada was lying back on the uncomfortable sofa. Sharp bits of crab shell jutted into her back. Decima settled on her lap and wiggled to get comfortable. Aunt Ada gazed wistfully around the pebbly copy of her old library, a faint smile playing on her gray lips. Everything was a bit of a blur since she'd lost her glasses. "Oh, I do miss my cozy house on land. The worn furniture, the faded wallpaper, my collection of porcelain cats..."

She flickered back to reality with a small shake of her head. "Well, no use dwelling on the past, I suppose. This is my home now." She leaned back with a sigh, a faraway look in her milky eyes. "Still, I'd give anything to sip tea from my chipped china one more time." She stroked the squid in her lap absently. "You're a cute little thing, Decima, but you're not Mr. Wiggums. How I miss burrowing my fingers into his soft fur and listening to his rumbly purr."

A slight quaver entered her voice at the end.

"Cute? Decima's the ugliest looking pet I ever saw," Faustina said, sneering, her bloodshot eyes bulging grotesquely. She gnashed her jagged teeth at the squid.

Decima scuttled closer on Ada's lap, fury in her beady eyes. Ada felt the squid's body tense, ready to unleash a torrent of inky rage.

Faustina loomed toward them, tattered fin claws outstretched. Foul seawater seeped from her shredded flesh, kelp strands swaying as she moved. Ada noticed hints of envy behind the zombie's sunken, hateful gaze.

The purple squid squirted a jet of midnight liquid right in Faustina's face.

"Ack! My eyes," Faustina shrieked, clutching her face. "I've been assaulted by a deranged cephalopod."

Decima shot another stream of ink for good measure, staining Faustina's hair and ragged seaweed bodice in the process.

"Just look at me. I'm an absolute disaster," she wailed, colliding with the coral coffee table as she flailed.

"Decima, heel!" Ada scolded half-heartedly, unable to keep the amusement from her voice. She gently pried the overprotective squid away. "There, there, no need for such displays."

Faustina wiped at her eyes, leaving dark smears across her pallid cheeks. "Just look at me. I'm a mess." She gasped dramatically, clutching at her ruined bodice.

Aunt Ada couldn't help chuckling at Faustina's freakout over some ink. "Calm down, you're already shredded. What's a little staining?"

Faustina shot her an annoyed look. "A classy lady's gotta look her best, even as a zombie." She examined a stained chunk of hair sadly. "Do you know how hard it is to find style down here that isn't chewed up?"

Aunt Ada hid a smile and handed her a sponge. "Here, let's clean you up. Honestly, you two bicker like little kids."

Faustina huffed but started dabbing herself. "Keep that ink-squirting punk away from me," she grumbled.

On Aunt Ada's lap, Decima was still shaking, angry. Aunt Ada gently calmed the upset squid. "There, there," she said softly.

Faustina swam around them, tail swishing. Bitterness and envy twisted her skeletal face into a freaky mask. Aunt Ada felt bad for the miserable zombie. Being undead had not been good to Faustina.

"I told you I needed help growing our group," Faustina suddenly yelled, gross dead bits dangling from her lips. "But you've been useless, barely keeping up."

"It's true. I'm not as spry as I once was. Being undead takes some getting used to."

She shifted on the sofa, rubbing at the stiffness in her back. "You forget, I was already ancient when I turned. I'm not as adaptable as you young folks." Ada shook her head wistfully. "My bones creak, my joints ache. I'm lucky if I can manage a slow drift most days, never mind the chase and chomp."

She met Faustina's gaze. "I want to help build your community, my dear. But you must understand this under-water world...it's still so foreign to me." Ada gave a sad, apologetic smile. "Honestly, making the sea rise made me so tired, I could barely crawl up the lawn. And since then, I've thrown out my back."

"I'm sorry about that," said Faustina. "But you know what they say: fake it till you make it. Just try to bite anyone who happens to be swimming by. Have you tried surfers? They're quite vulnerable when they wipe out."

"They look a bit tough in the flesh." Aunt Ada wrinkled her nose.

"Suffer through." Faustina gritted the few teeth remaining in her mouth. "Just until we have enough people to get the school and community up and running."

"You're not listening to me," protested Aunt Ada. "I will try, but I can't promise anything. And right now, I'm tired and need a nap. You need to recruit young blood."

"Don't I know it. I'm starting to wonder why I turned you into a zombie. I was desperate, I suppose. I was lonely. I wanted you because you're family. I guess I was out of my mind."

"I'm sorry things aren't working out the way you thought they would," Aunt Ada said, petting Decima. "But I wish you'd stop yelling at me."

"Sorry," Faustina said. "I find it hard to control myself sometimes." She flopped beside Aunt Ada; her hand dangled over the edge of the couch. She allowed the sand to run through her fingers.

"You'll love this one," Aunt Ada said, breaking the tension. "Why do mermaids live in salt water?"

"I don't know," Faustina said crossly.

"Because pepper makes them sneeze."

Faustina chuckled.

Aunt Ada smirked proudly, sitting up and leaning forward. "You liked that one?"

"It was pretty good, I gotta say."

Faustina began spiraling through the water, sniffing intently.

"What is that delicious smell?" Faustina murmured. "Is it...a limb from a rotting surfer?"

She paused, inhaling deeply again. Her eyes lit up.

"No, it's something better! That's the smell of metal and stone. It must be the ruby necklace."

Aunt Ada tensed, her grip on Decima tightening. She knew exactly what Faustina was searching for now. The ruby necklace, hidden just a few meters away on the library shelf.

"I've got a strong feeling that necklace is around here somewhere. Am I crazy?" Faustina shouted.

"You might be. Why ever would it be down here?" Ada replied casually, trying to throw Faustina off the trail.

Lately, Aunt Ada had been hanging near the surface whenever Selena walked around up top. She worried for the girl and wanted to keep watch. Recently, the necklace had plopped down right on Ada's head. Not wanting Faustina getting her evil hands on its power, Ada had stashed it behind some books in the underwater library.

But now, Faustina was sniffing around for the necklace, and Ada grew anxious. She stroked Decima for comfort, the squid's tentacles curling around her wrist. Ada knew if

Faustina found the necklace, big trouble would go down. She had to keep it hidden, no matter what.

"Tell me where it is, right now," Faustina yelled, zooming out the door in a blur, her nasty tail trailing gunk.

"Faustina, get back here," Ada called desperately, following slowly on creaky old joints.

Faustina popped her head back in, skin peeling to reveal bone. Her creepy, glowing eyes and pointy teeth glinted. "You know something. Where is it?" She hissed ominously.

"I don't, I swear!" Ada cried, sweat beading as her hair floated in the current.

Decima tugged Ada's hand urgently. Ada's back cracked painfully as they raced after Faustina's trail of bubbles.

FAUSTINA

Faustina was frothing with rage as she stormed through the underwater rooms. The house creaked and groaned around her, its walls made of piled stones and coral fragments. She kicked aside a table carved from twisted driftwood, not caring as relics and treasures scattered across the sandy floor.

"Where is it?" She seethed, overturning a giant clam chair. The mollusk inside snapped its shell shut in fright.

Behind her, Aunt Ada clung to Decima, struggling to keep up. "Faustina please, control yourself," she called.

But Faustina was deaf to reason. She tore down the hallway, ripping artwork from the kelp-woven walls. The stolen ruby necklace had to be here somewhere. She would demolish the entire house if that's what it took.

Bursting into the kitchen, Faustina grabbed handfuls of colorful pebbles from the countertop and hurled them in every direction. Clown fish darted away in terror. The pearl cupboards trembled as she slammed them open, one after another.

Faustina darted through the rooms at breakneck speed, colliding with objects, sending armchairs spinning into the glowing water, and ripping paintings from the walls. Drawers were upended, their contents sprayed in all directions.

"It's here somewhere, I just know it!"

"Do you really want to smash up all your hard work? How about we sit down and drink a nice cup of algae tea?"

"You can stuff your algae tea," Faustina hissed, racing toward the library, and pulled books from the shelves.

Aunt Ada followed, pulled along by Decima, seaweed swirling and flying in all directions. Faustina's fingers relentlessly plucked books from the shelves when suddenly she gasped. Just then, right at the back of a shelf, Faustina's fingers made contact with hard metal. Heat rocketed through her, and she jerked and twitched as warmth flickered up her arm.

"Well, slap my fins and call me a sea cucumber, it's only my long-lost ruby necklace!" Faustina exclaimed, gazing reverently at the jewels in her palm. "You hid it, didn't you, you silly old woman?"

"Yes, because it'll do you no good to have it."

"But it's mine." Faustina beamed. The ruby necklace that had been stolen from her hundreds of years ago. It was hers once more. She held it up and gazed at it, dazzled and so full of joy she thought she'd burst. It was going to change everything. The scales of power had finally shifted. She'd be able to do whatever she wanted, to control anyone she pleased.

"Hey, give that back," Aunt Ada said in a disapproving tone.

"Look, the necklace found me. Maybe the necklace wants me to wear it. Did you think of that? And anyway, it's not yours. It originally belonged to a pirate wizard called Zlotan."

"Except you stole it from him."

"I don't care," Faustina screeched. "It's mine now."

"Listen up, kiddo," Aunt Ada said, her voice kind but serious. "That necklace has been in my family for generations, and it's got some powerful magic. You know the story about the mermaid who used it to torment her enemies through their dreams? Well, it didn't work out so well for her—she ended up being possessed by a wicked spirit and died."

Ada waved her hands in Faustina's face as she spoke. "The lesson here is don't mess around with enchanted objects. They can get you into trouble if you're not careful. And you're a good kid—don't let this temptation of power lead you astray. Believe me, there's plenty of other things that are worth chasing after." She held out her hand. "Promise me, alright? I don't want to see you hurt."

"Spare me the gloomy tales, Auntie A," Faustina snapped, clutching the ruby necklace tightly. "This treasure's been in your family for ages? Well, now it belongs to me. Get a load of this mind control juice," Faustina snapped. "I can see sleepy little Selena right now, just waiting for me to mess with her head."

Joy blazed through her as an image of a sleeping Selena appeared.

"The little darling's ripe for my influence," Faustina purred. She pictured the girl sleepwalking into the sea's hungry jaws at her command.

Ada looked concerned. "You won't bite her, will you?"

"As if! I just want to hang with her." Faustina whispered, "Come, Selena...don't be afraid. I'll let you breathe underwater. Come to me..."

From within Selena's sleeping thoughts, Faustina focused her will, taking control of the girl's body. Selena stiffened then relaxed as Faustina seized command.

Like a puppet, Selena rose from bed in her nightdress, eyes glazed as Faustina directed her. She sleepwalked through the house, down the stairs, across the drawing room, and out into the night.

Selena's bare feet left prints in the wet grass as Faustina compelled her toward the cliff. Moonlight glinted off the waves crashing below.

Bracing herself, Faustina mentally pushed Selena over the edge. Helpless within her own hijacked body, Selena stepped off the precipice, plunging toward the waiting sea below.

30

SELENA

Selena was enveloped in darkness, the black water around her lit only by the soft glow of jellyfish and seaweed. Their neon blues and greens cast an eerie light as she sank deeper. The water grew steadily warmer, taking on an orange cast as she continued her descent. Sand particles floated by, also glowing orange in the strange light.

Desperately, Selena fought against the current pulling her down, her lungs screaming for air. She thrashed, trying to kick upwards, but some mysterious force kept dragging her into the deep blue depths. The lack of oxygen made her head spin, and dots flashed before her eyes. Still, she forced them to stay open, determined to remain conscious.

The saltwater stung and blurred her vision, but she could make out the roof of a large mansion coming into view below her. It looked identical to Aunt Ada's place. Strange mollusks and starfish clung to the shingles, their soft bodies brushing her feet as she sank lower.

Selena's lungs were fit to burst. Just as her vision started going black, her body went limp, no longer able to resist the relentless tug into the mysterious, orange-lit mansion beneath the sea.

The pressure eased, and she was becoming less light-headed. The underwater world was different and yet familiar. The house had the same layout as Aunt Ada's house. Selena floated through the front door, into the bright foyer, and along the ugly purple corridor with the massive portraits. The fish-like eyes of relatives inside their frames followed her as she glided down the hall and through the staircase—up or down, she no longer knew—swimming through doors and up and down halls.

Maybe this house is upside down, a mirror image of the one above.

Her body scraped against one of the rock walls as she drifted out of a window, tumbling straight into a clump of seaweed. Adrenaline spurted through her as the danger increased. Something was clutching at her throat.

"Help," she cried, gulping down water while she tore at the seaweed wrapped around her throat, but it just spun tighter and tighter. Hands grabbed at the seaweed and pulled.

"It's all right. I've got you," said the mermaid, her red hair fanning out. There was a cloud of green sulfurous water around her. It was the same zombie mermaid who had terrorized her that first night. Faustina.

Selena kicked out in fury through choking breaths. The edges of her vision started to blur. "Chill out," Faustina told her impatiently. "You can breathe underwater, don't freak. My magic will keep you safe down here, trust me. Anyway, thanks for swinging by, and sorry we had to meet like this. Soon as you moved in, I wanted to say hey. I'll admit I came on a little strong trying to bite you and pull you down here." Her voice was smooth as silk, inviting. With one last tug, Faustina ripped off the seaweed wrapped around Selena's throat. She put two bony fingers on each side of Selena's neck. "Just relax. You can breathe easy. I've got total control over you." Despite Faustina's reassurances, Selena continued to panic. Dizziness fell over her until she was light-headed, like all her limbs were dissolving. She lost feeling in her fingers and toes, then she blacked out.

When she came to, she was breathing. How was that even possible?

"Thanks," Selena said, dread rising inside her. She was underwater, at the bottom of the ocean. Panic seized her, and she thrashed about, grabbing at Faustina's arm. Her fingers sank into the spongy, rotting flesh. "I have to get out of here. I'm going to drown!"

"Don't worry. If you're with me, you won't have any trouble breathing underwater. I'm four hundred years old, so I have heaps of mermaid experience."

Numbness grabbed hold of her. Had Faustina bewitched her to not be afraid of her? "How did I get down here?"

"You sleepwalked into the sea," Faustina answered. "But it was all me messing with your head. Before I found this necklace today, my powers were kind of weak and rusty, you know? That's why things got messy when we first met. But now..." She got all excited. "After three hundred years, I finally got this necklace back. It made it way easier to control your mind and bring you down here. I really do want to be besties, for real. What do you think?" Faustina's eyes were blazing, and Selena wasn't sure she could trust her to be for real.

"I'm not so sure..." said Selena, deciding to stall for time. "This is all moving kind of fast." Selena stared at the ruby necklace shining around Faustina's throat. "You stole that," she said, reaching for it. "Jamie chucked it into the sea. But before that, it was mine."

Faustina swam away, leaving a trail of bubbles in her wake as she flapped her tail. Selena chased after her, struggling to keep up as Faustina entered the house.

"I told you already. It was originally mine, and you ain't getting it back," Faustina snapped, her voice getting all stern. "Take a good look around. This is gonna be your home when you go undead—"

"That's not happening soon, right?" Selena asked, freaking out.

"Who knows? But since you're scared of water, I figured it was high time you got used to it," Faustina said. "Can you imagine being a zombie mermaid who's afraid of water?" She giggled. "Have you ever heard anything so nuts?"

"It is weird. What's happening? Am I not scared of water anymore?" Selena asked, confused.

"That's because I control your fears, dummy. Look, why don't I show you around? You're gonna love it here."

Selena swam as fast as she could, but Faustina twisted and turned effortlessly and zoomed ahead. They entered a cave-like room with the same patterned, red-flock wallpaper made of coral as Aunt Ada's drawing room. The red sofa was there, too, with rainbow-colored coral growing out of it. When Selena reached up to the ceiling to touch the red chandelier, the crystals moved in her fingers. When she looked closely, red fish wriggled in the palms of her hand.

"Look, it was cool to really meet you, but I just wanna grab the necklace and leave," she told Faustina. "I don't wanna live down here, so I should probably get back."

Faustina grabbed her arm. "Don't go. Stay for a bit. This is your home under the sea, and you can stay as long as you want. As for the necklace...you're right, it's yours. But it's also mine. I'm part of your family. We go way back. Isn't it nice we're related?" She grinned, flashing her brown, rotten teeth.

Selena was starting to lose her temper. "Look, I didn't come here for a family reunion. The first time we met, you freaked me out."

"Don't worry. I promise I'll be good. Wearing this necklace has calmed me down." Selena thought it was true. Apart from the rotting tail and pus-filled wounds studding her skin, she looked far more serene than the time Selena had first seen her.

Faustina swam across the foyer and entered the library. A gray-haired mermaid lolled on the sofa made of crab shells, a purple squid on her lap. "Aunt Ada!" Selena cried in surprise.

"Selena, my dear! So wonderful to see you again," Aunt Ada replied melodiously. "I've thought of you often since we last met. It's truly a shame your mum never brought you to visit when I was alive."

Selena nodded understandingly. "I know, and I'm sorry about that. Mum can be a bit distracted sometimes. But I would have loved getting to know you back then." She smiled warmly. "That said, as long as you promise not to attack or infect anyone, I'm thrilled to become friends now."

"How can she promise that?" Faustina said crossly. "She's a zombie mermaid. She lives to infect the living."

"Not totally true," Aunt Ada corrected her. To Selena, she said, "Like I was telling Faustina before, I just don't feel the need to sink my teeth into people." She shrugged and motioned to her rotten body. "Try to look past how I look. We're family, and I want us to be close."

"I'd like that." Selena couldn't be angry with a nice old woman like Aunt Ada. Faustina, however, was another matter.

"I'm worried about your mother," said Aunt Ada. "I think Faustina is working on getting her mind under her control and is trying to lure her here."

"Of course, I am," said Faustina. "Fiona *is* under my

control, but it's hard to get her to turn all the way zombie because I only scratched her. Luckily, I now have the necklace to help me."

"You leave my mum alone," said Selena. "Stop trying to control her and turn her into a zombie. I need my mum to be well… to be with me on land."

"Fat chance of that," said Faustina.

"Look, Faustina. Stop being so mean," said Aunt Ada. "Stop messing around with Fiona's mind and give back the necklace."

"Come on. I need it. My life is falling apart," Selena choked out. "I get bullied all the time, I have like no friends, my mum doesn't care enough about me to get a real job, my dad doesn't wanna see me…it's all too much. When I wore it for just one day, I was protected. I didn't get bullied and Cindy was nice to me. Maybe my goodness unleashed its powers, I dunno. But when you wear it, I feel like you don't have good intentions. And that could make everything worse. I mean, are you trying to harm people?"

"Of course not. I'm a reasonable mermaid. I just want them to do exactly what I tell them to do. Like bringing you here."

"But I want to go back."

"You're right." Faustina paused as if thinking Selena's request over. Reaching back and unclasping the necklace, she said, "Maybe I'm the wrong person to have the necklace." She held it out before shrieking with laughter. "Just kidding. Of course, I'm the right person, and you're not going to get it." Her face softened. "Look, how about we make a deal? Just stay awhile and keep me company. Then I'll let you go. It gets lonely down here."

"My heart bleeds…" Selena said, crossing her arms.

"There are other zombie mermaids down here," Aunt Ada pointed out to Faustina. "Why can't you be friends with them? Share a pun, make a friend. Why did the mermaid look the other way? Because the sea weed."

Faustina rolled her eyes. "Enough! Look, they're boring, all right? They go on and on all day about how many humans they've infected and how many they intend to infect next week. It's just about fulfilling a death quota for them. That's fine and all, but they don't know how to have any fun."

"I'm sorry the undead life isn't all it's cracked up to be," said Selena. "But I need to get back up to dry land. So, hand over the necklace."

"I can't give it up. Or rather, I don't want to."

"I don't care." Selena grabbed for the necklace, but Faustina pushed her away.

"When I found this necklace in the library, everything changed. I feel reborn. Like I've been to a spa or something. Why don't you relax and enjoy your stay? I said I'd take you home eventually."

"Because I don't trust you," Selena said.

"I've asked you nicely to stay here," Faustina stated, securing the necklace around her neck. "Now, if I promise not to bite you, will you play nice?"

"No," Selena said, swimming away with all her strength. Faustina pulled her back by her ankles. Selena fought back, but Faustina's grip was too tight. Selena tried punching her in the arm.

"You can fight me all you like," Faustina said. "I don't feel pain, so I'll always win."

Selena squirmed away, trying to get free. Fury built inside her. She didn't have to worry about hurting Faustina. She just wanted to get away from her. When Faustina lunged at her with those bony fingers, Selena kicked her in the tail. The rotten flesh split open and black blood leaked into the water. Faustina freaked out, all disoriented in the plumes of blood.

Selena saw her chance to escape and took it.

31

SELENA

Back above ground, Selena was disorientated. It was as if she wasn't part of either world: neither the world above ground, nor the world under the sea, which mirrored her world in some dark and disturbing way.

She'd miraculously been able to breathe underwater until the waves heaved her onto the beach, leaving her sopping wet and freezing. She had no idea if she still had that ability now, and she didn't intend to find out. She thought about telling Chloe what had happened, but it was all so weird and hard to take in. So, she decided to keep the adventure to herself for the time being.

Selena dragged herself through the school day in a tired haze after her all-night swim. She could barely keep her eyes open in class as teachers droned on. At lunch, she laid her head down on the cafeteria table, not caring what anyone thought. The food on her tray looked totally unappetizing anyway.

Between classes, Selena shuffled along the hallways in a trance. She stifled yawns and tried not to collapse against the lockers. The night swim had drained every last drop of energy from her body. All she wanted was to be home in bed.

When the final bell rang, Selena normally would've felt relief. But instead, an icy knot formed in her stomach. She had play rehearsal next, which meant seeing all her bully classmates again. She took a deep breath and headed to the auditorium, bracing herself for what was to come.

"You shouldn't show your snout around here," said Jamie when she came through the door.

Unbelievable!

"This isn't a farm, you know," Cindy said, starting to snort.

Selena did her best not to react, but the insults continued. It was a relief when her mum came in, though she was late. That was peculiar. She was never late. Her hair was in a terrible state, bunched up and wild like a scarecrow.

"Let's turn to scene three," Fiona said without any greeting or introduction. Everyone leafed through their scripts. Selena peered at her mother. Was her neck more... sinewy? Did her skin have a weird, greenish hue?

Selena tried to focus on the play. It was the part where the children had been wrecked on the island for four weeks, barely surviving on fruits and berries. Things went okay until the night they realized the island was full of zombies that only came out after dark.

"So, Cindy," Fiona said. "Make sure you look like you're properly asleep when you hear two zombies coming out of the woods. Last time, your eyes kept opening."

Cindy stretched out on the stage. When Selena's mum hobbled over, she had a strange gait.

"Andrew and Jamie, get in position as the zombies who discover Cindy and want to bite her."

"This girl looks like she might be a tasty snack," Andrew said, doing a shambling walk around the sleeping Cindy. "What do you think?"

"Yum, yum. Let's just go for it," said Jamie.

Selena ran toward them. "No way are you gonna eat my friend. Get away from her, you nasty zombies!" She clapped her hands right in their faces.

"Get away from her," Chloe cried as she joined them. "Leave her alone!"

Cindy woke up and stretched. She rubbed her eyes. "What's going on?"

"We haven't had a taste of human flesh for years," said zombie Jamie. "We'll go away if we can have a nibble. Then we'll leave you alone."

"I gotta say," said Chloe, looking scared, "I don't think we can reason with these beasts."

Andrew roared and lunged at Chloe.

"I think you're right," said Selena. "Run. Run!" And with that, the girls fled from the zombies.

Fiona scratched hard at her head and face. Her nails left

red claw marks in their wake. "I'm sorry," she said. "I just feel so itchy all over."

"I think she's got fleas," Jamie whispered to Cindy.

"She does not," Selena said, seeing red.

"All right, Selena," Fiona said. "Let's try to concentrate on the scene. I'm feeling really odd right now. But the show must go on. Let's try that scene again."

Everyone regrouped on stage, and Fiona went around, gently prodding people into their correct positions.

As Selena and Chloe walked home along the seawall that ran along the coast above the beach, Chloe glanced over with concern. "You look exhausted. Have you not been sleeping well?"

Selena stifled a yawn. "Yeah, I didn't get much sleep last night," she replied grimly. "It was the freakiest thing. Last night, Faustina like, controlled my mind and forced me to jump into the sea. I'm scared to even think what else she can make someone do..."

Chloe's eyes went wide. "What? That's insane!" she exclaimed. "How did she even do that?"

"No clue," Selena replied, shaking her head. "I just woke up in the middle of the night and felt compelled to creep to the end of my garden and leap into the ocean."

"You just jumped into the water in the middle of the night? Weren't you totally freaking out?" Chloe asked incredulously.

"Oh my gosh, yes," Selena said. "You know I'm terrified of water. As soon as I hit the surface, I started panicking. I thought for sure I was going to drown."

"So, what happened? How did you not drown?" Chloe pressed.

"This is the craziest part," Selena continued. "Right as I started to black out, Faustina somehow found me and used her powers so I could breathe underwater."

Chloe's mouth dropped open. "No way. You could actually breathe underwater? What was it like down there?"

Selena shuddered at the memory. "It was so weird and scary. But also kind of magical. She's built a house, stuck together with pieces of rock. It's like my house, just upside down."

"She's trying to entice you by building it, I guess. Except you don't even like the version you're living in on land, so it won't work… right?"

"Not with me. But I think she built it more for Aunt Ada, who doesn't seem happy down there, to be honest."

"She seemed pretty pissed off when I saw her in my garden," Chloe said, giggling.

"That's not the real her. She was just hunting for humans because Faustina told her to."

"Still, I don't feel safe being in my garden at night in case she decides to make a return visit."

"I don't think she'll come back, but maybe Faustina will make an appearance."

"No, thanks." Chloe pulled a face.

"On top of everything, Faustina has the necklace and refuses to give it back."

Chloe whistled. "It's a lot to take in."

"Did you notice at rehearsal my mum was starting to look weird again?"

Chloe shrugged and looked down at the pavement. "I guess."

"Don't you get it? My mum was getting sicker and sicker until the day I wore the necklace. When I had it, the zombie infection paused. Now that Faustina has the necklace, the poison is spreading again. My mum's going to turn into a zombie mermaid unless I can get the necklace back." Selena sighed. "But how on earth am I going to do that?"

"I don't know. You don't want to dive back into the sea, do you?"

"No way. The problem is Faustina has total control over me. Her powers reached me when I was sleeping. There's nothing I can do."

The girls fell into silence, and Selena wondered if there was anything she could do about Faustina. Selena stared down at the beach from the seawall, shielding her eyes from the glare of the sun. She spotted Jamie and Andrew playing in the waves below. Cindy was running along the beach. Selena's stomach knotted at the sight of her bullies.

As Selena watched, a dark, triangular fin broke the surface of the water, gliding ominously toward the oblivious boys. Her heart dropped.

Forgetting her anxiety, Selena leapt into action. She raced down the stone steps, stumbling in the soft sand.

"Shark!" She yelled breathlessly. "There's a shark. Get out of the water!"

Andrew and Jamie stared at her blankly.

"You should get out before you get attacked," she yelled desperately.

Andrew just laughed and shook his wet hair. "We'll be fine. We aren't scared of sharks." But his chuckle sounded nervous.

"Andrew, seriously, you should get out," Chloe pleaded. "It's not safe."

"Relax, we're okay," he replied casually.

Selena turned to Chloe. "Maybe it's not a shark after all."

Chloe gave her a knowing look. "That's what I'm afraid of, too. They're annoying sometimes, but they don't deserve to be bitten. And if it's not a shark, the bite could turn them undead."

Just then, Cindy piped up, "It's probably not even a shark. It's just a silly old dolphin playing."

Selena bit her lip uncertainly. She wanted to believe Cindy was right, but that fin looked dangerous. Still, Jamie and Andrew clearly weren't going to listen.

Finally, she nodded to Chloe. "Come on, let's leave them to it." The girls turned and headed back up the beach, hoping the boys would be okay. Selena glanced back over her shoulder, unable to shake her foreboding feeling as the fin glided closer.

When Selena got home, she waved at her mum and Mr. Bottomley, who were sharing a bottle of wine in the garden. She tried to ignore his stupid toupee and oily smile. Their relationship could be whatever they wanted it to be. The reality was her mum was dying, so she deserved a bit of happiness in her final days.

FAUSTINA

Faustina drifted through the gloomy underwater caves, utterly alone. Aunt Ada lingered nearby, but she was poor company—either napping, mumbling puns, or fawning over that ridiculous pet squid of hers.

Faustina sighed, running her bony fingers over the ruby necklace encircling her throat. After so many years, she had finally recovered her precious treasure. But it brought her little joy. What good was it when she had no one to share it with?

The few zombie mermaids who lurked in these shadowy caverns avoided Faustina. She couldn't blame them—with her flesh rotting away to reveal bone, tangled seaweed hair, and glowing red eyes, she made for a terrifying sight.

Still, Faustina longed for a playmate. Spotting two young zombie mermaids swimming ahead, she propelled herself forward excitedly.

"Beatriz! Leilani! Remember me?" She called, giving her friendliest gross and ghastly grin.

The girls turned back, seaweed dangling from their rotting flesh. They didn't look terrified, just uninterested.

"Um, yeah hi," Beatriz rasped dully, her bright blue hair drifting around her.

"We know who you are," Leilani added, her vivid pink tresses floating like silk in the currents.

Faustina beamed. "Great. We should totally hang out and play Scrabble sometime."

Beatriz made a retching sound. "I'd rather barf up my own entrails, thanks."

Faustina's smile faded, but she tried again brightly. "Well, I'm also re-opening the Undead Academy. Wasn't it fun back in the old days?"

"Hard pass," Beatriz said flatly. "Your school sucks, just like you."

Annoyance flickered through Faustina. "Well, I suppose it was a bit advanced for certain students," she said loftily. "We can't all be brilliant academics like me. I'm smarter, prettier, more successful—"

"Ugh, shut up," Leilani groaned. "We don't want to play with you or go to your dumb school. Just leave us alone."

"Remember the good old days before my sister was eaten?" Faustina asked wistfully.

"How could we forget?" Beatriz said through a fake smile. "But ever since, you've been...a lot."

"I can't help incessantly reciting dirges," Faustina cried. "It's part of grieving."

Leilani winced. "We know, but most people don't sing funeral marches at midnight outside our cave."

"It provides comfort," Faustina insisted. "But fine, I'll work on more constructive coping."

Just then, Aunt Ada's nasal voice screeched out, "Faustina! Leave them alone and follow me to the library."

Faustina gave an irritated sigh before following Aunt Ada, leaving Beatriz and Leilani behind. She swam into the front door of the house.

"They're the worst friends ever," Faustina muttered sullenly. "I wouldn't even talk to them if they were the only zombies around. If it wasn't for me biting them when they were nobodies, they wouldn't even be zombie mermaids."

Aunt Ada spun to face Faustina once they were in the library, glaring sharply. "That's enough of your nonsense," she scolded. "You don't know how to be nice at all."

"I was trying," Faustina insisted defiantly, arms crossed. She twirled angrily in front of a wall of books.

"By insulting them?" Aunt Ada shot back.

Faustina lifted her chin. "I can't help it if I'm the prettiest mermaid in the bay, with the biggest brain and sharpest teeth. It's not my fault the others can't beat me at Scrabble."

Aunt Ada groaned, smacking a clawed hand to her forehead. "You're impossible. Unless you learn some manners, you'll never make any friends."

Faustina opened her mouth to retort, but Aunt Ada barreled on.

"Instead of screaming at people, try expanding your horizons for once. I found some books on manners in an underwater cave that are still legible. I put them here," she said, gesturing to the shelves groaning with books. "Go read them and learn something."

Faustina wrinkled her nose, but Aunt Ada wasn't finished yet. Her face suddenly lit up with inspiration.

"Ooh, I just thought of the perfect pun. Which of Santa's reindeer needs to work on his manners the most?" She paused for effect. "Rude-olph!"

Aunt Ada cackled. Faustina just stared, unimpressed. Was this supposed to be helping?

With a dismissive flick of her tail, Faustina turned to swim off. "I'm leaving. Have fun talking to yourself."

Aunt Ada's giggles faded to a scowl. "Fine, go. But don't come crying to me when you have no one to play with."

Faustina paused, considering. As much as she hated to admit it, she needed all the help she could get making friends. Reluctantly, she turned and approached the bookshelf.

"Hmm, these are from the Undead Academy," she mused, scanning the titles. "I wondered where they ended up."

Aunt Ada perked up, swimming over eagerly. "Yes, this whole wall is filled with books on manners, mermaid mind control, building societies—everything an undead mermaid could want."

She grabbed a heavy tome and pushed it at Faustina. "Here, this covers zombie lore and colonies all over the world. Since you are one, you should learn about your people."

Faustina flipped through the pages with mild interest before snapping the book shut decisively. "Fascinating, yes, but right now I need to focus on luring Selena and Fiona down here." Her eyes gleamed. "With them under my control, I can regain power over the zombie merkingdom."

Aunt Ada frowned disapprovingly. "You just want mind control and power. But you'll only drive them away, too, with your manners."

"Nonsense," Faustina cried, clutching her ruby necklace. "I hoped you'd understand, but you're as idiotic as the rest." She turned up her nose. "Go be in charge of the school if you insist on whining. It would give you something useful to do."

Aunt Ada just moaned, draping herself lazily upon the sofa. "Too tiiirrred..."

Faustina threw up her hands in exasperation. Honestly, it was like no one grasped her vision.

"You can't nap all day."

"All right. I'll try to get it going if it'll get you off my back," Aunt Ada droned.

"Excellent." Faustina clapped her bony hands together. "Recruit staff and students right away. This is happening."

Aunt Ada just let out a long groan, sinking lower on the sofa.

Faustina's nose twitched as she caught a whiff of something tasty. "Ooh, I smell humans somewhere above," she said eagerly, licking her lips. "I'll just nip up and bring some fresh meat—I mean students—back down here."

"Absolutely not, Faustina," Aunt Ada scolded. "You can't go around biting every human you smell."

Faustina pouted. "But making new friends is so hard when you're an undead mermaid. What do you expect me to do, start a book club?"

Aunt Ada gave her a stern look. "You need to find a better way to connect with others that doesn't involve chomping on them. That's no way to make real friends."

"I can't help that biting is the only way I can make friends," Faustina protested. "What else am I supposed to do?"

Aunt Ada wrung her hands fretfully. "I don't know...it doesn't sit right, but there's so much I don't understand about all this." She shivered. "Like when you convinced me to slither around in Chloe's garden, ugh."

But Faustina was no longer listening, trembling with excitement as the human scent filled her nostrils. "I'll be discreet, I promise," she said eagerly. "I think they're swimming near the beach."

"Oh, alright," Aunt Ada reluctantly agreed. "Just be careful."

Before she had even finished speaking, Faustina zoomed off, leaving a bubbling wake behind her. Nothing could stop her from sinking her teeth into that delicious human flesh.

33

FAUSTINA

Faustina's tail propelled her quickly towards the scent, her undead instincts urging her on. The temperature of the water became colder as she left the warm depths of the zombie merkingdom.

There, just beneath the surface, two pairs of young legs dangled carelessly in the churning waters. A wicked grin spread across Faustina's face as she bared her razor-sharp teeth in anticipation. It was feeding time, and nothing would stop this zombie mermaid from sinking her hungry jaws into those succulent limbs.

Slamming into one of the boys from below, her claws and fangs sliced through flesh with wet ripping sounds.

"Jamie! Help! Help!" The boy cried, kicking with all his might to break free from her biting grip. His scream sang sweetly in her ears.

"Andrew!" The other boy cried out in horror. At last, hot

blood rushed over her tongue as she tore savagely into Andrew's leg.

"I'm coming, hang on!" Jamie plunged toward them. Dimly, she registered his cries nearby. But this feast was hers alone. She wrenched her head back and forth, sinews and gristle tearing between her teeth.

Someone grabbed her tail fiercely. "Let him go, you monster!" Jamie shouted. Faustina snarled, furious at the disruption. Whipping around, she glimpsed her attacker – Jamie was a foolish boy, brave or stupid enough to challenge her.

With a flick of powerful muscles, she sent him flying. "Get off him!" Jamie screamed. But the interruption soured her pleasure. She curled her lips in a frown, displaying her bloody, wet chompers. Let him remember - this was her turf, and anyone here had to play by her rules.

Faustina bit the flailing Andrew in the neck and pulled him under the red-tinged water. His screams turned to muffled gurgles. With each passing moment, his resistance faded in her grasp.

Soon, all movement ceased. Faustina loosened her jaws and let the limp body drop. She licked her lips. Damn, Andrew was tasty, like a roasted chicken. But instead of feeling full, she still wanted more blood. When she surfaced and saw Jamie's horrified expression, she couldn't help but grin. His face went pale and his eyes were bulging out of their sockets in pure terror. His mouth gaped open in a silent scream.

Every muscle in his body seemed frozen, yet underneath

Faustina sensed a coiled tension, like prey ready to explode into flight. When their eyes met, that's exactly what Jamie did - with a jerk he spun around and propelled himself through the water at lightning speed.

Kicking her tail with all the zombie mermaid strength she had, Faustina gave chase.

As she gained on Jamie, the ocean came alive around her. Weird whale songs and creaky fish noises echoed all around. Shadowy ghosts danced and swished beneath the waves. It was like the ocean itself knew something weird was happening.

Faustina's heart—or whatever was left of it—was doing a crazy dance of its own, as excitement swirled inside her.

She was filled to the brim with excitement, as a jolt of electricity surged through her veins, the adrenaline rush of the pursuit overpowering any other sensations.

As Jamie's kicking legs came within reach, her fangs erupted with savage want. With lightning speed, she lunged. Her teeth sank deep into Jamie's thrashing flesh, drawing a strangled cry.

The taste was weird - it was this crazy flavor she couldn't figure out. And then, BAM! Memories came flooding in. Jamie's taste reminded her of that hearty venison stew her mum used to cook for her ages ago. But then she got lost in her thoughts and he pushed her away with some crazy force and took off swimming. Where did he get such power? Fury overtaking her, she took off in pursuit, tail lashing.

She caught sight of Jamie clinging to a piece of drift-wood ahead, his chest heaving as he tried to catch his breath.

When he threw a petrified glance in her direction, Faustina momentarily felt a twang of regret. But her hunger soon reared again, more ferocious than before after being denied her feast.

"What are you?" Jamie managed to stammer.

Faustina hesitated, contemplating the question. Then, with a whimsical smile, she responded, "Oh, just your friendly neighborhood zombie mermaid having a casual swim."

Jamie's confusion only deepened. "Zombie mermaid? Seriously?"

"Yep. But don't worry, I'm only after your brains if they're made of chocolate," Faustina teased.

A nervous chuckle escaped Jamie, but before he could fully catch his breath, Faustina lunged again, her eerie laughter joining the symphony of strange sounds in the depths. "Catch you later, alligator!" she added with a wicked grin.

As Jamie swam away, Faustina trailed after him, her predatory instincts battling with a strange mix of amusement and regret.

Closing the distance between them, Faustina bared her pointed teeth in a hiss. Jamie wouldn't escape her this time. As he glanced over his shoulders, eyes wide with panic, Faustina descended upon him with lightning speed. Her jaws opened wide, ready to take what was rightfully hers. This time, nothing would stop her from feeding her endless appetite.

Faustina bit into the side of Jamie's head. With one

vicious tearing motion, she wrenched her head back, ripping a chunk of his scalp away. Blood sprayed in a warm wash over her face, and she shuddered with unholy rapture. He squirmed and yelled, and everything felt way too intense.

As she chomped on his brains, she noticed the flavor was way more complex than just the typical iron taste. It was a mix of sugary candy floss and salty peanuts. She slurped it down, feeling her mood lift instantly. Gotta love that fresh brain boost. Plus, she could definitely go for another serving.

Finally, the horrible gurgling in his throat stopped completely. She sucked up a little more brain, the yummy texture of custard, before pulling Jamie over to his friend Andrew, who had sunk beneath the waves. Now the fun could start. She watched eagerly as their transformation began.

Their skin paled to a sickly white, eyes glazing over into vacant deadness. Faustina trembled with wicked delight—she had a good feeling about these two.

The last spark of life flickered from Andrew's eyes. "What...where's Cindy?" He mumbled in confusion.

Ah yes, the girl who had been with them. "She ran off shrieking when I bit you," Faustina explained calmly. "But don't worry about her. I'm your friend now."

Faustina did wish she could've sunk her teeth into the girl, too, but no matter. There would be other chances to feast. For now, she had two new zombie playmates.

Gazing at their lifeless faces, Faustina could hardly contain her excitement. Such fun they would have together in her underwater kingdom.

Jamie's head fell backward. His eyeballs rolled about in his head, and he let out an anguished moan.

Faustina beamed at the two boys. "Hey guys, welcome to the world of the undead. Now we're all zombies, want to come hang at my underwater lair? It gets a little lonely down there."

Andrew's eyes bulged. "Are you insane? You bit us and now we're freakish mutants!"

"Psh, details," Faustina waved a hand dismissively. "We'll play pranks on old sailors and hunt humans for burping contests. Guy stuff."

"This is a nightmare!" Jamie wailed. "I can't go home like this. My mum's gonna kill me herself."

Faustina patted his arm. "Forget about parents. Just stick with me. We'll trash every sunken ship and devour whoever we want."

Andrew gaped in horror as his legs began bubbling with black ooze, fusing together.

Jamie let out a distressed cry as cartoonish green plumes of stinky gas seeped from his rapidly growing zombie wounds. "I don't wanna be a zombie freak," he said.

Faustina grabbed his arm. "Get it together, man. Just follow me."

Andrew scowled at Jamie. "Phew, you reek."

"You're one to talk," Jamie shot back.

Faustina tutted. "Now, now, that stench you're referring to is simply the distinctive musk of zombie merfolk. A heady blend of rotten seaweed and decaying flesh. Trust me, it'll grow on you."

The boys paused their bickering to gag dramatically.

"Enough squabbling, let's go." Faustina led the way, the boys reluctantly kicking their new fishtails to follow. They soon left the cold water behind and entered the magical warmth of the zombie merkingdom at the bottom of the ocean.

Once inside her underwater mansion, the boys zipped around exploring, before collapsing exhausted onto the big bed in the upper bedroom with pink coral walls.

"I'm zonked," Andrew groaned.

"Me too," Jamie agreed wearily.

Faustina grinned down at them. She remembered how tiring those first days as a zombie were. Her new friends would need lots of rest.

Soon they'd be ready for all kinds of terrifying underwater fun. Faustina could hardly wait to get started.

After three endless days of waiting, Faustina couldn't take it anymore. She swam over and roughly shook the boys awake.

"Rise and shine, my zombie merlads," she said. "I'm thrilled you're enjoying your rest, but it's time for your first lesson."

Andrew opened one rotting eye. "Ugh, go away..." he groaned.

Faustina persisted. "As one of the undead, you're now part of an elite legion. Let me tell you about your role."

"Elite legion?" Jamie asked skeptically. "What do we even do?"

Faustina grinned wickedly. "You get to hunt fresh victims before moving in for the kill."

At this, both boys jolted awake, staring at her in alarm.

"Whoa wait, we have to hurt people?" Andrew asked nervously.

Faustina waved a hand. "Oh, it's not so bad to suck people's brains out once you acquire the taste. Now come along, we've got a lot of training to do."

Andrew cringed. "Brains? No way, that's gross."

Faustina cackled. "Don't knock it till you try it. Anyway, fun fact: sometimes when people turn zombie, they get a whole new personality."

Andrew raised an eyebrow. "What do you mean? Why does that happen?"

"Eh, zombie brains are weird." Faustina shrugged. "Some people turn nicer, some get nastier. It's a toss up."

Just then Aunt Ada swam over eagerly. "Great news, guys! We're starting up a new Undead Academy."

Andrew looked skeptical. "A school? I thought being a zombie was all about snacking on brains."

"Yeah, hard pass," Jamie grumbled. "I hated school up top, but down here? Forget it."

"It will help us zombies bond and find purpose," Aunt Ada insisted. "It's mandatory, I'm afraid. So, shape up or ship out."

34

SELENA

Two weeks had passed since Andrew and Jamie's mysterious disappearance at the beach. Selena didn't care much for them, but their vanishing still plagued her thoughts.

"You look dreadful, dear," Mr. Bottomley remarked to Selena's mum at dinner. "Perhaps you should see a doctor."

Fiona dismissed his concern with a wave of her hand. "I'm fine, just a bit run down."

But Selena noticed the dark circles under her mum's eyes, her messy hair, the pulsing blue veins on her neck. Things had been tense at home ever since the incident. The news ran the story incessantly, interviewing students endlessly.

Selena and Chloe told reporters they'd warned the boys to get out after they'd seen a shark. Even Cindy, who normally acted so mean, came up to Selena afterwards. "I feel awful," she'd confessed. "I should've made them get out when you warned us. Watching them get pulled under...it was so scary. I couldn't do anything to help."

Selena was surprised to feel sympathy for her long-time bully. But they were all rattled. She couldn't shake the uneasy feeling that Faustina had snatched them.

After Selena told her mum about her conversation with Cindy, Fiona said, "Since Cindy has confirmed a shark got to the boys, I think it's game over." She waved her fork. "Talk about a bad time to get eaten."

"Hey, that's not very nice," Mr. Bottomley said, serving himself some salad.

"I'm just trying to be honest. We're *this* close to the performance for *Zombie Island*, and two of my actors go missing." She slurped up some strands of fettuccine, eyes bugging out.

"Don't you think you should be worrying less about your play and more about what happened to Jamie and Andrew?" Selena asked. "They're *dead*."

"Why do you care? You said they were bullying you."

"Really?" said Mr. Bottomley, stabbing at a meatball. "I didn't know that."

"Well, it doesn't matter now, does it?" Selena mumbled.

"They might still be found. The police don't yet know for sure," said Mr. Bottomley.

"I did manage to get two boys to take on their parts," Fiona went on as if she hadn't heard what they were saying. "But it isn't going to be easy getting them performance-ready."

"Mum, they've been eaten," said Selena. "And all you can talk about is your play."

Selena thought Faustina had probably gotten them, not some shark, and they were fully zombified. Honestly, she pitied them.

"Yes, you're right, Selena. It's a tragedy." She patted Selena's hand. "I'm sorry. I don't know what came over me. I hope they're found. Oh"—she buried her face in her hands—"I feel like my head is going to explode." Selena wondered if her mum's headache was from the stress of the play or if it was because Faustina was always controlling her thoughts.

Selena couldn't sit there for another second. Faustina was controlling her mum's every move, changing her personality so she didn't even have a shred of sympathy for two boys who were probably undead. Selena had to do something.

She knew the necklace was the key to stopping Faustina's power. If she could get it away from the mermaid, the zombie poison slowly seeping into her mum could be halted.

Right now, the thought of facing Faustina in her underwater lair paralyzed Selena with dread. Not only was she scared of water, she dreaded coming face to face with Faustina's cruel eyes and her razor-sharp fangs.

Selena imagined Faustina's seaweed hair coiling around her ankles, dragging her down into black oblivion. A shudder went through her.

But then she pictured her mum's warm smile and sparkling eyes. Selena knew she had to be brave, for her sake. She couldn't let the mermaid's poison continue seeping into her mother.

Once Selena retrieved that necklace, Faustina would lose her hold. Her mum would return, and their lives could go back to normal.

35

SELENA

After Mr. Bottomley left and her mum fell asleep, Selena lay in bed, stroking her hair in a futile effort to calm her rattled nerves. Maybe if she could just drift off, Faustina would possess her mind and draw her into the sea again.

But sleep evaded her. No matter how she tossed and turned, the mermaid's influence did not come.

Finally, Selena sat up with a groan. Clearly, Faustina wasn't going to force her into the waves tonight. That meant Selena would have to gather her courage and enter the ocean herself.

She shivered at the thought. The dark, churning water filled her with primal terror. But this was the only way to save her mum from Faustina's control.

Selena slowly got to her feet. Faustina wasn't going to

make this easy. If she wanted that necklace, she'd have to overcome her deepest fears and venture into the sea alone.

Selena snuck out of the house, went through the garden, and crept to the seawall, peering over the steep edge into the pitch black ocean. As she sidled along, sea spray misted her face and waves smashed against the rocks below.

How could she ever dive into that icy abyss? She'd surely die or become bait for Faustina. Selena's knees shook as she inched along the slimy seawall top.

But she steeled herself, knowing there was no other way. She had to be brave, for her mum's sake.

Reaching the wall's end, Selena paused, looking down into the churning void. With a scream, she leapt into the air, hitting the water in an explosion of foam. Icy water enveloped her as she plunged deep into the midnight sea. Terror gripped her heart, but she kicked downward.

The icy water stabbed into Selena like a thousand knives. She kicked and struggled but only sank deeper into the freezing abyss. Her lungs screamed for air as the cold seeped into her bones.

This was a mistake. She was going to die down here. Selena's mind spiraled with panic. She thrashed violently but her limbs were leaden and numb. Shadowy darkness closed in around her.

Just as her vision started to fade, Selena felt the water shift. A gentle warmth enveloped her, the glow of mystical light illuminating the sea around her.

Shivering uncontrollably, she peered around. The cold's

vice-like grip had released her. She inhaled deeply, floating suspended in the strange underwater glow.

Selena's pulse pounded as feeling slowly returned to her limbs. She had made it past the freezing upper waters to the mermaid's realm below. But the real danger still lay ahead.

Steadying her nerves, Selena propelled herself onward through the warm illuminated sea. She had to find Faustina's lair. The necklace—and her mum's last hope—waited some-where in this eerie world.

The smell hit Selena first—rotten eggs and moldy salami. She gagged as the grotesque faces loomed out of the glowing water. Sunken eyes, gnashing teeth, stringy hair. Clawed hands reached for her legs and arms.

Selena twisted away with a cry, swimming frantically as the nightmarish forms gave chase. Their bone-chilling moans echoed all around her. Bubbles trailed from empty eye sockets.

Panic flooded Selena's mind. She pumped her arms furiously, the hideous swarm snapping at her heels. There, Faustina's house emerged ahead.

Selena rocketed through the entrance, not daring to look back. She swam until her lungs burned, finally collapsing on the stone floor of a winding staircase.

The zombie wails still echoed from below. Selena's breath came in ragged gasps, her legs trembling too much to stand. But she had to keep moving.

Scrambling up the steps on shaky limbs, she barricaded herself within an attic that reminded her of the one above her bedroom at home. The horde pounded on the trap door, howling hungrily.

Curled up in the corner, Selena shook. The nightmares were real and they wanted her flesh. Faustina's lair held only terrors...nowhere was safe here.

A bone-chilling screech echoed from below as zombie tails smashed against the trapdoor. Selena dove into an old rock tub, its exterior encrusted with shimmering crushed pearls. She buried herself beneath the smelly seaweed inside.

The trapdoor splintered open, and the nightmarish mermaids flooded the attic. Selena squeezed her eyes shut, praying the seaweed hid her within the pearlescent tub.

The zombies prowled around, snarling hungrily. But somehow, they didn't spot Selena curled up in her hiding spot. Finally, the mermaids left, still searching for their prey.

Selena cautiously emerged from the tub, its iridescent pearls glinting in the dim light. She knew she had to find Faustina now. Steeling herself, Selena swam back down the staircase and out the front entrance, emerging into the open sea.

Selena swam cautiously through a gloomy cave, focused intently on finding Faustina. She didn't see the obstruction ahead until she barreled right into it.

Bouncing back, she found herself tangled in stretchy, ropy tendons. Looking up, she stifled a scream as a mutilated creature loomed over her.

"Hey, great to see you," said a familiar voice.

Selena squinted at the figure floating there. Wait...those were Andrew's eyes peering out from the exposed skull.

"Andrew?" Selena gasped. "Is that you?"

"In the flesh. Or what's left of it anyway." The zombie merlad chuckled.

Selena recoiled as his skeletal arm reached to untangle her.

"Sorry about that," Andrew said. "It's so hard to steer this new zombie tail. I'm still getting the hang of it."

"I figured Faustina got you when you were dragged under," Selena said, backing away from Andrew's outstretched hands.

"Yeah, we live down here now," Andrew replied casually, as if becoming undead was no big deal.

Selena shuddered then paused as she heard a rumbling from above. She glanced up just as Jamie came crashing down through the cave ceiling in a shower of rock and sand.

Selena screamed as the zombie merlad landed with a splash at her feet. Jamie flashed a grin, part of his brain poking grossly out of his broken skull.

"Hey Selena, long time no see," he said. "Like my new zombie digs?"

Selena's pulse quickened as they approached her with cheerful grins. Since Andrew and Jamie used to bully her constantly back on land, their friendly behavior now put her on edge.

"This place is great, you'll love it," Jamie said, oblivious to her discomfort. "Faustina has all kinds of fun planned."

Selena cringed internally. Their idea of fun likely differed greatly from hers.

"Uh yeah, sounds awesome," Selena lied. "But hey, I'm looking for Faustina, I really should really get going, so..."

She trailed off, slowly backing away from the merlads. Their smiles never wavered, but Selena's heart still pounded. With those two, things could turn nasty in a flash.

"No problem, catch you later," Andrew said amiably.

Selena wasted no time turning to swim off at top speed. She had to get away while the merlads were in a good mood. Who knew how long that would last?

Selena swam on through the creepy glowing waters, searching every nook and cranny for Faustina. But all she found were the kooky creatures of the mermaid realm.

Ghostly shipwrecks loomed out of the dimness, their wood nibbled and gnawed. In rocky crannies, skull spiders and squids peered out, watching her pass. A mermaid skeleton pirouetted past in the current, still grinning cheerfully.

The scary sights made Selena jumpy, but she pushed onward until her legs and arms ached with tiredness. She stopped to rest in a nice little cave but couldn't relax enough to sleep.

After hours of hunting with zero luck, Selena started feeling hopeless. That sneaky mermaid knew how to lie low all right. Finally, she had to give up and kick back to shore as the sun woke up.

Back on land, Selena snuck inside and took a steamy shower to get warm. She sure hoped Mum wouldn't notice she'd been out all night on a crazy zombie mermaid quest.

Despite the hot water, Selena still shivered a little. She had searched her hardest, but Faustina had won this round.

She texted Chloe.

Selena: *I'm knackered. Went under the sea on my own this time. No magical powers!*

Chloe: *Did you get the necklace?*

Selena: *Nope. But I did bump into Andrew and Jamie.*

Chloe: *How is Andrew?*

Selena: *Undead.*

Chloe: *Lol.*

Selena: *Nicer dead than alive.*

Chloe: *Shouldn't we tell some grown-ups about this? Their parents must be frantic.*

Selena: *Think. Who's going to believe they've turned into merlads?*

Chloe: *I guess. Look, you've got to stop chasing that necklace. Faustina is nuts. She could do you some serious damage.*

But Selena couldn't let it go. Her mum's survival depended on her getting her hands on that necklace.

36

FAUSTINA

When Faustina swam back to the underwater house, Jamie told her Selena was looking for her. But Faustina already knew that. Ever since she had brought the boys down from the surface, she had been watching everything happen. She knew the police were searching for Andrew and Jamie, hoping they might still be alive somewhere. How daft humans were. Andrew and Jamie belonged to Faustina now.

Faustina still didn't know what to do about Selena, though. She kept trying to get the necklace for herself. Although she had to admit, there was a certain pleasure in watching Selena search but come up with nothing. If Selena didn't want to join the undead voluntarily, Faustina would have to take a bite out of her relative. But now wasn't the right time, even though there was a strong smell of human tickling her rotten nostrils.

Faustina rocketed up from the ocean depths, powered by her strong mermaid magic. She swam up and down the coastline, filled with restless energy. As she zoomed around, she spied her target—Mr. Bottomley, strolling down the beach. She still hadn't forgiven him for almost cutting her in half with his shovel. Now here he was, walking along, singing tunelessly as he picked up seashells. What a doofus. But even so, his teaching skills could be useful for her undead mermaid army.

Faustina grinned, flashing her mouth of sharp fangs. She was so making this fool part of her zombie staff. With her mermaid mind control, he'd be hers in a splash. Then he could teach all her creepy mer-zombies about algebra or poetry or whatever. It was going to be fantastic.

Mr. Bottomley made a face and waved his hand in front of his nose. Faustina could see her own scent, appearing as green fumes, wafting off the water around her. She sighed. Of course, the smell didn't bother her, but it would be easier if humans weren't so offended by it. It made it harder to sneak up on them.

He rolled his pants up above his knees, wading through the water, when a wave swept in hard, rushing against his legs. He lost his balance and fell. The waves seemed to want to pull him into the deep, and a strong current sucked him backward.

Faustina watched as the sand beneath his feet collapsed. He flailed his arms, desperate to stop himself from being buried by the sea and managed to regain his footing. Breathless, he stumbled back to the beach. He started to run, the waves lapping at his heels, their roar deafening. He scrambled up the bank of pebbles, but the uneven surface slowed him down. Faustina saw her chance and pounced.

Grabbing him by the ankles, she yanked him back. His face smashed down into the pebbles. He screamed, but there wasn't anyone else taking an evening stroll on the beach to hear his cries.

Faustina pulled him back across the bumpy pebbles, along the slick, wet sand, and into the sea.

"Wait. Stop." His hands gouged into the sand.

Faustina grinned at him, showing her sharp teeth, then jabbed her claws into his ankles. He yelped in pain. It would be a lot easier if he'd stop struggling.

She tugged him under the water, deeper and deeper under the surface, but he thrashed wildly, managing to break free and bob back to the surface.

Not so fast. Faustina gnashed her jaws as she gave chase. As Faustina bit into his shoulder, he screamed, pushing her face away.

"Stop fighting me," Faustina wailed. She was losing her patience. "You've been infected now." Faustina reached out her arms, showing the flesh hanging off and the bones of her hands and rotting nails. She grabbed Mr. Bottomley's hand and pulled.

"I don't want to come with you!" He cried. Blood poured from the wound in his shoulder, turning the sea foam red. "I have to go to work tomorrow. I'm the headmaster at Madderly Academy."

Faustina gave him an evil grin, her sharp teeth glinting.

"Well, congratulations! You've just been promoted to my zombie mermaid staff."

She cackled as she dragged the struggling teacher under the waves. He was going to be perfect for her underwater classroom of doom. She just knew her creepy mer-zombie students would love having a real teacher around. And with her magical mermaid mind control, he'd be a phenomenal minion in no time.

37

SELENA

When the police arrived at Madderly Academy, Selena knew it was bad news. Her suspicions were confirmed at the morning assembly.

A constable made an announcement. "A toupee has been found at the beach." Snickering from the kids ensued. "We believe the toupee belonged to Mr. Bottomley." A hush fell over the children. "We are treating this as a drowning. Anyone who has any information about this incident should come forward."

As soon as the assembly ended, Selena found her mum, who was in the art room surrounded by piles of fabric, wigs, and half-assembled costumes. She hunched over a sewing machine, sewing furiously.

"Why weren't you at the assembly?" Selena shouted over the whir of the machine.

"I've got too much work to do," she shouted back.

"Ouch. I've just run the needle through my finger." She popped it into her mouth.

"The police found Mr. Bottomley's toupee on the beach."

Her face crumpled, and she dropped her face into her hands.

"Did you hear me?"

Fiona looked up, a blank expression on her face.

"That's it then, isn't it? He's gone."

"We don't know that for sure," Selena said, but she didn't sound convincing, even to herself.

"If the toupee was found at the beach, Faustina must have gotten to him," Fiona said, a glazed look on her face. "And in that case, he'll be undead and can't come back to life. I'm never going to see him again."

Guilt engulfed Selena. She'd taken the necklace, then lost it, and had gotten herself into a big mess.

"I need to tell you something, Mum," Selena said, sinking down in a chair beside her and putting an arm around her shoulder. "That night we were planting flowers in the cemetery, I found Aunt Ada's necklace in a stone planter by her grave. I tried wearing it to see what it could do for me."

"What?" Selena's mum's face flushed with blood. "You knew how much I needed to get a hold of that necklace, and yet you decided to keep it for yourself?"

"I'm just telling you what happened. I only had it for a day. Jamie grabbed it off me after school, and it accidentally fell into the ocean. Faustina got hold of it. She used its powers to control my mind and made me jump into the sea one night. Mum, it was amazing down there. But Faustina is crazy. She's been controlling your thoughts. That's why you've been acting strange these past few weeks."

"That might explain it. My thoughts have been buzzing. And I have a throbbing headache all the time. I can't think straight, and I don't know what I'm going to do or say next. And at the same time, I'm always in a panic, knowing I'm slowly turning into a zombie."

"That's what I'm worried about, too. I think we could stop her if we could get the necklace, but she doesn't want to part with it. I can't even find her."

"How are we going to get it back?" Fiona stood and picked up a costume with sleeves of different lengths. "I should never have brought you to live in Aunt Ada's house. I never dreamed Faustina would turn me into a zombie. I don't know what to do. What can I do? Just stay focused on the play, I guess." She held the costume up to Selena. "Let me see if this is the right length." The skirt was *way* too long. "This will need taking in a bit if it's going to fit you," she mumbled.

"You think?" Selena flung the costume down beside the sewing machine. "Look, we need to get real here. I've got to find Faustina. Maybe there's something she can do to reverse this curse."

"No, it's too dangerous for you to go down there again. And besides, I need you in this play. It's been hell for me. I've been up for days sewing costumes and making props."

"And you've done a great job," Selena said, although that wasn't exactly true. Some of the palm trees created out of cardboard to fit on the island resembled a kindergarten project, with leaves made of torn tissue paper, and the costumes were badly sewn. "But why don't we just focus on getting you better?"

Fiona reached for Selena's hand. "That's sweet, but I need you to promise me you won't jeopardize your own safety."

"I won't," Selena said, giving her mum a quick kiss on the cheek.

Selena had to find Faustina and soon. She guessed her mum was taking so long to turn because she'd only been scratched rather than bitten. But it was clear they were running out of time.

38

SELENA

Selena was restless all week. Going back to face Faustina was a risky move, and she'd probably end up dead. One bite and she'd be a member of the undead club.

But she couldn't sit around and watch her mum become a zombie mermaid. Her mum was getting crazier and crazier. And Mr. Bottomley's disappearance was disconcerting. Everything pointed to him having become the latest of Faustina's victims. She had to find out what had happened to him and get a hold of the necklace.

That evening, after her mum went to bed, Selena snuck out of the house and down to the ocean. She felt nauseated and afraid, but she swallowed those feelings down. Taking a deep breath, she jumped into the waves.

As Selena dove under the surface, she was surprised to find she could breathe normally, just like the last time. It didn't make much sense, but she had a feeling Faustina was somehow behind it.

Selena swam deeper into the inky black depths, propelling herself forward in search of the necklace. She wondered why Faustina was still helping her. Surely, the mermaid knew Selena wanted the necklace for herself. So why provide magical aid? Selena didn't understand Faustina's motives, but she intended to take full advantage of this temporary power. With the mermaid's protection, she could keep looking as long as it took to find the treasure she desired.

Once she had swum down to the orange glowing area, the magical warm bubble inside the freezing sea, she entered the house. She swam into the drawing room, where Andrew and Jamie were lolling on the red sofa playing Go Fish.

"Hi, guys," she said. "I'm looking for Faustina. Have you seen her around?"

"Not recently," said Jamie, slapping some cards on the table. "She's gone on a biting spree, so if I were you, I'd make myself scarce."

"Hey, how come you're down here again?" said Andrew, grinning. "You miss us? Did you know Mr. Bottomley's down here now?"

"Can't stand the guy," Jamie said, scowling.

"I thought he might have ended up down here," Selena explained.

"Faustina bit him," Andrew confirmed, fanning out his cards. "And as soon as Aunt Ada heard he was a headmaster, she was hell-bent on him run the Undead Academy. She wanted us to help him sort everything out. Like I'm interested."

"Ugh, Mr. Bottomley will not stop talking about his new curriculum," Jamie complained.

"From morning to night, it's nothing but lectures on viruses and zombie biology. He's super pumped about teaching us ghouls."

Andrew let out an exaggerated yawn. "Total snore-fest. I miss fun human stuff like gym class and pizza parties."

"Seriously, this dude is already getting on my last nerve after only a week here," Jamie said. "Yesterday I chomped his arm off just to shut him up for five minutes. Though I'll admit, scrawny Mr. Bottomley was surprisingly delicious."

Andrew laughed. "Dude, you can't just go around eating the teachers. Even if he is super boring."

"I know, I know," Jamie said. "But a mer-zombie's gotta do what a mer-zombie's gotta do. We need to liven things up around here before we all lose our minds."

The two undead boys exchanged a mischievous grin.

"You need to learn to control your appetite," said Andrew. "Like if you bite the head off, the person dies and can't turn into a zombie."

"I know. Faustina told me. If I destroy the brain, it's game over."

Selena gaped at them. It was weird that they were so chill underwater since they had tormented her on land. Maybe your personality could change once you went zombie.

"Anyway, he's super annoying," Jamie continued. As a

shark slid through the water toward Andrew, Selena shrieked. Its pointy silver nose bumped into the cards he was holding, making them disperse into the water.

"Who's a naughty boy, then?" Jamie said. "This shark is a pain, believe me."

"Oh, my God," said Selena. "What are you going to do about it? What if he bites me?" The shark's skin felt like sandpaper as it rubbed against Selena. She instinctively pulled her shoulders up to her neck, screwing up her face in the hope that he would soon swim away.

"Oh, he's okay," Jamie said, reaching out and rubbing him on the nose. "There you go, kitty, kitty."

Selena glanced up. She relaxed a little and started to back away.

"Sounds crazy, I know, to pet a shark," said Jamie, "but it puts them in a trance." The shark settled down beside him on the sofa, giving a contented grin.

Except Selena didn't want to find out if the big kitty's bite would take her hand off.

"See you guys," said Selena, swimming away. "I've got to go get that necklace from Faustina."

39

SELENA

In the library, Selena bumped into Mr. Bottomley and Aunt Ada, who were scrubbing algae from the covers of books.

"Oh, Mr. Bottomley. Great to see you down here." Selena tried to hide how freaked out she was by his grotesque appearance and the fact his right arm was a bloody stump. Black goo dripped out of his mouth, and his teeth looked like old gravestones. "I hear you've been busy starting up the school."

"Gosh, yes. When Aunt Ada first recruited me to run it, I wanted to run in the other direction. But the fact is I'm a zombie merlad now." He sighed. "I'm not going anywhere. So why not put my leadership skills to good use?"

"Faustina was a genius to find Mr. Bottomley," Aunt Ada gushed. "And now we're trying to get all the new students to pitch in and get everything in order. Faustina's been working overtime, infecting new zombie mermaids and merlads."

"Yes," said Mr. Bottomley. "It's going to be a job to keep this place clean, especially as people are going to be dripping blood all over the place."

"Don't stress, Mr. B. We'll keep this place spick and span," Aunt Ada assured him. She waved over a group of zombie mermaid girls. "Ladies, looking fabulous as always. Grab those buckets and brushes. It's time to give this place a proper cleaning."

The mermaids giggled as Aunt Ada cracked a grin. "You know, I just sold my vacuum since all it did was collect dust. Get it?"

Mr. Bottomley laughed loudly. "Good one, Ada."

"These ghoulish gals will be your new students," Ada explained. "They're just dying to get involved in zombie school."

As the mermaids started scouring away, Selena asked, "How are you finding life down here?"

Mr. Bottomley looked glum. "I'm trying to make the best of being a zombie teacher, even though it's pretty nasty. All the blood and biting isn't my style. But I'm trapped here, so might as well make it work."

"Guys, this is super urgent. Have you seen Faustina around?" Selena asked.

"Afraid not," Mr. Bottomley replied.

"That girl is always disappearing and leaving us with all the hard work," Aunt Ada complained.

"Got it, thanks anyway," Selena said. "I really need to

find her."

Selena hurried off, determined to track down the elusive mermaid.

All night, Selena hunted for Faustina. She looked through every room in the house and found nothing, so she decided to take her search far and wide. The sun moved along the surface of the water as she swam around the sea, searching for the wretched mermaid. She searched for hours in the surrounding caves and tunnels, but to no avail.

Just before dawn, she found Faustina up in the attic, lying in the bath. The ruby necklace glittered around her neck. A spider with red legs, a skull face and creepy fangs, raced above, building a web from the rafters, working his way back and forth and heading toward the floor.

"Listen up, Faustina. I don't have time for your games," Selena said. "I just need that necklace. It belongs to my family. It belonged to Aunt Ada."

"So what? I'm part of the family, too." She beamed.

"I need the necklace," Selena said, trying not to blow her top. "My mum…she's gone crazy since you scratched her."

"Oh, good. She'll wander into the sea any day now. She'll want to come down and be with us once she's undead. She'll join her people."

"Not if I can help it." Selena clenched her jaw. "Just how long will it be before she turns all the way? Since it was just a scratch."

Faustina stretched out in the bathtub and flopped her tail up on the edge. Putting her hands behind her head, she said, "It's been quite a while now. I don't think it'll take more than another few days until she goes zombie and utterly insane. In the meantime, she'll cause so much havoc up on land you'll be pleased when she comes to live down here."

"Never!" Screamed Selena. She hurled herself at Faustina, nails sinking into her mushy, rotting flesh.

"You should learn to control that temper of yours," Faustina muttered, smacking Selena in the neck. As they wrestled, some other mermaid zombies poked their heads through the trapdoor, intrigued. "You'll never win, you know. Even if you could beat me, I have a whole army. I can control their minds."

Obeying a silent order, the other mermaids held Selena down while she struggled. The skull headed spider continued to spin his web. Scurrying back and forth in the attic, he spun his slimy, sticky net until Selena was trapped underneath it, her hands shackled into the web.

"Let me go!" she screamed.

"Your mum warned you not to meddle with the necklace," said Faustina, peering through a gap in the web. "You should have listened. When you dug it up, you released a powerful energy."

"It only gave me good powers when I wore it."

"Yes, it did. It protected you from the bullies and made them be nice to you. But you didn't look after it very well, did you? You didn't even have it for a day before you lost it. Which is fine because it's much better for me to have it now. Problem is, right now I feel like I'm so evil, and this necklace is going to amplify my powers. So, thanks for doing me a favor and bringing it to me." She stretched her arms in the sea and threw back her head. "I'm going to be so evil. You have no idea."

"Let me go."

"No. You'll be my prisoner forever."

"That will never work. My mum will look for me. Chloe will look for me." Selena writhed about, trying to tear at the web with her teeth. She thought of Chloe. They were so close. Surely, Chloe would realize what had happened to her?

"So what? They can look all they want. They'll never find you. But who knows? If you calm down, eventually I might take you out of the web. Now relax. Let's enjoy the evening. How about a game of Monopoly?"

"How can we do that? My hands are all stuck to this web."

"Yes, I didn't think of that. I'll release your hands so you can roll the dice," she said, ripping the sticky strands off Selena's hands.

Faustina pulled a plastic board out of a box then put a spell on the board so it floated between them.

When Selena rolled the dice, they tumbled through the water and landed on the board as if governed by some magical force.

Selena's heart pounded as she tried not to panic. Even if Chloe realized she was missing, how could she possibly help down here?

Selena had no choice but to play along with Faustina's twisted games for now. The mermaid seemed obsessed with board games. So, Selena would keep rolling the dice, hoping it put Faustina in a good enough mood to let down her guard. Then, just maybe, Selena could break free of this underwater prison.

She took slow, deep breaths to stay calm. Panicking would only make Faustina angrier, and Selena needed the spiteful mermaid in a cheerful mood.

"Your turn." Faustina grinned, her mouth full of jagged teeth.

Selena forced a smile and grabbed the dice. She had to keep playing nice until she spotted her chance to escape Faustina's clammy clutches for good. Selena's heart thudded as she plotted her next move. This escape mission would take all her courage and cunning to pull off.

CHLOE

The next day before school, Chloe received a frantic phone call from Selena's mum.

"Selena's disappeared." Her voice was high-pitched and hysterical as the words tumbled out. "She wasn't in her bed this morning. Have you seen her?"

"What? No, I haven't seen her since yesterday," Chloe replied through sniffles.

"She was going for an underwater swim at night. I don't know if she told you…"

"Yes, she did. She was looking for Faustina and the necklace."

"Well, she's finally gone and done it," Fiona said miserably. "She's disappeared. Probably drowned." She started to cry.

"You don't know that. Just try to stay calm."

"Why didn't I do more to stop her from going down

there?" She said through sobs. "How am I going to cope? Do you think I should call the police?"

Chloe wondered if Selena's mum was so far gone that she didn't even know what to do in an emergency.

"Maybe," Chloe said. "They might be able to find her. I'm going to the beach to look for her."

"All right, but don't dive under the sea. Faustina's dangerous."

After Fiona had talked to the police and they'd spent the day looking for Selena along the coast, Chloe got a text from her.

Fiona: *So far, nothing.*

Chloe headed toward the room where the drama class rehearsal was about to start. She inhaled her nasal spray and walked in. She texted Fiona.

Chloe: *The rehearsal's canceled, right?*

She saw the cast assembled on the stage. They all sat perched on a large wooden cutout of the island, covered in wonky palm trees, a sandy beach, and a weird-looking monkey with a lopsided grin.

"Hey, snooty," Cindy hollered, sidling up to her. "What do you think of the set? Looks like someone vomited up their dinner."

"I'm sure Selena's mum did her best. I didn't see you volunteer to help."

"Where is porky today?"

Chloe frowned. "Can you not call her that?"

"Someone's touchy." Cindy rolled her eyes. "So where is... Selena?"

Chloe hesitated. "She's gone missing. She wasn't in her bed this morning, and her mum's worried sick."

"Oh, that's awful," Cindy said, taken aback, and staring at her, lost for words. It was an expression she'd never seen on Cindy before. "I wonder what happened to her. I mean, Andrew and Jamie... I think they were gobbled by that shark. But what about Selena? You don't think the shark got her, too?"

"I don't know," Chloe snapped. Although, of course, she had her suspicions that Selena was under the sea and might at that moment, be turning into a zombie mermaid.

Chloe was surprised to see Selena's mum bustle into the room.

"Oh, Ms. Flowers... I didn't think you were coming in, what with...." she trailed off. "Is there any news?"

But Fiona didn't seem to hear Chloe at all. She bossed the students around on stage, making them move props here and there in a robot-like way. Chloe felt worried as she watched. As one boy absentmindedly started whistling a little tune, Fiona suddenly shouted, "No whistling in the theater! It's bad luck."

The boy's eyes got huge, and he clamped his mouth shut. Fiona was going nuts, her voice echoing all over the room. Chloe could tell Fiona was majorly stressed. As she ordered kids about on the stage, she looked like she was about to lose it at any second.

"Ms. Flowers, we're all so worried about you being at

school right now," Cindy yelled, and everyone hushed. Cindy furrowed her brow with exaggerated concern. "What with Selena missing and all, you must be going through hell."

Chloe narrowed her eyes as she watched the exchange between Cindy and Fiona. *What is Cindy up to?*

Chloe thought the rehearsals would be a distraction for Fiona until Selena was found. But Cindy acted like they should be out searching instead.

Cindy gave a sympathetic smile. "I know if it was my child missing, I'd be an absolute wreck, so maybe you should go home in case the police call."

Chloe had to resist the urge to roll her eyes. Trust Cindy to find a way to be dramatic about the situation and make it all about her.

She probably just wants to get out of being in the play. Well, it's not going to work.

Fiona sighed, running a hand through her hair. "I appreciate your concern, Cindy. But the police are handling the search. And I have my phone in my bag if the police call."

Fiona started to pace and gestured vaguely with her hands. "I just can't sit still right now. I need a distraction, or I'll lose my mind." She stopped and put her hands on her hips. "You know, I'd rather keep busy instead of sitting here worrying. Let's rehearse the scene where Helena and Gracia build the wall. Cindy, you'll have to fill in for Selena for now."

Fiona grabbed a stack of heavy books from one of the bookshelves. "Here, we can use these as pretend rocks.

Work together to move them into a wall shape. I know it's not the same without Selena, but we can do it. The show must go on, right?"

Fiona clapped her hands together. "Chop chop, everyone! Places. Let's run through this wall building scene. It'll help pass the time until Selena comes home. I just know she will."

<hr>

After the rehearsal, Cindy came up to Chloe. "That was weird… playing Selena's part. What do you think happened? Do you think she's run away?"

"I don't know," Chloe snapped. "I'm just hoping she comes back." Chloe held her tongue, knowing Cindy would never believe her wild story about zombie mermaids, even if she told the truth.

When everyone had filed out, Chloe approached Selena's mum.

"What are we going to do? How are we going to get Selena back?" Chloe asked.

"We're going to wait and see what happens. What else can we do?" She said, hugging Chloe. Then, in a firm voice, she said, "And don't get any silly ideas of going down there to try to bring her back. Unless you want to put yourself in danger, too."

After school, Chloe wandered alone along the shore, absentmindedly licking her ice cream cone. Her thoughts raced as she tried to decide what to do. Should she try to find Selena herself? It would be dangerous—the sea was icy cold and the currents strong. But if she didn't at least try, would she ever see her best friend again?

Chloe's heart pounded as she stared out at the dark waves lapping the shore. She was a pretty strong swimmer. Could she gather the courage to dive into the frigid water if it meant having a chance of saving Selena? She hoped with all her might that she could. The only question was: could she survive the attempt?

SELENA

Deep beneath the waves, Selena's eyes glazed over as exhaustion set in. She had been trapped in this underwater Scrabble marathon for hours, to Faustina's smug delight.

Across the sea spider's immense web dividing them, the zombie mermaid lounged smugly in the bathtub.

A bunch of creepy skull faced spiders were all over Faustina's gnarly shoulders. Their gross red legs were moving in weird ways, like they were trying to give her a massage but failing pretty hard. Some of them were just wiggling back and forth awkwardly while others were making squiggles that probably didn't feel very nice. And then there was this one spider who thought it would be cool to do some acrobatics and climbed all over Faustina's head like it was a jungle gym.

Faustina cackled with glee as she tallied up her latest

triple word score. "Sure you don't want my spiders to give you a massage?"

"I'll pass thanks," Selena said.

"Then let's play another."

Selena stifled a groan. There had to be some way out of this underwater prison.

"*Bandura* isn't a word," said Selena wearily, looking at the letters Faustina had just placed on the board. "Do you mean *bandana*?"

"It's a Ukrainian lute!" Faustina yelled like everyone knew that. The board floated between them. "That's seventy-eight... no, wait a minute... eighty-two points—"

"I give up," Selena huffed. Her arms were hanging out of the web so she could place her tiles on the board, but they were aching from the marathon Scrabble session. "Have it. Have your Ukrainian lute." Selena flung the remaining letters to the side, but they bounced back onto her rack like a boomerang.

Selena let out a raspy cough, her throat feeling as dry as a desert. "Gimme some water," she croaked.

"Why didn't you say so?" Faustina snapped her fingers and her pet sea spiders scurried off.

Before long, they came back with glass bottles filled with fresh water. Selena guzzled it down hungrily.

"They got it from a beach tap," Faustina bragged.

"Big whoop," Selena rolled her eyes. "Don't act like you're taking care of me when I'm stuck down here against my will."

"Relax. You can't count on your mum to save you, you know."

"My mum loves me. She'll come looking for me!" Selena protested.

Faustina rolled her eyes and let out a disbelieving laugh. "Fiona only cares about herself and her fancy plays. She couldn't care less about you."

"That's not fair. She may have her flaws, but she cares about me."

Faustina's voice got softer. "I know your mum tries her best, but let's be real, she's kinda kooky." Selena shrugged, not wanting to admit it. "You're probably tired of moving all the time, right?" Faustina asked with a knowing look. "What if you didn't have to worry about that? You could just stay here with me and have a BFF for life."

Selena scoffed. "Hard pass."

Faustina leaned closer, and Selena had to hold back a gag. Her red hair drifted lazily in the water, wispy strands clinging to her graying scalp like tangled seaweed. But up close, it was matted with algae and infested with little shell-backed critters.

As she peered at Selena through the web, her clouded eyes seemed sunken deeper into her bloated face. Skin like spoiled fish clung loosely to her skull in peeling patches, revealing glimpses of viscous black goop beneath.

"I know we got off on the wrong foot," she gurgled, her ragged lips drawing back in a mockery of a smile. Black liquid dribbled from between her busted teeth, diffusing a foul stench through the water. "But I used my mermaid magic to keep you from sinking like a rock."

Selena had already figured that out, but she bit her tongue and nodded.

"And I want you to think of this as your home. The water's nice and warm around the house, isn't it?"

"Yes but—"

"You're floating around in a magical, safe pool of water, far warmer than the English Channel. Think of it as a Jacuzzi and let's have a spa day. Relax. Let your cares disappear and stop trying to escape."

"Woohoo! Thanks for the Jacuzzi party," Selena cheered unconvincingly. She sank into the warm water, eyeing Faustina suspiciously.

Faustina flashed an overly wide grin. "I'm just trying to help you chillax and be your best underwater self."

"Riiight," Selena was so mad she flailed around and got herself stuck in the giant sticky spiderweb. "Ugh, what is this gunk?" She opened her mouth in disgust, accidentally getting a strand of web stuck to her tongue. She spat it out.

Faustina chuckled. "It's my special sea spider silk wrap. Great for exfoliating."

"More like extra irritating," Selena grumbled, trying to peel the sticky threads off.

"It's the hottest new spa treatment," Faustina insisted. "All the celebrity mermaids are getting it."

Selena tore at the web with her teeth dramatically. "Blech! Tastes like old bubble gum mixed with squid ink. Worst spa day ever."

Faustina shrugged. "Fine, suit yourself. But don't come crying to me when you don't have glowing mermaid skin."

Selena rolled her eyes and kept struggling to break free.

Selena spit out another sticky glob of web, gagging. "I don't care what you say. I'm getting out of here."

Faustina snorted, absently fiddling with the ruby around her neck. "Good luck with that. Don't you get it? I've got all the power now, thanks to this little beauty." She flashed a sinister grin. "I can keep you trapped down here as long as I want."

Selena's stomach dropped, but she tried not to show her fear. "Yeah right, like I'd ever want to stay in this disgusting underwater prison."

"You'll come around eventually," Faustina said with a casual shrug. "Maybe I'll even turn you into a zombie mermaid, make you one of my minions."

"No way!" Selena thrashed harder in the web but only succeeded in tangling herself up more.

Faustina cackled. "Face it, you're not going anywhere. No one's coming to rescue you, either. You're stuck with me, princess."

Panic rose in Selena's chest. She had to get back above water, back to her mum. But the more she fought, the more ensnared she became, until she was wrapped up like a mummy in the silky trap.

Faustina smirked, clearly enjoying her despair. Selena glanced down at her hands. Were they starting to get webs between the fingers?

"Keep thrashing around like that and you'll end up a

human raisin," Faustina scolded. "Is that what you want? To be a prune-skinned freak forever?"

Selena scowled. "Better than being your prisoner."

Faustina pouted. "But we could have so much fun together. I've got board games galore. Ooh, we can have slumber parties and braid each other's hair."

"Gee, I wonder why you don't have any friends," Selena said dryly.

"It's not my fault," Faustina insisted. "I tried making nice with the other mermaids, but they think I'm weird."

Selena rolled her eyes. "Maybe because you're a mean, power-hungry basket case?"

Faustina ignored the jab. "But then I got this necklace and realized I can control them. I can make them help me keep you here." Her eyes lit up creepily. "I never thought of taking a human prisoner before. But it's brilliant, isn't it? You'll learn to love it here, just wait."

"In your twisted dreams," Selena spat. "I'm getting out, no matter what!"

Faustina's expression hardened. "We'll see about that. You'll stop fighting eventually. And when you do, you'll see this is for the best."

Selena suppressed a shiver at the mermaid's icy tone. She had to escape, and fast, before this psycho made her a permanent playmate.

CHLOE

At the dress rehearsal for *Zombie Island*, Chloe couldn't help but stare at Selena's mum. Fiona was racing around like a nut, trying to prop up the palm trees that kept tipping over and smudging the yucky gray makeup on all the kid zombies.

She looked totally frazzled, with sweat dripping down her face. Chloe felt kind of bad for her. It was obvious Fiona was barely holding it together.

Chloe's eyes widened as she noticed something weird about Fiona's right eye. It was slightly hanging out of the socket, and it had turned a gross greenish color, like a boiled egg that had been in the pot too long. Any day, she was sure to go all the way over to the dark side.

"Why don't I put some makeup on you?" Chloe offered.

"Oh, I don't know if I have time," Fiona said, flustered.

"It won't take a minute," said Chloe, giving a sniff. "I'll style your hair a little, too."

"Okay, but we need to get to rehearsal as soon as possible. I don't feel like anything's ready at all."

Once Chloe got Selena's mum looking a little more human again, the dress rehearsal kicked off. Cindy was trying her best with Selena's part, but she was no good at all.

"I can't hear you," Fiona shouted from the back row. "Cindy, you've got to project more. I can't believe I have to tell you that today."

Fiona hustled up the aisle toward the stage. "Don't you get it? This is my big debut at Madderly Academy. I can't let anyone down. My rep is on the line here."

"Don't stress, Ms. Flowers," Cindy said. "Just opening night jitters. I promise I'll chill out by showtime."

"You better," Fiona said. "I need everyone at one hundred and ten percent."

As Fiona climbed onto the stage, she dragged her leg behind her in a funny way.

Something's not right. Fiona was bent over as if she had trouble straightening her spine. Was Selena's mum turning into a zombie mermaid right in front of them?

"Ms. Flowers, are you okay?" asked Cindy.

"Thanks for your concern, Cindy," she said. "I'm feeling great. Let me show you one more time how to say your opening lines and how to project."

Chloe tried to focus on the rehearsal. Luckily, she had her lines down and could rattle them off no problem. Since she wasn't stressed about her role, her mind kept drifting to Selena.

She felt awful that she had no clue how to get her BFF back. Chloe hated not knowing what to do. There had to be some way to rescue Selena.

Chloe sighed, sneaking another peek at her phone. Still no texts from Selena. Where could she be? And how was Chloe going to be brave enough to get her back? She had to figure out something soon before it was too late.

43

SELENA

A week in this underwater deathtrap and Selena was wasting away. Her stomach gnawed with hunger after being force-fed nothing but soggy shellfish. Blech, she was sick of sashimi. She'd rather eat squid slime.

The web cocoon held fast no matter how she thrashed. Any rip or tear was instantly repaired by swarms of skull-faced spiders. Like Houdini in reverse, the more she struggled, the more stuck she became.

Selena floated limply, energy drained. She was sick of fighting. Doubts crept in that she'd ever break free of this nightmare. What if she was trapped with Faustina forever? The very thought made her shudder.

Selena glanced down at her freakish webbed hands and gulped. No doubt the rest of her was turning into a swollen, prune-skinned mess, too. Hard to know for sure without a mirror, but she could feel the transformation. Gross.

"Hey, Raisin Girl, high five those gnarly flippers," Andrew said, raising a hand.

Selena shot him a death glare.

"Someone's cheesed off." Jamie chuckled. "What's got her knickers in a twist anyway?"

Andrew shrugged. "Search me. Who'd take boring land over this brilliant zombie merlad life?"

They high fived their claw fingers.

"This is the bee's knees, surfing these waves forever." Jamie grinned.

Selena groaned. Were all zombie merlads this annoyingly cheery?

"Too right, this underwater world rocks," Andrew said.

"Let's go for a cheeky splash, shall we?" Jamie said.

Yep, apparently, they were. Selena facepalmed.

"I'm thrilled you're having a blast, but I need out," Selena yelled at the merlads. "What will it take for you to help me escape this web?"

Andrew winced. "Sorry, no can do. Faustina would roast us alive if she caught us freeing you."

"We want to help, really," Jamie added. "But that mermaid's mental. We can't risk getting on her bad side."

He poked the sticky web, his hand coming back coated in strings of gunk. "You'll need an underwater machete to hack through this thing."

Selena groaned. "How long does that nutter plan to keep me trapped here?"

"No telling with that one," Andrew said, shaking his

head. "She's a few seashells short of a necklace, if you ask me."

"Too right," Jamie snorted. "I can't stand her, either. She's always trying to make us do weird stuff, like advanced sudoku puzzles. No wonder she has to snatch 'friends'"

"She thinks I'll enjoy living in a web eventually," said Selena. "Talk about delusional. She wants me down here so I can be her little playmate. Meanwhile, I'm going to be down here until she decides to make me undead."

"Like I said, it's not so bad," said Jamie.

"There must be people up there who care about you," Andrew said gently. "Who else knows you're trapped down here?"

Selena perked up a bit. "Chloe and my mum. But it's too dangerous for them to attempt a rescue." She glanced at Andrew pleadingly. "Though maybe you could bring Chloe down? She's an incredible swimmer."

"We can try to get Chloe," Andrew said after thinking it over.

Selena's face flooded with relief. "That would be brilliant, thank you."

"But how will we find her?" Jamie asked, puzzled.

"Sometimes, she walks along the beach after school, near those beach huts, eating ice cream," Selena explained.

Jamie nodded slowly. "Okay...but will you be able to stop yourself biting her, Andrew?"

Andrew blushed a deep purple. "Of course, no worries there."

"We'll need to disguise her so Faustina doesn't recognize her," Jamie mused.

Andrew snapped his fingers. "I know, we can put her in a Halloween costume, like a Superman outfit with a full-face mask."

Selena looked at him flatly. "You don't think Faustina will find a random underwater Superman suspicious?"

Jamie laughed. "Good point, bad idea. What about covering her in seaweed instead?"

"Perfect," Andrew said. "Let's do this."

"Please be careful," Selena implored.

Just then Faustina burst in, gnashing her sharp teeth. The merlads jumped, exchanging a nervous look.

"Get away from her," she cried, pushing them away from the web. "She's my friend, and you're not meant to be talking to her."

"How about you give her a break?" Said Andrew.

Faustina floated up to the web cocoon, inspecting Selena with a smirk. "It's easy peasy. Promise you'll stay down here with me, and I'll turn you back and free you from this sticky trap."

Selena scowled through the thick ropes encasing her.

"Better decide fast, babes," Faustina said, her voice sickly sweet. "You're only getting more hideous under there by the minute. Doubt mummy dearest would even know it's you now."

She cackled, clearly enjoying herself. Selena pictured smacking that smug grin off her face.

"Why should I trust you?" Selena retorted. "You're probably lying to trick me into being your prisoner forever."

Faustina put a hand to her chest, feigning offense. "Me? Lie? I'm hurt you'd think so little of me." Her voice hardened. "But suit yourself. Enjoy slowly morphing into a freakish creature all alone down here. Last chance to take my very generous offer."

A bitter loneliness washed over Selena. As much as she hoped, she knew the chances of her mum or Chloe somehow finding and rescuing her from this underwater prison were slim to none. But still...she had to keep faith that Andrew would come through to bring Chloe.

"Why me?" Selena demanded of Faustina. "Of all people, why do this to me?"

Faustina sighed. "That first night at your house, the resemblance to my twin was uncanny. Your hair, your face, your voice—it was like seeing Starona's ghost."

Her tone grew wistful. "We did everything together. Two halves of one whole. From the moment I saw you, I wanted you to take her place."

The familial resemblance dawned on Selena. Beyond Faustina's gauntness from being undead, they could almost be sisters.

"But I'm not her," Selena said quietly.

"Close enough for me," Faustina replied with a shrug.

Selena changed tack. "Why don't you listen to Aunt Ada and let me go, like she's asked you to?"

Faustina snorted. "As if I care what that old bat thinks. In case you forgot, I'm the queen down here. I give the orders." She examined her clawed hands casually. "Ada has no power or bite. She'd rather chatter with her squid than bring humans to our side."

Faustina refocused her icy gaze on Selena. "So no, I won't be listening to her advice to free you. You're mine now. Got it?"

Selena suppressed a frustrated scream.

"Now, deep breath in," Faustina said serenely. "This'll all be much easier if you relax. Just embrace your new life down here."

44

FAUSTINA

As Faustina plopped herself into the bathtub and took deep, cleansing breaths, she tried to quiet the turmoil inside her. Having Selena as her captive was thrilling, but it wasn't enough anymore. She needed a new outlet for her destructive impulses. She longed to cause chaos and destruction, but how much damage could she do from down here? The real action was up on land.

Faustina couldn't help but grin at the thought of Fiona turning into a zombie. It was all thanks to Faustina's scratch, and it brought her immense satisfaction. She wondered if anyone on land would be surprised if she pushed Fiona to take things to the next level. With a touch of her necklace, Faustina released its toxic magic and felt a rush of exhilaration. This was going to be so much fun.

Suddenly the trapdoor on the floor burst open with an explosive splash. Before Faustina could even react, Aunt

Ada came rocketing up through the opening at inhuman speed.

With a massive belly flop, Ada's bloated bulk crashed directly into the tub on top of Faustina. "Oof!" She grunted as Ada's swollen carcass mashed her under waves of putrid flesh.

"Get off!" Faustina snapped, shoving at her aunt's distended form. Somehow Ada's lolling body had twisted them face-to-face, jaws gaping wide to expose blackened teeth stumps.

"You need to let Selena go." Ada gargled, jelly-like skin quivering. Faustina grimaced at the foul waters lapping her face, reeking of long decay from Ada's swollen middle. With a squelch and heave, she tossed Ada's flailing mass onto the slick floor.

"Ew, you're ruining my whole vibe here!" Faustina growled. But it seemed Aunt Ada wouldn't leave empty-handed.

Selena cried out from within the giant spider's web, "Aunt Ada, help me!"

Ada rushed over and placed a clawed hand against Selena's cheek. "I wish I could child, but this is beyond my powers," she rasped. Faustina smirked at the useless display.

"It's quite alright, Ada," Faustina called with a grin, inspecting her jagged talons. "I thought she might want to stay underwater by choice...but whatever, I'll go full zombie on her. I only mean to take a nibble of the girl. Once turned, she'll be pleased as plankton down here among our kind."

Selena's eyes went wide with terror. Faustina licked her

lips slowly, savoring the taste of fear on the air. One prick of her fang was all it would take to make Selena one of them.

But Ada fixed her with a hollow glare. "You'll not lay a rotting digit on her, Faustina," she hissed. Faustina threw back her head and cackled, amazed Aunt Ada thought she could stop her from doing whatever she craved. The games were only beginning.

Faustina flashed her sharp teeth at Selena's horrified face. "You need to take a chill pill. It won't hurt much—just a quick chomp on your arm ought to do it. Then you and me will be best zombie pals forever. We can shuffle around the ocean together. It'll be a blast, you'll see."

She lunged toward Selena, ready to infect her with her zombie bite. This was going to be epic.

"No way," said Aunt Ada, sliding her slimy body between them. "Let Selena be, let her live above the waves. Not everyone wants the zombie mermaid thing. I miss being on dry land all the time. It's hard to adapt when you're old like me. I miss Mr. Wiggums..."

"Zip it," Faustina snapped. "I don't wanna hear your grumbling. I want Selena to stay underwater, and the only way that'll happen is if she goes full zombie like us."

Faustina rushed at Aunt Ada, shoving her creepy fingers right into the old mermaid's neck. "So, get out of my way, you old hag. I'm biting Selena no matter what."

"Never," said Aunt Ada, grabbing Faustina's arm. "I won't let you. Get rid of that spiderweb now—you're torturing the poor girl. Your ego is out of control just because you got that ruby necklace."

Faustina let out a growl. She was filled with evil power and shook Aunt Ada's frail body violently.

"Don't tell me what to do," Faustina snarled. "I'm the original old school zombie mermaid. Me and Starona were the first ones Zlotan put that freaky spell on. If we hadn't gone around biting humans, there wouldn't even be a zombie mermaid crew. So, I can do what I want." A wave of sadness rushed through her as she choked back tears. "Yeah, after Starona got eaten, I was totally bummed. Couldn't see the point of unliving anymore. But I finally realized it's time to get over the self-pity and take charge again. So, if I want to keep Selena here and make her my zombie prisoner, that's my call."

Faustina grabbed a hunk of Aunt Ada's scraggly hair and yanked hard. But Aunt Ada fought back, throwing punches with her bony fists. She whipped her big fish tail, thrashing and kicking for all she was worth.

The two mermaids tangled and spun.

"You'll never get your zombie fangs in her," Aunt Ada declared, even as Faustina continued her vicious attack.

"Come on, Aunt Ada," shouted Selena. "You got this!"

"I'm going to kill you!" Shrieked Faustina, biting into Aunt Ada's wrist.

"How can you kill me," asked Aunt Ada, clamping Faustina's head under her arm, "when I'm already dead?" She laughed.

"Shut up," Faustina fumed.

"Oh, for crying out loud. Kill me already!"

"Watch me," said Faustina, kicking Aunt Ada in the tail

and pulling herself free. Reaching into her bodice, she pulled out a long knife. Faustina pressed the blade to Aunt Ada's throat, and light bounced off the metal. "I'm going to finish you off. Once I cut your head off, you won't just be *un*dead. You'll be *dead*-dead."

Aunt Ada tackled her.

"You'll regret this!" Faustina shouted. The two mermaids thrashed around, fighting for the knife. At the last second, Aunt Ada shoved Faustina away hard, sending the blade spinning through the water.

Faustian watched in rage as wimpy, old Ada made her escape. The knife twirled down right by Selena. Faustina darted for it, but quick as a fish, Selena slipped her webbed hand through the web and snatched the knife first.

"Give that back, you little brat," Faustina howled.

But Selena slashed the web with all her might. Before Faustina could react, Selena plunged the blade into the side of her scaly neck.

Faustina felt the knife scrape against bone. Though she felt no pain in her undead state, a horrible chilling sensation shocked through her decaying body. It was as if every nerve had been flooded with ice, overwhelming her senses. She tried to scream, but only a hollow raspy sound came out. The awful feeling intensified, like her very spirit was being stabbed. Faustina's vision blurred as the chilling agony became too much for her undead mind to handle. She collapsed in the water, limbs spasming uncontrollably. The knife remained lodged in her throat, continuing to radiate its paralyzing supernatural energy through her.

Through the swirling black blood, Faustina could see Selena pausing, trying to figure out her next move. Faustina groaned, furious she had let her prisoner get the upper hand. This wasn't over. She'd get Selena and Aunt Ada back for this.

45

CHLOE

The performance of *Zombie Island* was in full swing, and excitement rushed through Chloe. When she stepped on the stage, all her nervousness melted away. Her parents, in the front row, stood and clapped at the end, their faces radiant with pride. Chloe's skin tingled with the thrill of it all. Maybe they'd finally believe she could make it as an actress.

But she couldn't stop thinking about Selena, especially after watching Cindy doing such a terrible job with Selena's role. Even then, when she should have been basking in the glory of her first performance ever, anxiety gnawed at her insides.

The applause went on as the actors came out to take a bow. Selena's mum hobbled out after them. She looked like she was having trouble supporting her body. Her head lolled, and her right arm nearly scraped the ground. The audience didn't seem to care. Maybe they thought it was part of the play.

"I want to thank everyone so much for coming to see *Zombie Island*," said Fiona, her eyes rolling back in their sockets. "This has been such a success. I never dreamed I'd pull this performance together all by myself. I've overcome so much. I had no money to put on the lavish production you see before you." She gestured at the badly painted island. "I despaired. I worried. I cried and begged for somebody — anybody — to bring me the money I so desperately needed to make this show work. But I didn't receive a penny from anyone. In the end, I had to pull it all together myself. Working tirelessly night and day to make it work." Her tone was bitter, but she kept a smile on her face.

The audience started to clap again, nervously.

"I hope you all don't mind if I say a few words about our late headmaster, Mr. Bottomley. Oh, my Pookie Bear, how I miss him so..."

Fiona paused awkwardly as confused murmurs spread through the audience.

"Of course, I mean Mr. Bottomley. He was the best headmaster this school ever had. In fact, he was the greatest headmaster in the world, No one could compare to my darling Pookie..."

People shifted uncomfortably in their seats as Fiona rambled.

"If only he were here now to see this performance, I just know it would bring tears to his eyes. But alas, he was taken too soon."

There were murmurs in the audience as people began to wonder what was going to happen next.

"I'm so pleased to be here celebrating this wonderful performance. Though I must say, some of you were utterly dreadful up there."

Fiona scowled, peering around the auditorium. "Cindy Crane, your acting was atrocious. I've seen better skills from a toddler! You ruined the entire show with your bumbling."

Standing beside Chloe, Cindy looked down, blinking back tears as the audience whispered.

"Luckily, we had some real talent to make up for the hopeless cases." Fiona put her hands on her hips. "Chloe Partridge, you were utterly brilliant. A star is born."

Chloe shook off the weird feeling Fiona's speech was giving her and bowed again. Despite everything else Selena's mum was saying, Chloe was thrilled she'd singled her out for a job well done. Especially since it was in front of her parents.

"Thank you all so much," Fiona said, taking a final bow. The audience started another round of applause when her arms suddenly jerked up above her head like a puppet master was pulling her strings. She started to spin, faster and faster, her head hanging back, her mouth open in a silent scream.

Some of the clapping died out, the audience uncertain whether it was some grand finale. Chloe stood with the other actors in a line across the back of the stage, staring.

Cindy leaned toward her and tapped her on the arm. "I wonder what's going on…"

"It doesn't look great," said Chloe miserably.

The clapping stopped, and all eyes were on Selena's mum as she started muttering something over and over again.

Is it some kind of spell?

Fiona stared up at the stage lights, the bright beams illuminating her crimson hair fanning out behind her as she spun around like a mechanical toy. Then a light exploded. Then another. As the lights popped and shattered and glass crashed to the floor, the audience started to scream. Fiona's feet lifted off the ground, and she spun in the air like a bright red leaf.

"Oh, no!" Chloe ran across the stage, trying to dodge the broken glass. All around her, people screamed, and glass shattered.

The last thing she remembered was Fiona crashing against a wall, blue sparks flying from her body as if she were short-circuiting before slumping to the stage. Then a security guard dragged her away.

46

CHLOE

Chloe sat in her room at dusk in her pajamas, turning over the events from the previous night. She should have been getting praise for her stellar performance, but no one remembered anything about the whole night apart from Fiona's light-smashing performance. Her mum even told her she wasn't allowed to hang out with Selena anymore because her mum was a nut job. Well, she'd gotten her wish.

Chloe pulled open the curtains, pushed open the glass doors, and sighed as she stepped out onto the balcony. As the breeze rushed over her face, a gnawing sense of loneliness covered her. She missed Selena.

She stared out over the garden toward the sea. What if Selena had drowned? What if she'd been bitten by a zombie mermaid? The police would never figure out what had happened. She would never know the truth.

The sea roared beneath her, and a rush of seafoam rose in front of her in a massive wave. Chloe gasped as she saw a figure riding it. He grabbed the railing of the balcony, his rotting hands covered in greenish flesh. As the water hissed and fizzed, Chloe yelped. She was face-to-face with Andrew. It was weird and exhilarating and gross all at the same time. It was Andrew's familiar face with the jutting-out ears, except some bits of his face were hanging away in strips of flesh. He grinned and ripped off a frond of seaweed tangled around his neck.

"Hey, Chloe. What's up?" Andrew said in an attempt to sound casual.

"You scared the life out of me!" A horrible scent filled the air, like rotten meat. She sneezed. "Yuck. What's that smell?"

"It's the smell of zombies." Andrew shrugged. "It's rank, but you get used to it."

"What happened to you?"

"Faustina bit Jamie and me while we were swimming. I'm a zombie merlad now. It's been a wild ride. I've missed you, though."

Chloe mumbled, "I missed you, too." She blushed and looked away.

"Look, I can't stay long. I just promised Selena I'd try to convince you to come rescue her. Faustina's trapped her."

"How's she coping?"

"She's going out of her mind. Faustina's keeping her prisoner in a spiderweb."

"Why haven't you rescued her?" She guessed it was a

silly question. He was a jerk when he was alive, so why would he have changed?

Andrew gripped the balcony railing, his knuckles turning white. "To be honest, we're too scared of her. She told us if we ever tried to free Selena, she'd turn us into zombie shrimp."

Andrew took a deep, shaky breath before explaining. "Jamie and I tried to warn you when we saw you on the beach. We shouted that Selena was in trouble, but you didn't hear us. I guess normal humans can't always hear zombie voices."

Looking directly at Chloe, he continued urgently, "I'm too scared to face Faustina on my own. But with your help, I think we can save Selena. Will you come with me? We don't have much time before..."

"I appreciate you're trying to help Selena. But meeting Faustina freaks me out. What if she turns me into a zombie shrimp?"

"You've got to try. You're gutsy, and you can stand up to her."

The crashing waves swelled higher, spilling over the balcony ledge and soaking Chloe's slippers. She shivered, the sea wind piercing her thin pajamas. Somewhere below, unseen creatures moved in the inky depths.

Chloe's heart pounded. She wanted to scream out her frustration and fear, but only managed a choked whisper. "How can I survive underwater?"

A rolling wave drenched the balcony, the salty spray stinging Chloe's eyes. She coughed as the foul scent of sulfur filled her nose; she almost gagged on the noxious fumes.

The sea itself churned in violent reply. Shadowy tentacles breached the surface, writhing in the dim light before slipping back into the frothing abyss.

"Just dive in," Andrew told her.

"I can't. I'll drown."

He held out his hand. "Just grab my hand. I've been reading those mermaid books… I'm going to try to harness my own mind control powers so you can breathe. Just let me concentrate." He raised his eyes to the sky and pursed his lips to take a big intake of breath. It *really* didn't look like he knew what he was doing.

"I don't know if I trust you," said Chloe, her heart pounding. "What if you can't help me breathe? What if I drown?"

"You won't. I'll bring you back up before that happens. What have you got to lose?"

Chloe gulped nervously. She was terrified, but thoughts of Selena trapped underwater forever made her resolve harden.

Chloe looked up at Andrew, her face set with determination. "I'm ready," she said, grabbing his shredded hand. "Let's do this."

Just then, a large wave swelled behind them. As it crested over their heads, Chloe took a deep breath and shut her eyes. She held tightly to Andrew's hand as the wave carried them swiftly under the dark, roiling sea.

47

CHLOE

Chloe knew the water was cold, but she could barely feel it. She was heated from within. Andrew imparted a searing white energy that swirled within her. Now her blood rushed through her veins, faster and faster. He pulled her down, his strength propelling them like a speed boat slicing through the water. It got easier to swim the farther down they went, then a magnetic force dragged her deeper toward the ocean floor.

Eventually, they came to an area where the water was warm, glowing yellow and bright blue. Chloe gasped when she saw the house in the sea. It was just like Aunt Ada's, but it seemed to grow from the ocean floor. She was even more surprised to see Mr. Bottomley—minus his toupee and with only one arm—floating around outside the entrance.

"Chloe! So glad you could make it to Undead Academy," Mr. Bottomley said, waving his one remaining arm at the house. "You're going to get an amazing deaducation here. I promise it'll be killer!"

He grinned widely. "For newbie zombies, I recommend starting with *I'm Undead, Now What?* to get your bearings. Then you can take *Zombie Slaying 101* to learn all the best techniques."

Mr. Bottomley leaned in conspiratorially. "And once you've got some experience under your belt, maybe try *Advanced Brain Sucking for Undead Dunces*. It's not easy when you first become one of the swimming dead, let me tell you."

He chuckled while Andrew rolled his eyes behind him. Chloe forced a polite smile.

"Sounds great," Chloe gushed, trying to humor him. "Not planning to go the zombie route right now, though. Sorry. Have you happened to see Selena?"

Mr. Bottomley looked at her blankly. "Selena? I didn't even know she was down here. I've been so busy with the school. I don't think she's registered for classes, or I would have seen her name… I do miss her mum, though. Fiona is such a talented woman. How's she doing these days?"

"Not good," Chloe said flatly. "She's acting all strange and seems like she's falling apart. She's morphing into a zombie mermaid right before our eyes. Still, she hasn't grown a tail. I think Faustina has her completely under her control."

Mr. Bottomley looked concerned. "That's terrible. What's your plan to save Fiona?"

"I'm stumped, no idea what I can do. I just need to find Selena right now."

At that precise moment, Jamie swam by with a sense of urgency, snatching Andrew's arm and tugging him away from Chloe.

"Sorry Chloe, but he's gotta get out of here," Jamie said. "Faustina's really pissed off. She somehow knows you're down here." He turned to Andrew. "She's super mad and she's threatening to put you in the spider's web with Selena." Jamie tugged Andrew's wrist impatiently.

As the boys turned to swim away, Andrew's face twisted in fear as he turned to look at Chloe.

"Don't be scared," Mr. Bottomley reassured them. "Faustina's bark is worse than her bite." Chloe's heart raced with panic, a sense of sadness consuming her.

"No, don't leave me," she pleaded with Andrew. "I'll drown without you."

Chloe choked down mouthfuls of seawater, thrashing in panic. Andrew glided over and gently put his arms around her.

"It's okay, just try to stay calm," he said soothingly.

Chloe felt his mystical energy surround her like a warm, calming glow. Her racing heart began to slow down as her fear melted away.

Andrew gave her hand a reassuring squeeze, then let go and drifted over to Jamie. Chloe called out to him, but they were already swimming away.

Without hesitation, she kicked her legs and followed them, shouting, "Wait! Where do I find Selena?" But it was too late; they had disappeared into a cluster of waving seaweed.

Bioluminescent creatures swam by, their glowing bodies casting an eerie blue and orange light over the water. She tried to swim towards them but found her movements sluggish and heavy, as if she was being weighed down by invisible lead weights. Panic began to set in as she sank further into the magical depths.

Gazing downward, she glided towards the sandy plain, coated in grains of orange shifting sand. She scanned for the entrance to the house, her eyes landing on it with ease. She closed her eyes and inhaled deeply, allowing a sense of peace to envelop her. It was a gift from Andrew, still shielding her even though they were apart. She could still breathe comfortably thanks to him.

Why is everyone so terrified of Faustina? As she pushed open the door and swam into Aunt Ada's house, she gagged at the overwhelming stench of foot fungus. She was glad she could breathe underwater, but she could do without the smelling part. She also noticed she wasn't sniffling or sneezing anymore, which was a relief.

Chloe poked her head into the library and gasped. Golden walls shimmered all around, glowing like sunlight filtered through waves. Rows of desks were packed with zombie mermaid students hard at work. Their stringy manes of swaying seaweed hair reminded Chloe of underwater forests. Balanced on scaled tails, the mermaids scribbled away busily in their notebooks. Too focused on lessons to notice Chloe gawping at them.

Shelves bursting with bright corals and kelp hosted a rainbow of reef critters. Jellyfish floated near the high ceiling in a lazy dance, their pulsing glow casting an eerie blue-green sheen over the class.

Next, Chloe walked right into the living room, where a bunch of zombie mermaids sat at coral tables doing science experiments. They were totally oblivious to Chloe, focused on mixing their weird bubbling potions.

She shuddered. Were they cooking up an evil plan in there? Maybe a potion to turn humans into sea slaves? Or give them fish breath for life? Chloe didn't stick around to find out.

The walls were striped yellow and green, made up of bazillions of shiny sea beetle shells. It was like insect bling. Chloe wanted to stare at the sparkly shells, but she had to stay focused. Selena was in trouble somewhere in this house.

As Chloe swam down the hall, she passed a window. Whoa. Outside it looked like Fish City - fish of all shapes, colors and sizes swam by. Chloe saw schools of fish, lone ranger fish, blowfish puffed up like spiky balloons. For a second, she got distracted by the underwater scene. She loved fish, she'd admit. If only they weren't next to zombie mermaids.

Get it together. She couldn't forget why she was in this freaky place. Got to find Selena.

Chloe took a deep breath and kept moving. *Don't worry Selena, I'm coming. Just as soon as I get past all these weird glowing plants and hypnotic lights.* Dang, this place was distracting. *Focus, Chloe, focus. And what had Andrew said about a web?*

She swam up the curved staircase to where Selena's bedroom would have been on land. Pushing open the door, she was surrounded by pink, flowery walls made entirely of overlapping fish scales that glimmered in the filtered light. The scales formed floral patterns that mimicked wallpaper. The room contained a bed covered in a quilt made of woven seagrass, but Selena wasn't in it. A dresser stood against the wall. Chloe curiously pulled open one of the drawers...only for some orange sea worms to wriggle out. She shrieked and slammed the drawer shut fast.

She was about to leave when she heard shuffling from above. The attic. She'd forgotten the access was through Selena's room. She swam up to the trapdoor and pushed it open.

But as soon as Chloe entered the attic, cold claws clutched her shoulders, digging into her flesh.

"Get off me!" Chloe yelped, bubbles escaping her mouth, and spun around. A nightmarish mermaid with stringy red hair loomed before her. The zombie mermaid's sunken eyes bored into Chloe as she bared her jagged, yellowed fangs.

Chloe stared in horror at the mermaid's rotting, undead face. Even though she was as small as a child, Chloe knew this had to be Faustina, the oldest and most terrifying of the zombie mermaids.

Chloe grabbed Faustina and threw her across the attic room, which was filled with slimy strands of spiderwebs. As Faustina flew through the water, her arm snagged momentarily on the spiderweb, sticking to it before she pulled herself free with a big squelch.

"I'm here for Selena," Chloe said. "Where is she?"

A webbed hand pushed its way out of a gap in the web.

"I'm right here," shouted Selena, pushing her face up against the web. Chloe recoiled at the sight of Selena's bloated face and her nose that had swollen up to the size of an orange. "How did you find me?"

"Andrew. He came to my house and told me you were trapped under the sea."

"That idiot boy shouldn't be messing with forces he doesn't understand!" Screamed Faustina, who was swimming toward Chloe.

"It's so good to see you," Selena cried.

Chloe's eyes locked onto the glinting necklace around Faustina's mottled green neck. The zombie mermaid stroked it possessively with a gnarled hand.

"Give back the necklace," Chloe demanded. "It doesn't belong to you."

Faustina's bloodshot eyes narrowed. She bared her sharp teeth and let out a hollow, rasping laugh.

Over Faustina's hunched shoulder, Chloe spotted Aunt Ada slithering into the attic, trailing strands of kelp. The zombie swam with agonizing slowness, milky eyes fixed on the necklace.

"You're the last one who deserves it," Chloe shouted, trying to keep Faustina's attention.

"That's where you're wrong," the mermaid hissed. She clutched the necklace tighter.

With a sudden burst of speed, Ada lunged, her greenish arms outstretched toward the treasure hanging around Faustina's neck.

Faustina jerked away and smacked Aunt Ada. Chloe

took advantage of the confusion, diving toward Faustina and wrapping her fingers around the giant ruby.

"Get off me." Faustina kicked her tail in Chloe's face.

The blow hurt, but Chloe held on. "Give it back."

"You'll never get this necklace back," Faustina shrieked. She grabbed a fistful of Chloe's hair and yanked viciously.

Chloe yelped in pain. As Faustina's bony finger jabbed toward her eye, Chloe reacted instinctively, driving her knee into the mermaid's slimy stomach.

"I'll scratch your eyes out," Faustina snarled, clawed hands swiping at Chloe's face.

Chloe seized Faustina's scrawny arms and pinned them behind her back with all her strength. But the mermaid thrashed wildly, nearly breaking free.

"Help me hold her," Chloe cried to Aunt Ada.

"I'm coming, dear," Aunt Ada called back. She swam over with a loop of tough seagrass and tied Faustina's wrists securely.

Faustina let out a piercing howl as Chloe unclasped the necklace, pulling it free.

"Oh, come on, Faustina. There's no need to be so dramatic. How about some of those deep cleansing breaths you're always on about?" Aunt Ada said.

"Quick, get me out of here," Selena cried.

Chloe swam over to the web, trying to clasp the necklace around her own neck.

"You shouldn't have taken that," Faustina said, growling. "Now Selena's going to have to pay. I'm going to bite her and turn her into a zombie."

Aunt Ada looked furious. "It doesn't look like you're going anywhere right now."

Faustina wiggled against the seagrass handcuffs, but the moment Chloe fastened the necklace around her neck, an electric shock jolted Faustina. She flew back, crashing against the dresser. Chloe frantically scanned the ocean floor for something to cut the web's thick strands. She spotted a jagged-edged oyster shell and grabbed it. Positioning the sharp shell like a knife, Chloe feverishly sawed at the elastic fibers.

Each time she managed to slice through one cord, it suctioned back together with a wet squelch. But Chloe kept hacking away unrelentingly. The razor-sharp oyster shell eventually carved a hole just big enough for Selena to scramble free.

Chloe reached through the gap and grasped Selena's hand, pulling her safely out of the web's grip. Clutching the makeshift oyster shell blade, Chloe led Selena away swiftly before the opening could reseal itself.

Immediately, Selena's body began to turn back to normal. The webs between her fingers receded, and her misshapen face shrank back to its usual proportions.

Chloe and Selena watched Faustina, who was slumped against the dresser, her hands still tied behind her back. She looked drained, shrunken. The heat and power that once gave Faustina energy throbbed through Chloe's body.

"You know when Faustina got shocked just now?" Chloe said. "Something super similar happened to your mum last night after the play, too. I bet Faustina used that necklace along with her freaky mind control to make your mum go all spinny and make the lights explode."

Selena's eyes went wide. "Wait, so my mum's gone zombie now, too? No way."

Chloe nodded. "Yeah, I'm worried we're too late to change her back..."

"We *have* to try," Selena begged. "Now you've got that necklace, can't you like, magic her back to normal?"

Chloe squeezed Selena's hand. "I dunno if it'll work, but we can totally try. But your mum looked bad. First, we've gotta get back up to land."

Selena took a shaky breath. "Please let it not be too late to save her," she whispered.

"We'll do everything we can, I promise," Chloe said. "With this necklace, maybe we can reverse Faustina's zombie curse and turn her back to her old self."

"That would be beyond amazing," Selena said. "Now let's hurry and fix this."

The two friends hugged quickly then set off, determined to use the necklace to try and save Selena's mum.

Selena grabbed hold of Chloe's hand and led her over to Faustina, who was lying limply against the rock, opening and closing her mouth like a fish out of water.

"Let's tap into Faustina's mermaid magic," said Selena. "If we harness her power, she can turn my mum back into a human. I know we can do it." Carefully, Selena unknotted the seagrass from around Faustina's wrists.

Chloe looked skeptical. "I don't know if this is a good idea."

But Faustina didn't attack.

Instead, she started to babble incoherently. Chloe wondered if she'd lost her mind. "It's no good, Selena," Chloe said. "She doesn't know what's going on."

"It must've been the necklace—it totally destroyed Faustina," Selena said. "But she's got like centuries of magic power left in her. This is our only chance. We gotta move!"

Chloe nodded. "If we focus really hard, maybe we can get some of Faustina's magic to flow into us. Then we can use it to fix your mum."

The girls swam away fast as Faustina lay limply on the ocean floor. They zoomed through a tunnel of sparkling turquoise stones toward a bright glow.

Suddenly, a swarm of skull-faced spiders streamed at them, gnashing their pointy teeth. They sank their fangs into the back of Chloe's neck.

"Owww," Chloe yelped, writhing around. The bites burned like hot needles stabbing her skin.

"Just keep swimming," Selena urged. "We're almost there."

The water fizzed and bubbled around them as Chloe screamed, "Get these spiders off me!"

Selena frantically brushed away the spiders crawling all over Chloe's skin, but they kept hopping right back on, nibbling her earlobes with their snapping jaws.

Chloe's hand flew to her neck as she thrashed around. "The necklace—it's gone!" She shrieked. She caught a glimpse of spiders skittering away down the tunnel, carrying the ruby necklace back toward Faustina.

As Chloe and Selena spun around to chase after them, the spiders rushed from side to side, spinning furiously. A thick, gluey web rapidly formed, blocking the tunnel.

"They're Faustina's pet spiders," Selena said. "They're trying to stop us and return the necklace to her."

"We can't let them get away," Chloe cried, clawing at the sticky blockade preventing their pursuit.

48

SELENA

Selena's heart pounded as blood rushed to her head. She thrashed and twisted manically, feeling the web fibers stretch and strain around her. Putting all her adrenaline-fueled energy into her movements, Selena tore a ragged hole in the resilient blockage.

Selena kicked furiously, propelling herself through the torn hole in hot pursuit of the necklace. Her muscles burned but she couldn't let it get away.

She heard Chloe shouting behind her, but Selena kept swimming full speed ahead. She had to catch that necklace before it returned to Faustina.

But she was too late. Swimming back to where Faustina was sprawled against the rock, Selena watched in horror as the ruby necklace clasped itself back around Faustina's neck. The mermaid's eyes glowed red as a sinister smile twitched at the corners of her mouth.

"It's mine... It's mine..." Faustina said in a low, croaky voice. "I called it back with the power of my mind. You can't have it, you greedy girl."

As the glowing necklace poured Faustina's magic back into her, Selena saw her chance. She grabbed Faustina in a headlock from behind. Faustina thrashed and flailed, beating her fists against Selena's arm as Selena desperately tried to unclasp the necklace. She had to regain its power to save her mum from the zombie curse.

But amidst the swirling limbs and Faustina's violent struggles, Selena couldn't get a grip on the slippery necklace. Suddenly, a purple and gold patterned squid appeared, watching pensively. One of its arms shot out, wrapping tightly around Faustina's mouth to muffle her shrieks. Another arm encircled her waist, holding her still.

Selena realized it must be the same squid that hung around with Aunt Ada. With the mermaid immobilized by the squid, Selena was finally able to unhook the necklace from around Faustina's neck and put it on herself.

The squid proceeded to crush Faustina in its powerful arms. The suction cups made horrible squelching sounds against Faustina's rotted flesh as it squeezed tighter and tighter. Eventually, a dazed, defeated look came over Faustina's face.

Selena swam with determination back through the tunnel, her muscles aching. The thick spider web still obstructed her path, a gluey barricade. Chloe floated behind it, trapped.

With a graceful wave of her hands, Selena channeled the

necklace's energy. Beams of blazing white light sparked from her fingertips, searing a smoldering hole in the web's center. Screeching spiders poured out toward her face in a frenzy. Selena batted them away in revulsion.

"You got it back, awesome," Chloe said as Selena emerged through the web's ragged opening.

Selena grinned. "Yup. That web was crazy sticky. And those spiders—blech."

"I'm wiped out," Chloe whined. "Can we take five?" Her eyelids drooped heavily.

"Not now. Quick," Selena said, grabbing Chloe's hand. "Let's get out of here. I think without the necklace, Faustina's not going to have the energy to chase us, but we need to get out of here just in case."

As they emerged at the other end of the tunnel, they plunged into an area of the sea that pulsed with a bright orange glow.

Selena was dying to get back home and see what state her mum was in, but Chloe's strength was sapped. Luckily, holding Chloe's hand, things went a little faster. Selena's body was supercharged from the necklace, spluttering with bursts of energy. Selena couldn't help worrying about her mum and whether the necklace mixed with Faustina's magic would be enough to save her from transitioning into a zombie mermaid.

As fast as she could, she swam toward the surface of the sea, dragging Chloe behind her.

49

SELENA

Dripping wet, Selena and Chloe sprinted into the library. They found Fiona lying motionless on the sofa.

"Mum, are you alright?" Selena cried.

Fiona didn't respond. She weakly grasped for a glass of water on the floor, barely able to lift it to her parched lips. Her skin was cracked and pale.

Though she looked ill, Fiona appeared more human than last time. Selena felt a rush of hope. Maybe their positive thoughts had halted the zombie virus.

"I'm so glad you're back, Snookums," Fiona said, drawing Selena weakly toward her and staring at the ruby necklace. "You got the necklace back. You're such clever girls. What happened last night? Something went wrong at the performance, but I can't remember what."

Chloe shook her head. "It doesn't matter. The main thing

is you're doing better, Ms. Flowers. You're not as sick, right?"

"I think I can totally heal her," Selena said, eyes closed. "There's like this weird tingly magic flowing all through me. If I direct it at you, Mum, I bet I can do this." She sighed. "I wish I'd tried this when I first had the necklace. But I was too wrapped up in my own drama."

"You got this," Chloe encouraged. "Focus your mind and make the magic happen."

The walls started shaking a little. Then they rumbled harder, raining plaster bits from the ceiling.

Selena kept concentrating, scrunching her eyes tight. She mumbled to herself, trying to channel the power sparking under her skin.

"C'mon magic...do your thing..." She whispered. "Heal my mum...heal my mum!"

The necklace glowed brightly as Selena put all her mental energy into activating its healing powers. She had to make this work.

Selena had the overwhelming sense that as the house trembled, it was giving up energy and magic and filling Selena up to the brim. The house had her back and was fighting for the Flowers family to survive.

A warmth spread across her chest and zoomed up her arms, igniting her fingers and turning them into burning matchsticks.

"I'm hot!" Selena shrieked. "I'm on fire! What's happening to me?"

"It's alright," said Chloe, sneezing uncontrollably. "That just means it's working."

There was an almighty rumble in the bookshelves. Selena opened her eyes as books tumbled down, forming dusty heaps. They zoomed to the ground like a flock of geese, landing with a thud. Some books opened their yellow musty pages and fluttered like parachutes onto Fiona's face.

"What's happening?" Fiona wailed, coughing and covering her ears.

"I think she's almost there," said Selena, opening her eyes and taking the books off her mum's face. "I just need to give one more little push."

Selena held her palms over Fiona's face and squeezed her eyes shut. Using all her powers and concentration, she focused on changing her mum all the way human. Gradually, her mum's skin turned from gray to pink, and her bulging eyeballs began to shrink back into their sockets. Her sores faded and melted seamlessly into her skin.

At last, the plaster stopped falling. There was a rustling as the flapping pages settled on the ground. As the heat left her body, Selena knelt beside her mum. Fiona opened her eyes.

"I feel so different," she said. "I can't thank you both enough for saving me. I think I was part zombie. For a while, I thought I was going to turn all the way. And now, I'm so relieved I'm back to myself again." She swiped a cobweb from her face.

Selena reached out and touched her mum's hair. "It's over," she whispered. "The virus has left your body."

"I can tell," Fiona said. "I've felt so out of control, so full of poison, ever since Faustina scratched me. And now, that feeling's gone."

"Faustina was totally obsessed with controlling your mind," Selena said.

"Yeah, but now we've got her necklace. I think she's powerless," Chloe added.

"Let's hope so," Fiona replied. "It's great she's out of action. But what if she comes back someday?"

Selena shrugged. "We'll make sure she can never get to us again."

"I'm so ready for that fresh start I promised when we moved here. I really hoped things would work out with Roger..." Fiona trailed off.

"Sorry, Mum...he's a zombie merlad now," Selena said. "Faustina turned him."

"Oh, how awful!" Fiona exclaimed.

"Don't feel too bad, though," Chloe said. "He's running a school underwater and seems happy. Plus, Andrew and Jamie are there, too."

"Well, that's a lot to take in." Fiona laughed. "Makes me glad I'm done with all that zombie excitement. I'm looking forward to a nice, normal life now. And you two clearly had quite the underwater adventure. Are you over your water fears, Selena?"

Selena nodded. "I hope so! It was awesome down there, except for Faustina. I'm just glad it all worked out. But this necklace is too much power for me." She removed it and handed it to her mum.

Fiona turned the glinting ruby necklace over in her hands. "Now that we've got this back, what should we do with it?"

"No way, Mum. That thing is trouble," Selena warned.

"Oh, come on, think of the fun we could have," Fiona said mischievously.

Selena and Chloe exchanged a knowing grin. "Bury it!" They shouted in unison, and all three dissolved into laughter.

ABOUT THE AUTHOR

Ella English, the talented writer behind the Merblood Saga, has created an enchanting middle-grade fantasy series that will send shivers down your spine. Although she was born in London, Ella currently resides in Baltimore, USA. Her inspiration for the series can be traced back to her childhood memories of exploring the tidal pools near her family's holiday home on the Kent coast. It was during these vacations by the sea, that she first got the idea that bloodthirsty zombie mermaids dwelled in the ocean's depths.

In the first book in the Merblood Saga, *Selena Flowers and the Cursed Ruby*, you can join Selena Flowers and her friends on their thrilling and terrifying journey beneath the waves. Keep an eye out for the second book in the series, which is coming soon.

instagram.com/ellaenglishauthor

tiktok.com/@ellaenglish